I0775709

Cutler's Legacy

a John Cutler mystery

by Colin Conway

"No matter where you go,
there you are."

Buckaroo Banzai (Peter Weller)

Cutler's Legacy

2008

Chapter 1

A car rumbled into my neighborhood. Its engine sounded worse the closer it got. I could speculate any number of reasons for the sound—a broken piston or misaligned timing, for example. It would have been nonsense, though. I don't know anything about motors yet pretend to understand every word from a mechanic's mouth.

When the vehicle slowed in front of my house, I filed the paperwork on a recently finished case. Over the years, I've learned to document my actions better. Back when I was on the job, writing a decent report was necessary for a successful prosecution. Now, it was important for covering my ass—too many details might come back to haunt me and not all of them through the court system.

From my desk, I had an unobstructed view of A.M. Cannon Park if the front door was opened. The noisy car had stopped, but it wasn't visible from where I sat.

Two little boys ran through the park, dragging kites behind them. Their mothers stood with their arms crossed. The women were engaged in a conversation, too bothered with their story to help the struggling boys launch their toys into the air.

A heavy door squeaked. It was the long metallic shrill old steel cars develop. When it slammed closed, my dog barked. Corporal was in the backyard. It was a comfortable spring morning—too nice for an aging Shepherd to spend it lying indoors.

There was a shushing sound I couldn't place until a woman came into view and headed up the sidewalk toward my house. The heels of her untied combat boots dragged as she walked.

She was a tall, thin woman with dark hair. Her faded jeans pooled into the scuffed boots. Her hands were shoved into a tattered green Army jacket she kept wrapped tightly around her.

Corporal continued to bark.

Unseen hands were a cause for concern even from an attractive woman, and I pulled open my desk drawer. A .40 Glock lay there. I wasn't one of those paranoid types who carried a gun wherever I went, but I wasn't a fool either. An ounce of precaution as they say. I rested my hand on the gun.

The woman and I made eye contact through the screen door, but I remained seated. She ascended the front concrete stairs in two long strides.

"You John Cutler?" she asked with her nose almost to the screen.

"I am."

"Mind if I come in?"

"Help yourself."

She removed a hand from a pocket and opened the door. When she stepped inside, she pulled the other hand free of its pocket and the jacket parted to reveal a Queen half-shirt. A thick chain ran through the loops of her jeans and a padlock secured it in place. The metal belt appeared uncomfortably tight, and several links dangled down between her legs.

I lifted my hand from the gun and pushed the drawer closed.

Dark mascara highlighted her darting, green eyes. She scanned my office. There wasn't much to see—just a desk and a couple of metal folding chairs. Outside of the occasional internet search, the computer was for show. I did most of my paperwork by hand. The office doubled as my home, but the bedroom at the back of the house wasn't much to brag about either.

She had a strange allure, much the way danger emits a siren call to attract the foolish. Too many things threw me when considering her age. Baggy clothes hid most of her thin frame, but the half-shirt revealed a flat stomach. A younger woman seeking attention likely would have dumped the jacket in this weather and shown off the body under that cutoff shirt.

Besides the mascara, the woman wore no other makeup. Faint lines creased the edges of her mouth and a hint of crow's feet played at her eyes. We might have been the same age, but her hair appeared unnaturally black. Perhaps she colored it. Gray speckled my hair now that I was pushing forty. I gave up guessing and assumed we were the same age.

"What can I do for you?" I asked.

She stopped checking the room and her gaze settled on me. She shoved her hands back into her pockets and pulled the coat tight once more. "You ever search for a missing person?"

I nodded.

"You find them?" The way she asked it carried more than a hint of challenge.

I nodded again. I didn't bother to mention the person I found had been murdered. It didn't seem the time for such a revelation, especially with her undercurrent of provocation.

She looked down and tapped the toe of her boot against the floor.

Something held her back from just spitting out what she came for, so I tried easing her into a conversation. "What's your name?" I asked.

She stopped tapping her toe. "Daisy." As if almost an afterthought, she added, "McLaughlin." She straightened, pulled her shoulders back, and thrust her chin out. "Daisy McLaughlin." The Army jacket was from a generation before her, but perhaps she had served in the military.

"All right, Daisy," I said. "Do you live around here?"

She shook her head. "Up in Metaline."

When I cocked my head, she shrugged.

Metaline was two hours north of Spokane. There likely weren't any private detectives in that small town but coming this far for help seemed excessive. "Is someone missing?"

"My boyfriend, Nick." She cleared her throat. "Nicholas Gossett."

She stared at me as if I should have recognized the name. Or perhaps her expression was because I hadn't written anything down. I grabbed a pad of paper and jotted the missing man's name. "How long has Nick been missing?"

The woman continued to watch me.

"Daisy?"

She blinked and looked away. "Three days."

"Have you gone to the police?"

"You said you could find a missing person."

"If he's missing you should notify the cops."

Disappointment crossed her face and her legs stopped moving. "They won't help."

"How do you know?"

"They'll say…" Her fists dug into the pockets. "They'll say he's on a bender."

My pen hovered over the notepad. "He's an alcoholic?"

"He doesn't drink anymore, but you know how cops are."

"Is there anyone who might have wanted to hurt him?"

She watched me with unfocused eyes as she tapped the heel of her boot against the toe of the other.

"Daisy?"

"Will you help us?" she asked.

"You didn't answer my question. Is there anyone who might have wanted to hurt him?"

"I don't know."

"He's your boyfriend."

"He's made his mistakes. I've made mine." She flashed an awkward smile. "We both have pasts."

"What does that mean?"

"It means I don't know."

I made a lot of past mistakes that I wouldn't share with my girlfriend. Maybe some of those mistakes would come back to haunt me. I left the question alone. I could always circle back to it later.

"Have you fought recently?" I asked.

"Me and Nick?"

"That's right."

"We don't fight." Her knees rubbed together. "Never, in fact. We're lucky that way."

"Has he seemed depressed?"

"Not usually." Daisy's hand slipped out of its jacket pocket and the flaps parted. She grabbed the padlock and twisted. The chain link belt tightened further around her thin waist. Her face contorted in pain and her knuckles whitened. When she let go, a peacefulness returned to her features.

Since starting my private investigation business, I've learned to screen clients. Early on, I accepted too many cases that turned out to be wastes of time. I got paid, but I spent countless hours chasing my tail. Clients could create many stories which required the aid of a detective.

My spouse is cheating on me.

An employee is stealing from my business.

Our child wants to kill us to get their inheritance.

When I discovered zilch in those investigations, not only did the client feel I failed, but I squandered my time on their bullshit stories. I liked getting paid, but I also enjoyed feeling as if my work mattered.

Several things seemed wrong about Daisy McLaughlin.

Right out of the gate, nothing seemed to add up about her story. For a concerned girlfriend, she didn't know much about her partner or, at the very least, she was dancing around the truth. One meant she wasn't aware. The other meant she was lying.

Daisy also gave off some strange vibes. The undercurrent of danger remained. Even though the loose Army jacket and floppy combat boots detracted from her figure, something hyper-sexualized was going on underneath. She wrenched the lock with the intensity of a mechanic trying to break loose a stuck bolt.

She watched me with an odd curiosity in her eyes. It wasn't the way a cat watches a mouse, but it was close. Her gaze was closer to the way a lioness observes a zookeeper. The former depends on the latter for its food and safety, but the lioness would kill the zookeeper even to the detriment of its own life. It was in the big cat's nature.

Daisy McLaughlin would surely turn out to be a client I'd regret keeping. It would be best if I ended the interview. I set my pen down and interlaced my fingers. "I can't help you."

She blinked. "Why not?"

"Because I'm not familiar with Metaline." It wasn't a lie, but I'm sure I could have worked around it well enough. It was a convenient excuse to get out of the work.

Daisy shoved her hand back into the jacket pocket. "He told me to never contact you." Her mouth puckered as if trying to contain her words. "But I figured you would understand."

"Who?"

"I'm breaking a promise by being here."

"Lady, I have no idea what you're talking about."

Daisy pulled back her shoulders and defiantly thrust her chin out. "You're not even half the man he is."

"Who are you talking about?"

"Your father." She turned and slapped the screen door open. "Thanks for nothing." Daisy hurried down the stairs. Her boots scuffed along the sidewalk as she ran.

The words stunned me. *Your father.*

I stared at the screen door's mesh as it went out of focus, blurring everything. The sounds of the neighborhood warbled, suddenly becoming irrelevant. It was as if the world shook.

Your father.

I sat there for a moment, testing the words on for size. When my wits returned, I realized she was getting away. I hopped to my feet and knocked my chair over with a clatter.

Outside, a metallic door squealed.

I jumped around the desk and banged through the screen door.

A late '70s Chevy pickup started and its engine revved. The truck lurched forward. As it drove by, Daisy extended her hand toward the passenger window and flipped me the bird. Even though I couldn't hear her, I could read her lips.

"Asshole!"

***

I never met my father, but his name wasn't Nicholas Gossett. It was Gabriel Baldwin.

At least that's what my birth certificate said. Gabriel Baldwin never married my mother and left her about a month after my birth. As a result, she refused to say his name or say anything nice about the man. When I was a boy, my mother referred to him only sparingly as "your father." This was often said with a curled lip and a contemptuous tone indicating he ranked below something she had scraped from the bottom of her shoe. The abandonment and most of the hurt occurred before my mother began her climb into polite society. An unwed mother wouldn't have fit nicely into the narrative she created. She never discussed my absentee father with others.

Your father wasn't a good man, Johnny.

My childhood was the reason she resented the revelation of my own out-of-wedlock daughter. Maria and I had a short-term relationship that ended up with an unplanned pregnancy. I offered to marry Maria, but she realized it was a poor decision for many reasons that I couldn't understand at the time. Had she chosen an abortion, I would have supported her. Thankfully, Maria chose the baby. Yet, she didn't want anything from me other than to let her raise the child her way. Even though we didn't have anything court sanctioned, I regularly paid support. That was easy while I was on the job. It got sticky for a bit after my termination, but I've been back to timely payments for a while now.

I mostly see Erin in the summers. The two of us used to write letters to each other when she was younger, but now our communication was limited to text messages until our summer vacations. Erin's a newly minted teenager and she's got a life, but I'd be lying if I said I didn't miss those handwritten notes.

My mother accused me of repeating my father's actions. She had drilled certain behaviors into me as a child. There were deeds that 'real men' did not do and having an out-of-wedlock child was one of them. For a woman improving her station in life, my actions were the height of embarrassment.

You're just like your father, Johnny.

As I've grown older, the relationship with my mom has strained to where we speak only three times a year—on our birthdays and Christmas. We don't bother with the pretense of gifts or greeting cards. The calls are obligatory and free of affectionate words. We barely pretend to care about the other and say whatever pleasantries are required for the moment. The calls last only as long as necessary.

So I didn't pick up the telephone to call my mother and ask if she'd heard the name Nicholas Gossett. And I certainly had no intention of asking if she knew the whereabouts of my father. The last time I asked was in junior high school. When you're told 'no' long enough, you learn to quit asking.

I sat at my desk and opened the big drawer containing my files. I found a dog-eared folder labeled *Personal* near the back and pulled it out. Inside were certificates memorializing various events of my life. My high school and college diplomas. A certificate for graduating from the police academy. A photocopy of Erin's birth certificate.

At the back of everything was my birth certificate. I don't know why I needed to see his name; I already knew who my father was. I'd stared at the certificate enough as a child. *Father—Gabriel T. Baldwin.*

My mother never told me what the T stood for. Maybe she didn't know. Somewhere down the line, I decided my father's middle name was Thomas. I couldn't imagine my father being the type of guy who answered to Gabriel or Gabe, so I imagined him responding to Tom.

Gabriel "Tom" Baldwin was my father, not Nicholas Gossett.

Daisy McLaughlin was a loon. There were a fair amount of them in this business.

I tucked the papers back into the folder and decided to do something to take my mind off the entire business.

***

I threw the gnarled tennis ball as hard as I could. The German Shepherd sprinted after it.

He seemed to have gotten slower over the past year. Maybe it had been going on longer. I don't know. What I know is the dog couldn't go for as long or as hard as he could in the past.

Corporal brought the ball back and dropped it at my feet. Slobber covered it. I threw it again, and he raced away.

If I thought too long about the ramifications of his slowing, it would depress me. I pushed the thoughts away. Corporal had belonged to a friend who was murdered. I took the Shepherd in, and he'd become my best friend. I didn't know how old he was, but maybe he was older than I estimated.

The dog overran the ball, then circled back to get it.

A late-forties man in a blue T-shirt and khaki cargo shorts crossed the park in my direction. He had longish gray hair that made him look like an aging surfer. He raised his hand and yelled, "Hey yo, Cutler!"

"Remo," I muttered and turned my attention back to the dog.

Corporal started back but stopped with the ball clenched tightly in his teeth. His gaze was trained on the interloper.

Remo Lightly noticed the Shepherd and froze mid-stride.

"Keep walking," I called.

"I will not!" Remo's eyes remained locked on the dog.

"He's not going to bite you."

"He looks hungry."

"If you keep standing there, he's going to think you're lunch."

Remo's head snapped to me. "I'm not edible."

"Walk like you're not afraid."

"But I am."

I waved him over.

He started moving again. "That beast is a menace."

"He's a dog. Get over it."

"He's a shark in the park." Remo pointed at the dog. "And Dr. Seuss would not approve."

Remo Lightly was a weed dealer, but he didn't sell to the lowly residents of my neighborhood. He handled an upscale clientele on the South Hill. His sister lived a few blocks away. Since I didn't see his car, I figured he was visiting her. He stopped by whenever he was in the neighborhood.

I had helped Remo with a problem last year. Ever since then, he imagined we were friends. He had a strange sort of charm and wasn't a bad guy overall, so I tolerated the occasional visit.

"Fall in," I hollered.

The dog ran toward us.

Remo squealed and hurried to my side. He lifted his knees unnecessarily high as he ran, as if his feet were burning, and his light blue shoes blurred from the effort.

Corporal sat in front of me and dropped the ball.

"A trained killer is what you've got," Remo said. "I don't trust it."

"He's a him," I said. "How would you like it if I referred to you as an 'it?'"

Remo's face pinched. "Why are you always so mean?"

I scratched behind the dog's ear. "Did you come over for a reason?"

"Elva went to the bar, and I was bored." He shrugged. "I thought maybe you could use some company."

"That's why I've got a dog."

Remo studied Corporal. "Or maybe you could use some help. You know, on one of your cases or something?"

"I don't need any help."

He shoved his hands into his shorts and looked down. "You never know."

"Remo."

"What?"

My gaze dropped to his blue rubber shoes. "What're you wearing?"

"Crocs." He lifted his head, but his brow had furrowed. "Why?"

"They look like grandma shoes."

"They're not." He stuck one out to model it. "They're comfortable."

"That right there is Exhibit A why you can't help."

"Because of my shoes?"

I nodded. "Detectives don't wear grandma shoes."

He smirked. "That *Murder, She Wrote* lady does. What do you say to that?"

"I say you're not reliable."

Remo appeared hurt by the truth. "I could be."

"Why do you want to help?" I asked. "You've got clients to take care of."

"Maybe I'm looking to diversify."

"And be a weed-selling private detective?"

He shrugged. "There are worse jobs."

"Not on my license," I said.

"Why won't you teach me?"

"I've got other work to do."

His lips pursed. "Like what?"

"Anything but that."

"Sometimes you can be an asshole, Cutler."

"So I've heard. Today, in fact."

"Well," Remo said, "you should probably listen to the people telling you that."

He turned and walked off.

***

When we returned to the house, Corporal curled up next to my desk. He didn't seem interested in going out in the backyard, and I didn't force him.

The front door remained open. A breeze blew in and rustled some papers. I shuffled some items to make sure nothing fell off, then I started the computer. The monitor flickered, and the disk drive whirred. I absently stared at the machine as it rattled to life.

There were times I missed being a cop. This was one of them. Asking a dispatcher to run a name was far superior to what I was about to do. Not only was delegating the task nice, but the radio operator had access to NCIC. The National Crime Information Center was operated by the FBI and interlinked all police agencies. On my own, I couldn't even access Washington State's Department of Licensing.

I could use Google. It wasn't much but, if I had patience, it could get me pretty far. A former girlfriend was a wizard at the computer. Our relationship ended, though, and so did her help. I had to adapt or die. I chose the former.

When the computer finally allowed me to control it, I started my browser and entered 'Nicholas Gossett.' The search results were plentiful, but I didn't find any in Metaline. There was, however, a MySpace result for a Seattle resident named Nicholas Gossett. Out of curiosity, I clicked it. I spent less than two seconds on the page. He was younger than me.

Facebook provided results for Nikki Gossett and Nico Gossett. I hadn't considered the nicknames and clicked on them. Nico was a twenty-something black man stationed at Travis Air Force Base. Nikki Gossett was a woman.

I returned to the search engine and added the city to the search criteria—Nicholas Gossett Metaline. This limited the search results considerably. There were five, and none of them concerned Metaline, Washington. I clicked the back button and returned to the browser.

There were companies that offered help with online name searches for a monthly subscription. I considered subscribing to them in the past, but they felt like a scam. Especially since the people I was likely to contact fell into two categories.

The first were the ones who had a digital footprint to follow. They signed up for things like MySpace and Facebook. They shared photos of themselves with friends and family. Perhaps those pictures were always the best of the best—a false representation of their lives—but it still presented something of them. Those folks wrote happy posts about their favorite activities. Maybe they participated in team sports or group hobbies which had their own websites. Whatever their extracurricular activities, those people had an online presence. They weren't trying to hide. Those folks stood before the world and exposed themselves. Those online flashers essentially said, "Look at me! This is who I am." They were easy to find, and I didn't need a subscription to locate them.

The second type of person I usually contacted was the antithesis of the online flasher. They didn't want to be found. For whatever reason, they knew the complications that came with a digital footprint. Perhaps they had a jealous former lover who stalked them in the real world as well as online. This hard-to-find person might have thought the U.S. Government tracked citizens, so they stayed away from modern advances. Or perhaps this type was wanted by the law, and they knew better than to get online and give the cops one more avenue for tracking them.

If Nicholas Gossett was of this suspicious variety, it wasn't out of the question that he didn't have a digital profile. No subscription service would help me find him. However, those online businesses would gladly take my money and let me feel foolish in the process.

I cleared the search bar and entered *Gabriel T. Baldwin*. My pinkie hovered over the Enter key. I had never looked for my father. Could it be as simple as this? Would I find him now by letting Google do the heavy lifting?

When I was a boy, my mother did her best to discourage me from ever looking for him.

"Your father didn't want us, Johnny." When she was really upset with something I'd done, *us* became *you*. "He didn't want you, Johnny."

By the time I entered high school, I resented my father. He abandoned me. Had I met the man, I would have punched him in the mouth. So much anger built up inside me by the time I graduated. I'm lucky the internet wasn't around back then. I would have wasted a lot of time searching for him.

By the time the internet became ubiquitous, I no longer cared. I had my own life, and I was making a damn fine mess of it. Looking for Gabriel T. Baldwin was no longer a priority.

But Daisy McLaughlin had shown up saying another man was my father.

Daisy McLaughlin, I thought. I emptied the search bar and entered her name along with the Metaline modifier.

This time I got a result. Daisy owned a used bookstore—Sturdy Goats Reading Company. She was mentioned in an online article promoting the previous year's Small Business Saturday, the day after Black Friday. The post's author didn't quote Daisy nor provide a picture, but it listed the store's address in Metaline.

I leaned back and stared at my computer. Was I wasting time with this?

Daisy might simply be crazy. Lunatics owned businesses as well as the sane.

Why did she choose me, a detective two hours south of where she worked? Why would she mention my long-absent father, even if the names were all wrong?

I scratched my chin as I stared at the article for Small Business Saturday.

Damn, I thought. I wish I still had access to NCIC.

But I did. Sort of.

I picked up my phone.

Chapter 2

Sergeant Gary Ackerman closed his eyes and pinched the bridge of his nose. His hair was mussed, and he wore a wrinkled blue T-shirt. He had a five o'clock shadow and bloodshot eyes, but it was late morning. He worked the graveyard shift and got overtime this morning because of a shooting his guys were on. I first met Ackerman when he was a Major Crimes detective, and he investigated the murder of my friend.

"Tired?" I asked.

"You wouldn't believe."

I wiggled the handle of my coffee mug. "I've been there."

"You're living banker's hours now."

We were at Dolly's Cafe at the corner of Washington and Indiana. The small restaurant served a busy breakfast and lunch crowd. Due to its proximity to the Public Safety campus, it was a favorite spot for cops and deputies.

Ackerman mopped the remaining hash browns through some egg yolk and stuck them in his mouth. He pushed his plate away and grabbed his coffee.

"Working the night shift sucks," I said.

"Stop buttering me up." He sipped his coffee. "Get to why we're here."

"I need a favor."

"We talked about this."

"This is different."

He set his coffee down and put his hand over the top of the mug. "Different, how?"

"It's about my father."

Ackerman cocked his head. "I didn't know you had a father."

"We all have fathers."

He rolled his eyes. "You never mentioned yours."

"Was nothing to mention."

Ackerman turned his mug. "Now there is?"

I nodded.

"He in trouble?"

"I don't even know if it is my father."

Ackerman's eyes narrowed. "I'm too tired for you to mess with my head."

"I never met my father."

He tapped the table with his cup. "Okay, slow it down."

"A woman came into my office—"

"Why do all your troubles start with a woman?"

"Not all of them."

"Most."

I sipped my coffee.

"Well?" he asked.

"Are you finished?"

"I asked a reasonable question any investigator would ask."

I sipped my coffee again.

"Fine." Ackerman crossed his arms. "Tell me a story."

I told him about Daisy McLaughlin's visit and how her accusation related to my past. "But my birth certificate says Gabriel Baldwin is my father."

"Maybe she's a one-oh-five."

"The hell is that?"

"A crazy."

Cops have all sorts of slang. Who knew how SPD developed the verbal shorthand that a 105 is a person having a mental crisis? Maybe Ackerman didn't even know.

He slipped his finger through the coffee mug's handle and dragged the cup around the table. "And what are you asking of me?"

"Run this guy's name through NCIC. Tell me what you find."

"I could get in trouble for doing such a favor. There are policies against running names for personal reasons."

"Nick Gossett might be missing."

"Did she contact the sheriff's office up there? Which county is that, by the way?"

"No idea. Doesn't matter because she didn't reach out to them. She said they'd only accuse Nick of being on a bender."

"He's a local drunk?"

"According to her, he doesn't drink anymore."

"Anymore," Ackerman parroted.

"That's right. So you can see why I'm trying to determine how much energy to expend on this."

He stopped playing with his coffee cup. "And you want me to spend my energy on it?"

"Well."

"And put my neck on the line for you?"

I grimaced. "That's not how I'm looking at it."

"That's how I am. Policies and procedures, remember? Besides, you don't know anything about this woman or who this Gossett character is. Maybe you should do a little homework on them first. I'm not risking anything for something that might be nothing."

My eyes widened.

He groaned. "Gimme a break. I'm tired, but you get my point."

I did, even if it wasn't solidly landed.

"Thanks for breakfast, though." Ackerman lifted his cup. "We should make this part a habit."

***

"So, he's not your father?" Stacy Mathers said. "Hailey, don't do that."

The five-year-old shoved yet another tater tot into her mouth. She looked like a chipmunk preparing for winter. She wore a pink T-shirt with stars and rainbows that read *Grrl Power!*

"Do what?" Hailey looked in my direction and her eyes sparkled with mischief. She smiled and revealed a mouthful of fried potatoes.

"Gross," Ethan muttered. Her brother returned to nudging his tater tots with an undressed hot dog. Its bun lay in ruins; the boy had shredded it earlier. No ketchup or mustard lay anywhere on the plate. He wore a green T-shirt with a G.I. Joe logo and some character I didn't recognize.

The children were a year apart. He was the oldest and had recently turned six, yet their personalities diverged wildly. Hailey was outgoing and loud, while Ethan was quiet and reserved. She seemed to enjoy when I was around, but the boy couldn't have cared less if he ever saw me again.

"Chew with your mouth closed," Stacy said. Her eyes shifted to me. "Not you."

My hot dog hovered in front of my mouth. "I hope I always do that."

"You have nice manners."

I bit into the hot dog.

We were at Stacy's house. I'd been staying there most nights now over the past two months. We'd been dating for almost a year, but Stacy was fiercely protective of her children. I had to earn my way into their lives. Prior to that, we were a secret.

I allowed my daughter to meet my previous girlfriends. I never thought of the ramifications until she grew close to one. When that relationship ended, Erin blamed me for it. She created parallels between her mother and that girlfriend that didn't exist. Children are best kept in the dark when it comes to affairs of a parent's heart.

It was a big deal when Stacy let me meet her kids.

Hailey raced a tater tot around her plate and left a trail of ketchup in its wake. "You don't have a daddy?" she asked.

"Hailey—" Stacy started, but Ethan interrupted.

"Don't be dumb."

"*Ethan!*"

His head jerked up, but his gaze morphed into puppy dog eyes so quickly I couldn't believe it. It was straight out of Parent Manipulation 101.

Stacy's face softened. "We don't say that word."

"Dumb," Hailey muttered as a second tater tot joined what appeared to be a chase around her plate.

"*Hailey!*"

The girl ignored her mother as the fried potato pieces zoomed through a puddle of ketchup. Two more trails of ketchup spread across the plate. The kid was making a masterpiece. "Vroom."

"Stop playing with your food," Stacy said.

Hailey plopped both tater tots into her mouth. The chipmunk had returned and so had her mischievous grin.

"You, too," she said to Ethan. "Stop poking your tater tots and just eat them already."

The boy dropped the hot dog and picked up a tot. He examined it the way a scientist might.

"Let's remember our manners," Stacy said. "Just because we get to eat with our fingers tonight doesn't mean we should act like barbarians. Okay?"

Hailey nodded as her attention settled on me. I winked at her. Ethan's gaze returned to his plate.

Stacy continued, "We're going to observe our manners if we want to have dessert, right?"

Both children muttered some version of "uh-huh." Hailey grabbed another tater tot. Ethan abandoned the one he was holding and wiped his hands together.

Stacy's gaze slid back to me. "So you were saying?"

I swallowed the last of my hot dog. "Where was I?"

"You don't have a daddy," Hailey offered.

"So dumb," Ethan corrected.

***

I leaned against the counter.

Stacy stood before the sink. She washed a plate, ran it under a stream of water, and handed it to me. "So, about your father."

"This guy isn't my father." I dried the plate and slid it into the cabinet.

"What are you going to do about it?" She rinsed another plate and handed it to me.

"Nothing."

"Nothing?"

I slid the dry plate into the cabinet. "I tried to find the guy on the internet and struck out. I met with Ackerman, too."

"What'd Gary say?"

"He said good luck."

Stacy washed a pot. "What's that mean?"

"He's not going to run a name for me and put his job in jeopardy."

"Checking someone's name would put his job in jeopardy? Don't cops do that all the time?"

"For official purposes. Not as favors."

"Oh. Duh." Stacy put the pot under the clean spray of water. "Can't say as I blame him, then. He's got a family and responsibilities."

"Yeah," I said. "Still, it would have been nice to have had some background on this Gossett guy."

"Maybe we should have Gary and his wife over for dinner one of these days."

"We've been saying that for a while now."

"You're the one that has to make it happen," she said. "Not me."

"Yeah."

She handed me the pot. "Well, get on it."

"You're not the boss of me."

"That's so cute you think that." She patted my butt with a wet hand. "You know who else you could call?"

I swirled the towel inside the pot. "I'm not calling her."

"One of these days, I'd like to meet her."

"You do *not* want to meet my mother."

"Yes, I do. What's the problem?" Stacy grabbed a sheet pan. "You've met mine."

"Your parents are perfectly normal." I set the pot on the stove.

"They are pretty great. I'll give you that."

"My mom is the opposite of great."

"We all have our crazy family members."

She didn't need to say anymore because I knew who she was talking about—her sister. Tanya and I had been involved in a sordid relationship. She was on the rebound and slumming with me while I bounced at Spokane's hottest nightclub. We weren't exclusive, although I would have liked us to be. I eventually ended it because I couldn't handle the hurt.

Stacy contacted me after her marriage ended. She did so under the pretense of getting my insight—a man's opinion. It turned out she wanted what Tanya and I had—a relationship without strings. I should have known myself better. No relationship works out that way when I'm involved. I fall in love too easily. It seems Stacy did, too.

She scrubbed the pan. "You and your mom have never had an adult conversation about your father."

"She won't talk about him."

"How do you know unless you ask?"

I rolled my eyes.

"So, you're going to let this thing stew."

"I'm not going to do that."

She cocked her head.

"I'll try not to do that."

"Why not go up to Metaline and poke around?"

I grunted, not bothering to hide my dissatisfaction with her plan.

She rinsed the pan. "You said the woman owned a used bookstore."

"That's right."

"Maybe you can get me something to read." Stacy raised an eyebrow. "You know what I like."

I stared at her.

"Don't consider it looking for your father—"

"He's not my—"

"Consider it buying me a gift." She smiled and passed me the sheet pan. "I like gifts, if you didn't know."

"So I've been told." I dragged the towel across the pan.

Stacy turned off the water. She dried her hands on a portion of the towel hanging below the pan. "And you know how I always show my appreciation when you buy me something." Her eyes sparkled with promises of carnal delights.

"I guess I could run up to Metaline tomorrow and check out a bookstore."

"Atta boy," she said. "Now remind me, who's not the boss of who?"

Stacy patted my butt once more as she left the kitchen.

Chapter 3

I awoke early the next morning without the help of an alarm. My watch said it was a couple of minutes after five. I slipped quietly from under the sheets.

Stacy continued to sleep while I dressed. She didn't try to encourage me to come back to bed. We had passed that point in our relationship where every moment held the promise of a tryst. We knew we would see the other again, so sleep was embraced without the fear of missed coupling. There was always later.

After closing the bedroom door, I retrieved Corporal. He slept in the house, but while the children were awake, he remained outside. Stacy was fearful the dog might hurt the kids, so I followed the rules. I assured her Corporal wouldn't touch them, but there's no getting past a mother's concerns regarding her offspring. As much as I loved the Shepherd, he remained on the other side of the sliding glass door until Ethan and Hailey went to sleep.

When I returned to my office, I put the dog in the backyard. I might shower and get a change of clothes at the house on Spofford, but it felt less like a home now.

After slipping into a clean T-shirt, a different pair of jeans, and a set of boots, I grabbed a coat and took the dog across the street for a game of ball. The sun was still down, but the park was bathed in a hazy yellow courtesy of pole lights. I wanted him to get a bit of exercise before I left.

I tossed the ball, and the dog sprinted away.

It was an eerie feeling, being in the park that early. No one else was there and only an occasional car drove by on Maxwell Street. We never played in the park at that time.

Corporal brought the gnarled tennis ball back. It was wet not only from his slobber, but from the dew. Droplets covered my boots. I tossed the ball again, but the dog didn't run. Instead, he growled at something behind me.

I turned and faced an approaching homeless man. A dark blanket was draped over his head, and he clutched it around his body. Dirt smeared his face, but the whites of his eyes shone brightly.

"Bum a five?" he asked.

"No."

I didn't sugar coat my answer with a white lie. Perhaps I could have said I didn't have any on me and that might have placated the man. However, the homeless traipsed through my neighborhood on a path from the river to downtown and back. They were an increasing plague in the city. If I encouraged them with handouts, they would return to this park. The homeless were like pigeons or mice—only worse.

Corporal snarled.

"The fuck is with your dog?" the man asked.

"He doesn't like strangers."

His eyes cut back to me. "I need money."

"No."

A hand slid from between the blanket. It clutched a knife. "Gimme some money."

My gun was at the house. I had stopped carrying it everywhere I went years ago. Right now, I regretted that decision. However, I still had my dog.

"Present Arms," I said.

Corporal barked wildly.

The man pointed the knife at the dog. "Stop!"

The dog continued to snap.

"I'll stab him!" he yelled.

A light flicked on across the street, then another.

The man sneered as his knife slowly disappeared behind the blanket.

"At ease," I said.

An immediate quiet descended over the neighborhood.

"You're lucky," the man said.

"You've confused me with someone else."

We stood there in the morning's darkness. A car raced toward downtown, probably someone late for work. They were followed by a patrol car with flashing lights.

The homeless man watched the cops leave the neighborhood. I never took my eyes off him.

His gaze returned to me. "Next time, I'm not asking. I'm just taking."

"The next time, I'm drawing my gun."

He shook his head. "Asshole." The guy slunk off into the darkness.

I waited until he was out of the park before eyeing the dog. "Get the ball."

Corporal stared at me.

"Get it."

The dog didn't move.

I motioned in the direction that I'd thrown it, but Corporal studied me like I was teaching him math.

"Let's go."

We headed off and the dog circled around me in bounding leaps. I didn't know where the ball was—it was still too dark. Corporal eventually alerted to it somehow, probably its scent. He ran and snatched it.

"No bragging," I said. "I helped you."

Corporal proudly wagged his tail.

"Whatever."

I didn't feel like throwing the ball anymore. We returned home, and I fixed us both breakfast. He got a bowl of kibbles, and I had a couple of eggs and some toast. Even though I didn't spend my nights there, I still kept a few staples. I read *The Spokesman-Review* while I ate.

Usually, I would have left the dog in the backyard for the day. Spring days were pleasant, and there was shade from a couple of trees for him to avoid the sun. I'd leave him a big bowl of water to drink throughout the day. However, the encounter with the homeless man bothered me. I didn't know what a person like that might do. Perhaps he hung around the park and watched us return home. Or maybe he would come back to the park and hear Corporal barking from the backyard. There were plenty of variables.

I wasn't normally a worrywart, but an ounce of prevention seemed a prudent measure.

When the dog and I finished eating, we both hopped into my truck.

Metaline was two hours north.

***

We made a couple of stops along the way. The first was to get gas. The second was to let the dog do his business at a rest stop. An elderly woman glowered at me as we walked back to the truck.

"You have to pick that up," she said, pointing in the direction we had come from. "It's the law."

I pulled the passenger door open for Corporal. "Okay."

The dog jumped inside, and I closed the door behind him.

The woman crossed her arms and waited. She stood at the front of a Toyota RAV4. A man with gray hair sat inside reading a book. He seemed untroubled by his wife's social activism.

"Well?" she asked.

"I've got a bag in my truck."

She cocked her head. "Well, go get it. I'll wait."

I walked around to the driver's side and climbed in. When the engine started, she shouted a word I'd heard several times recently.

I dropped the truck into gear and backed out of the stall.

***

Shortly after connecting with Highway 20 right before the town of Usk, we paralleled the Pend Oreille River north. The 20 turned west at the town of Tiger, but we kept north on Washington 31 and continued to run alongside the river.

I pulled into Metaline shortly after eight. A sign on the outskirts of town said the Canadian border was twelve miles away. I'd never been to Metaline before and, at first glance, it didn't look like much more than a one-road town. Washington 31 ran through its heart, and I didn't bother to get off.

Various political signs lined the edge of the highway. *McCain for President. Mitt '08. Vote Huckabee.* There was even one that just said *Rudy*. There wasn't a single sign for a democratic contender. Washington State leaned blue because of the population west of the Cascade Mountains. Everything east of the mountains was red— dark red.

Metaline had a fire department at its southern edge, and a U.S. Customs and Border Protection office near its center. By my second blink, I was through the town. I wondered if perhaps there might be more to Metaline, so I continued.

A little more than a mile up the way, I came to a bend and bridge into Metaline Falls. Highway 31 also cut through this town, but it seemed slightly more vibrant than its sister. I took a moment and wound through various neighborhoods before crossing back over the bridge.

Back in Metaline proper, I found a coffee shop across the highway from the border patrol office. I wanted a cup, but first went to find Daisy McLaughlin's bookstore.

Sturdy Goats Reading Company was on East Metaline Street. The city's original planners obviously weren't paid for their creativity in naming the town's roads. The bookstore was in a rundown house. An open sign hung in the window unlit. I stopped the truck and trotted up to the door. A computer-printed notice said the business wouldn't open until ten. I started back toward my truck.

A speed walker in her seventies hurried around the corner. She wore a pink tracksuit and white athletic shoes. A pink headband held her silver hair back. The woman's face tightened when we made eye contact.

"Good morning," I said as she neared.

"Don't bother." She picked up her pace as she passed.

"Have a nice day."

"Sickos," she muttered.

I watched her until she disappeared around the corner. She never looked back.

***

A Cup of Happiness sat just off Highway 31. Its small building didn't start life as a coffee house. More than likely it had been some sort of clinic, perhaps a small dentistry. The building's brick exterior had a medical shape and feel, and it didn't have a drive-thru like most coffee joints.

Its interior hid all indications of the structure's previous life. Hardwood covered the lobby floors, and the ceiling was painted black. Two fans sluggishly spun overheard while moody jazz played through unseen speakers. Behind the counter, a charming barista in her early thirties worked an espresso machine. She wore a blue T-shirt that read *Autumn Bloom 10k* and her jeans tightly hugged her thin hips. A sleeve of tattoos ran down her left arm.

I waited behind several customers, one of whom referred to the barista as Brooklyn. She cheerfully chatted with each customer as she filled their orders. It was pleasant banter, mostly harmless morning chatter, and everyone seemed to like the woman.

Several others sat in the lobby. They unhurriedly read newspapers or fiddled with cell phones. Conversation didn't happen away from the counter and that seemed just fine with everyone in attendance.

When it was my turn, Brooklyn smiled brightly as she wiped her hands with a ratty towel. "What're you feeling this morning?"

"Sixteen-ounce black coffee."

"Really testing me with that one."

My eyes cut to a nearby tray of baked goods. "And a bran muffin."

The barista looked over my shoulder. "That your dog outside?"

I followed her gaze through the window. Corporal sat in the passenger seat of my truck and watched an exiting customer head to their vehicle. "Yeah, he's mine."

"He's a handsome boy." She pulled a paper cup off a stack and filled it from a pumper. "I had a Shepherd once.

Best dog ever." Her eyebrows lifted as she looked back at me. "Passing through or visiting someone?"

"Visiting someone."

"Oh yeah? Who's that?"

I didn't see the harm in telling her. "Daisy McLaughlin."

She paused briefly before turning with my cup—a hitch in her stride. Brooklyn's smile faded, and she averted her eyes as she slid the coffee onto the counter. "Looking for a book?"

"No."

She didn't say anything. Instead, the barista lifted the clear plastic lid from the container of baked items.

"Something wrong?" I asked.

Brooklyn shook her head. She selected a muffin using a napkin in her hand and set it next to my coffee. When she stepped behind the cash register, her lips pursed. She still hadn't made eye contact since I'd told her who I was visiting. Brooklyn tapped several buttons and announced a total.

Her gaze remained down as I reached into my pocket. When she took my cash, she made change and closed the register with a thrust of her hip. She moved to another position and turned her back to me.

Our transaction was complete.

"Thank you," I said and pushed a dollar into the tip jar.

She raised a hand. "Have a nice day," she said to the wall.

***

I sat in an overstuffed chair and perused a copy of *The Newport Miner*. Someone had left it behind or the shop carried a subscription for its customers. I'd read the national news in *The Spokesman* back home, so I skipped it in *The Miner*. I skimmed the Metaline local news, but nothing caught my eye.

The *Opinion* section held my attention the longest. A local columnist prattled on about the upcoming presidential election. He made the case about how dangerous a Hillary Clinton presidency would be for national security. The writer made a similar case for a senatorial upstart named Barack Obama because of his inexperience. The author put his full support behind former Arkansas Governor Mike Huckabee and suggested the residents of Pend Oreille County do so as well. The governor would keep God in our country, the author argued. There was no mention of national security when it came to the Lord.

Now and then a door opened—another patron entering or leaving. When a shadow moved across my paper, I looked up.

A border patrol agent stood nearby and looked through the window. He was handsome, in his late thirties, with short dark hair and blue eyes. Thick biceps bulged against the short sleeves of his green uniform. A gun rode on his right hip and his name tag read *Young*.

"He thinks he's people."

I twisted in my seat. Corporal now sat behind the steering wheel of my truck.

Agent Young sipped from his coffee cup and let his eyes drop to the newspaper. "Mind if I take a gander at that when you're done?"

"Not a problem."

His jaw flexed, and his gaze returned outside. He didn't bother moving from his spot. His head swiveled as he took in the highway. "On your way to Canada?"

"No."

"From Canada?"

The barista wiped down the counter and didn't take any interest in either of us. At first, I suspected she said something to the border patrol agent, but now it wasn't looking that way. Young's gaze continued to sweep along Highway 31. He had the vibe of someone who felt his job gave him a certain leeway in life—that he could behave as a bully anytime, because the badge allowed him that authority.

I knew that type of man well. I had been one when I wore a badge.

Young's eyes fell to me as he waited for my answer.

"No," I said. "Just visiting."

"Family?"

It seemed strange for a border patrol agent to take such an interest in my activities. Once again, I looked toward the barista. She ignored our interaction and continued to wipe the back counter. Either Brooklyn didn't care about what was going on, or she had seen this behavior before from Agent Young. Maybe this happened often since the town was located so close to the Canadian border. Maybe this is what the agents were supposed to do.

I decided not to poke the bear. "I'm looking for a book," I said.

The border agent rubbed the coffee cup along the side of his face. "Only bookstore in town is the Sturdy Goat."

"That's the one I'm going to."

Brooklyn stopped cleaning. She turned and cocked her head. So, she had been listening.

"You're a reader?" Young asked.

"That's right." I closed the newspaper and held it so he could see the headline, but he didn't bother looking. Instead, he maintained eye contact as he rested his forearm on his gun.

"What book are you looking for?"

"Haven't decided."

"Uh-huh." He studied me. "Have you met Daisy before?"

I feigned ignorance. "That the owner?"

"Oh, yeah." The customs officer chuckled lasciviously. "Tell her Big Dog says hi."

Brooklyn rolled her eyes, then angrily threw her cleaning rag onto the counter. She walked into the back room.

Agent Young eyed the newspaper. "You done with that?"

I folded it in half and handed it to him.

The customs officer tapped my leg with the paper. "Good luck with the book."

"Thank you."

"And don't forget."

"Big Dog," I said.

He laughed. "That's right."

Young repeatedly slapped the paper against his leg as he left the coffee shop.

***

Metaline Riverfront Park sat at the north end of town. It appeared to serve as a regional boat launch into the Pend Oreille River. I let Corporal out of the truck, and we walked to a picnic bench.

The dog ran around and sniffed. I regretted not bringing a ball on the trip. There was no one else in the area and it would have been a nice place to play catch. I lay on top of a picnic table and let the morning sun warm my face while Corporal checked out the area. We had time to kill.

Perhaps I should have checked on the internet to see when the bookstore opened. I could have taken my time getting up here. Maybe I should have called Daisy and interviewed her over the phone.

Driving up to Metaline to speak with Daisy McLaughlin ran counter to my initial thoughts on her. Something was certainly off with the woman, but she held a strange allure. Add to it the mystery of Nick Gossett being my father and seeing her again in person didn't sound like a bad idea.

The interactions at the coffeehouse with the barista and border patrol agent lingered in my mind. The two obviously knew Daisy and had their own thoughts about her. It wasn't hard to determine what those feelings were.

I sat up and looked for the dog. Corporal sniffed near a tree. He seemed content, so I lay back on the table.

My thoughts drifted to my childhood. My friends had their fathers—either living with them or ones they visited every other weekend. My father's absence cheated me out of a sense of normalcy, and I blamed everyone for it—him, my mother, my friends. As I got older, I blamed God, too.

By the time I was a teenager, an absentee father was a badge of honor. I tossed that fact around whenever I got in trouble. Teachers and school administrators loved helping a kid with a sad story.

Potential girlfriends adored my runaway father story. I'd perfected it in high school and if a girl let me tell the whole spiel, it guaranteed me to score. "Oh, poor John," was often followed by my hand sliding up under a bra. My father never taught me how to throw a football, but he delivered a ticket to paradise.

At first, my father's absence wounded my mother, then she carried it like a cudgel. On bad days, I reminded her of the woman she'd been. *You look just like your father, Johnny.* She never talked about him. She refused to tell me anything other than he was a deadbeat, a loser, a liar. *He promised* was often followed by dead air. My mother never told me the promises my father failed to deliver. I only learned his name by seeing it on my birth certificate. He had a different last name than us, which confused me at first.

A grade school friend filled me in on the truth—he said I was a bastard. My mother said it wasn't true, she was a feminist and refused to conform to society's expectations that a woman had to take a man's last name. Therefore, she wasn't required to give her child the father's name, either. My mother changed her tune when I entered high school, though.

By then, she couldn't call me a bastard enough.

In moments of weakness, I dreamed about searching for and finding Gabriel T. Baldwin. He would confirm my suspicions that my mother kidnapped me, that she had whisked me away from my father in the dark of night. After we reconnected, my father would welcome me into his home. If that had happened, I could have left my angry mother behind to finish out my high school years.

Those were the foolish wishes of a child. I never searched for him, and he never came for me. When I finished high school, I no longer harbored fantasies about Gabriel Baldwin. If he didn't want me, then I didn't need him.

The dog trotted over and sat next to the table.

"Done?"

He panted.

"I'll take that as a yes."

I squinted against the sun as I checked my watch. It was a few minutes before ten.

Time to go.

Chapter 4

A brass bell dinged as I entered Sturdy Goats Reading Company.

Hazy morning sunshine shone through and around the front window's logo of a goat standing on a tower of books. The light splashed over faded paperbacks. Multicolored pendants hung from the ceiling and reflected rays of sunlight throughout the shop. The entire place smelled musty, as many old bookstores do. I moved deeper into the shop, the carpeted floor creaking with each step.

Four small stacks of hardback novels towered at the edge of the front counter. Several flat USPS boxes leaned against them, along with a roll of clear tape.

A woman's strained voice came through a heater vent above the counter. "No, he hasn't come home. Uh-huh. Three days."

Sturdy Goats Reading Company was in a large single-family home. Most of the first-floor walls had been removed and only a couple of support columns remained. Bookshelves lined the shop. A stairwell in the back went upstairs. It appeared there might have been a bathroom there, too.

"No family," the woman's voice drifted through the heater vent. "He doesn't own a car anymore. He borrows my truck if he wants to go anywhere. Because I drove it to the grocery store this morning."

I glanced out the window. My truck was the only one out front.

A gray cat sauntered down the stairs as if to investigate my presence. It neared me, turned a full circle before getting too close, then darted down an aisle of books labeled *Romance/Sci-Fi*. If I was looking for a book, that's an aisle I would never enter.

"Thank you," the woman said. "Yes. I'll be here."

A moment later, Daisy McLaughlin came down the stairs. She wore the same blue jeans and green Army jacket as yesterday, but her heavy metal half-shirt was different today. This one was faded gray and read *REO Speedwagon*. The chain link belt wrapped around her waist and the padlock was in place, but it seemed as if it might not have been as tight as the day before.

When Daisy neared the bottom of the stairs, she noticed me and stopped. Her eyes were red from crying.

"The police?" I asked.

She considered the cordless phone in her hand, then looked up toward the room she'd just left. "It's not polite to eavesdrop."

I motioned to the heater vent above me. "In case you didn't know."

"It's still not polite."

"Would you like me to leave?"

She approached the counter. "I was speaking with the sheriff's office. We don't have a police department."

"And they took a report?"

"They started one. They're going to send out a deputy."

"What made you change your mind about reporting him missing?"

"I didn't think you were interested, but it'd be nice if they showed some goddamned urgency." She tossed the phone onto the counter. "So why are you here?"

"To satisfy my curiosity." I lifted one of the hardbacks—Stieg Larsson's *The Girl with the Dragon Tattoo*.

"Is this a joke to you?" Daisy asked.

I flipped the book over. "No."

"Because my boyfriend is missing."

"Why did he think he was my father?"

Daisy set her hands on the counter. "Because he is."

I carefully placed the book back on the top of the stack. "How would he know?"

"A father knows."

I wondered about that. Would I know Erin existed if Maria hadn't told me? If I had never met her, would I be able to pick my daughter out of a crowd? I'd like to think I could, but was that a reality?

The gray cat briefly reappeared, then darted upstairs. Daisy watched him go. "Hagrid doesn't like people." She turned back to me. "How did you find me?"

I cocked my head. "It's my job."

"Right."

"I stopped for a coffee on the way in."

"And?"

"Seems like a few people know you."

"It's a small town. What did you expect?"

"Big Dog says hi."

"Macon." Her eyes narrowed. "He say anything else?"

"I take it you guys have history."

"Old friend." She grabbed the padlock and twisted it. It took a couple of extra turns today, but the chain tightened around her waist, and she grimaced.

I thought about the barista's reaction to my mention of Daisy but kept it to myself. Brooklyn got upset when Macon mentioned her name, too. Perhaps the barista had also been involved with the border agent. Maybe it was a love triangle. Like Daisy said, it was a small town.

Daisy studied me as she kept pressure on the padlock. Her knuckles whitened as her fingers reddened.

"Did Big Dog know about you and Nick?"

"Please don't call him that." Her hand shook on the padlock and the grimace worsened.

"Everything all right?"

Daisy released her grip and her expression relaxed. "Sorry."

"You okay?"

"I'm fine."

"So, Macon?"

Daisy looked down. "He and his friends didn't like Nick."

"His friends? Are they on the border patrol, too?"

She nodded.

"Why didn't they like Nick?"

Daisy twisted the lock again and pain registered in her face. "Because he was my boyfriend."

"What's with the—" I motioned toward the padlock.

Her hand relaxed. "It's a metal thing." Daisy flashed the devil's horns with her other hand.

"You keep twisting it."

"I'm nervous."

"Why are you nervous?"

"My boyfriend is missing, and a detective just showed up at my business."

"You asked for help."

"You said no."

I shrugged. "I changed my mind."

"Because he's your father?"

"He's not my father."

Daisy studied me for a moment. "I need to show you something." She reached under the counter and grabbed a set of keys. "It's at my house."

She headed to the front window and hung a sign that read Back in ten minutes. A phone number was below the sign. "We'll be gone longer than that, but no one ever knows when I left."

We stepped onto the front porch. While Daisy locked the house, I noticed Corporal sitting in the cab watching me.

Down the street, a red Honda parked roadside facing us. A man with silver hair was in the driver's seat. His hand was out the window, resting on the rearview mirror, a cigarette dangling between two fingers. The front license plate read *Beautiful British Columbia*.

"You know that guy?" I asked.

Daisy looked in the Honda's direction. "Never seen him before, but the Canucks come down here all the time. Don't worry about it." She bounded down the steps. "My house is around the block."

I followed her.

She paused near my truck. "That your dog? Bring him. He can play in my yard."

***

We walked southbound and Corporal trotted by my side.

"Thanks for making the trip," she said.

I glanced over my shoulder.

"What're you looking for?" she asked.

The guy sitting in the red Honda bothered me, but I didn't want to worry needlessly if it was just paranoia. "Street signs," I said.

"Is that a detective habit? Trying to orient yourself?" She swooped her arm along the road's path. "This is Main Avenue. We were just on Metaline Street." She pointed to the right. "That's Spokane Street." She motioned ahead. "And I live on Pend Oreille."

To the east was the Pend Oreille River.

The lack of creativity from the town's founders astounded me. I pointed toward the road running along the water. "What's the name of that street?"

"Riverside Drive."

"Of course it is."

With all the words available to the original planners of Metaline, they named the streets after their town, their river, and the largest municipality to the south. How hard was it to name city streets? Since Metaline was in the Pacific Northwest, the town's founders could have honored the wildlife by naming streets Grizzly, Black Bear, Gray Wolf, and Jack Rabbit.

Salmon Lane would have been a much cooler name for the road along the Pend Oreille River than Riverside Drive. Although, I had no idea if salmon actually ran in the river. Trout or Sockeye, then. And if none of those fish were in the water, then the town's founders could have named it Mountain Lion Lane and skipped the whole mess. It would still have been better than Riverside Drive.

And that was just animals. The town's planners had other options like flowers, trees, or Greek heroes from which to choose. The list was endless.

"Something wrong with the name?" Daisy asked.

I shook my head. Maybe she loved the town and my shitting on their street names wouldn't do me any good.

"We're here," she said.

Her Chevy pickup was parked along the property line. As she passed it, she patted its hood. "Hey, baby."

Daisy trotted toward the house, then bounded a set of rickety stairs to a porch. The extra links on her chain belt swung wildly.

Her Craftsman-style home was painted white with green accents. Several roof shingles had popped, and others were curling. The railing around the left side of the porch had twisted and fallen. A wood fence ran the perimeter of the small backyard. Its white paint was mostly flaked off and revealed sun-faded wood underneath.

She removed a set of keys from her jacket pocket and unlocked the door.

Corporal sat next to me, and I scratched behind his ear. "I thought people in small towns never locked their houses."

"In the fifties, maybe." Her eyes cut to me. "Too many people drive through here daily not to be careful. You never know who might swing through the neighborhood looking to steal something." Daisy pointed to a neighbor's house. "A couple days ago, my neighbor ran off some guy snooping around his house."

I straightened. "Anyone ever snoop around your house?"

"Not that I know of. Besides, what do I have they'd want? Books?" She pushed open the door and called, "Nick? Nick?" After a moment, she turned toward me. Sadness registered on her face. "Bring your dog if you want. He won't hurt anything."

Daisy opened the curtains, and sunlight flooded through the windows. Dust particles fluttered about, as did the stale stench of marijuana. "Don't mind the mess."

"At ease," I said to Corporal, and he sat near the door.

"Want some coffee?" She headed off toward the kitchen without waiting for my reply.

My gaze drifted about the living room. The home's exterior was indicative of its interior. Everything appeared heavily worn, as if it might have been purchased from a local thrift store. The pink couch seemed to have been made sometime in the sixties. Dark wood was inlaid into its arms and its cushions were threadbare. There were two chairs, both wing backs, of mismatched styles. Their excessive wear made them fit this room. A lamp with a dented shade and dangling crystals sat on a wooden end table. Books were stacked everywhere.

Daisy clanked around in the other room.

A bong and lighter sat on the coffee table next to a dog-eared copy of Stephen King's *The Stand*. There was no baggie to be found.

In the corner stood a stereo system and several crates of vinyl albums. Large speakers stood at opposite ends of the room. I flipped through the albums. There were bands like Montrose, Black Sabbath, and KISS. I'd heard of KISS and Black Sabbath, of course, but it wasn't my kind of music. I pushed the albums back into place. Since Daisy and I were roughly the same age, the music was from a generation before us.

I liked older soul and funk music, so perhaps she carried an affinity for classics, too. Music touched everyone differently. Why couldn't her preference be older rock and roll?

Daisy returned to the room and slipped off her Army jacket to reveal her thin frame. She dropped onto the couch. "Do you smoke?"

I assumed she wasn't talking about cigarettes. Even if she was, I had stopped a while back. "No."

Daisy dug into one of the jacket's pockets and pulled out a plastic baggie. She removed a pinch of marijuana and packed the bong's bowl. Once she was ready, she secured the baggie and returned it to the jacket. She grabbed the lighter and lifted the bong to her lips. Her eyes met mine.

"You've got cop's eyes," she said. "Judging eyes."

"I'm not judging."

Daisy held my gaze while she inhaled deeply. When she finished, she put the bong down. She moved her jaw around but didn't let any air out. Slowly, smoke escaped through her nostrils. Eventually, she exhaled.

"Feel better?" I asked.

"See?" She smiled, but it contained no joy. "You *were* judging." She straightened and rolled her neck. "All right. What do you want to know?"

"Are you from Metaline?"

Daisy motioned toward the highway. "Born and raised in Colville. Married too young. Divorced too late. Got into some trouble after that. How's that?"

"That trouble you got into. Was it drugs?"

Her thumb rubbed the padlock. "It's not polite to ask."

"Trying to get the lay of the land."

She grabbed the bong once more. "You must have been a good cop with those eyes." Her lighter flashed, and she inhaled. Smoke escaped from her mouth as she spoke. "Cannabis voyeurism. Ever hear of that? Me neither." She set the bong and lighter back on the coffee table. "Where was I?"

"Trouble in Colville."

"Right." Daisy rolled her hand. "Married, divorced, trouble. The story of every nice girl." Her lip curled. "I embarrassed my family. My mom and dad were sort of muckety-mucks. Big fish in a small pond, as some say. They tried to get me to settle down. When that didn't work, they helped me move here, so I could start over."

"Why not move to Spokane?"

"Big city, bigger problems." She absently tugged on the length of chain. "Metaline seemed a safer bet."

"What made you open a bookstore?"

"It was for sale. I saw an ad in the paper. I always liked to read and thought owning a business would be great. The lady who sold it gave us a deal."

I glanced around the living room.

"My parents helped with the house, too." She cocked her head. "That's what you were wondering, weren't you?"

I was.

"My dad was always smart with money." She sniffed dismissively. "Mom called him cheap. They inherited a bunch of money after my grandmother died—timberland money—and used it to help me. I've got a trust fund set up. It's not a lot, but it helps cover most of my expenses. My parents sold their house and moved to Arizona to beat the snow."

"But you stayed."

"They didn't want me to follow them." Hurt flooded her eyes, and she looked away. "Didn't matter 'cause I like the area. Besides, if I went anywhere, I'd always be there."

No matter where you go, there you are. I heard that in a movie once. We can't outrun ourselves, I thought. I tried it once. It worked out badly.

"How did you and Nick meet?" I asked.

"Your father—"

I held up a hand to interrupt her. "Nick."

Daisy kicked off her boots and brought her legs up onto the couch. She leaned her head against an armrest. "He came into the store. He wasn't looking for anything in particular, but he prefers science fiction. What about you?"

I ignored her question. "Is Nick from Metaline?"

"His car broke down outside town."

"And he came in for a book?"

"It was going to take a couple of days for the shop to fix his car since they had to order a part out of Colville. We're not exactly Spokane, so it's not like our mechanic has everything in stock. Since it happened before the weekend…" Daisy let her thought trail off.

"Why was Nick visiting Metaline?"

She looked at the ceiling. "He was exploring to see if it was somewhere he might want to live."

"What was he really doing here?"

Her head snapped back to me. "I just told you."

It still felt like a lie, but now she was indignant about it. Whatever reason Nick had to come to Metaline, it wasn't innocent.

"How old is Nick?" I asked.

"Sixty-two."

If Nicholas Gossett was my father, he would have been roughly twenty-three when I was born. Maybe twenty-two when he and my mother met. I still wasn't buying the story, but the math worked. There was a hell of an age difference between Nick and Daisy.

"So, Nick walked into your store, and you took up with him?" I asked.

Daisy coughed several times. She sat upright to get control of herself and put her bare feet on the coffee table. "I like to fuck more than the next girl, but even I'm not that bad."

If her words were meant to shock, they didn't. However, could that be why the barista eyed me with disdain? Was a rumor about Daisy's sexual activities running through the small town?

"You're judging me again," she said.

"It's not intentional."

She reached for the bong and lighter. "All you cops do it."

"I'm not a cop."

"Whatever." A flame burst from her lighter and she pressed the bong to her lips. Daisy inhaled deeply and held her breath for a moment. When she finally spoke, smoke drifted from her lips. "You were a cop, and that still counts. Geez, I need to get some better weed."

I cocked my head. "What'd you say?"

Daisy studied the bong. "I need to get some better weed."

"The other comment."

She shrugged. "What can I say? I know cops better than I should. You've still got the eyes."

"You said I was a cop."

"I used to hate the police. I think that all changed after my husband got arrested for smacking me around."

I snapped my fingers to focus her attention, but she continued to roll with her story.

"After that, I had these weird fantasies about them cops." She looked down the bong's tube. "Not weird *weird*, you know? But like weird *good*. Nice, I mean. The cops were buff and in tight uniforms, which I thought was super hot." She shook her head and set the bong down. "Maybe the weed's not as bad as I thought."

"How'd you know I used to be a cop?"

Daisy fell back onto the couch. Her thumb absently rubbed the padlock laying on her lower belly. "All those head trips probably helped me get out of that toxic marriage. My husband was a controlling son-of-a-bitch, and I didn't think I'd ever get free. So those fantasies helped in a strange way, but I'm sure they've led to a string of bad decisions. Like monumentally stupid. Don't get me wrong, there was some great sex involved, but in the end, what did I have? Nothing."

I stared at her.

Her brow furrowed. "You're judging me again."

"How did you know I used to be a cop?"

"Your dad told me."

"He's not my father."

Daisy waved her hand. "Fine. Nick told me."

"How would he know?"

Her hand dropped onto her leg. "It was in his scrapbook."

***

Daisy led me into a back room. Boxes of books sat on a twin-size bed. A dresser contained various framed photographs. All of them appeared to be of Daisy when she was younger with people that I suspected to be family.

"Do you have a photograph of Nick?"

She shook her head. "He dislikes his picture taken, but there's this." Daisy pulled open the top dresser drawer and removed a folded copy of *The Newport Miner*. She handed it to me.

On the front page was a picture of a two-vehicle collision along Washington 31. Standing near two officers was a man with gray hair and dark eyes. There was blood on his shirt, and he stared off into the distance. I checked the newspaper's date—it was from one week prior.

Underneath the photograph was a small blurb. *Nick Grossett helps some youths involved in a fatal collision on Highway 31 yesterday.*

"They misspelled his name," Daisy said, "but that's him."

And that's why it didn't pop up in my internet search. I searched for a resemblance in our faces but didn't see any. However, it was a newspaper, and Nick's face was turned. To be honest, I didn't want there to be any resemblance.

Daisy tapped the edge of the paper. "Your father—"

I looked up.

"He stopped to help the kids involved in that accident. It happened right outside town. The driver of the truck—" Daisy tapped the picture. "—had a heart attack and died. He swerved into oncoming traffic and collided with a car full of high school students. Nick was out for a run—"

"He runs?"

She nodded. "Not far, but he's working off the years of drinking and smoking."

"How long has he been clean?"

"About six months. He said he's getting too old to abuse his body like that. Plus, he wants to be around a while longer. For me."

I considered Nick and Daisy again. "Twenty years is a big difference in a relationship."

"He's nice to me. That goes a long way after the battle I've had."

"He's a regular boy scout."

Her expression hardened. "Don't talk about him that way. You don't even know him."

"He's clean but doesn't care you smoke weed?"

"He's no prude."

It was a jab at how I watched her with the bong. A part of me wanted to defend myself and say I didn't care what she did, that I knew growers and dealers. She could smoke weed until her heart was content. How would that help in this moment?

"Can I keep this?" I held up the paper.

Her eyes flicked to the newspaper. "It's my only copy."

"I'd like to get a scan of the picture."

She took the paper. "I'll make a copy. I have a scanner at the bookstore."

"You mentioned something about a scrapbook?"

"That's what I call it, but it's not really."

Daisy tossed the newspaper on the dresser, then headed toward the closet. "He doesn't have a lot of stuff, but he has this." She pulled a manila folder from the top shelf. "He showed me this one time. That's how I knew about you."

"What is it?"

"It's your life." Daisy flopped the folder onto one of the opened boxes of books. "Look."

Inside were old newspaper clippings, printed articles, and yellowing photographs. On the left flap were a variety of notes in various colors of ink and pencil. Some had dates associated with them. 1997. 1999. 2002.

I pointed to the entries. "Did Nick explain these?"

She shook her head. "Nope."

I couldn't make heads or tails of his notes and the associated years, so I gave up trying. I grabbed the grainy pictures and studied them. There were seven, and they were all small and square. I hadn't seen any like them in some time.

The woman in each picture was my mother, albeit many years younger and far less worried about her social status. In some photographs, she wore flared jeans and a billowing orange shirt. In the others, she sported a red shirt and white pants. Her long hair fell to the middle of her back. My mother was a beautiful woman when she was younger.

In each picture, she held a swaddled baby. Unless she gave another child up for adoption, that child was me.

Daisy's house phone rang, and she left the room.

I started to set the pictures down but studied them once more. They were all taken around a similar apartment building. My mother never looked toward the photographer. Whoever had taken the pictures was far enough away not to be noticed.

If Nick Gossett was my father, why didn't he approach my mother? And why were there only two days of photographs? I assumed two days because of the two outfits she wore. Perhaps she wore the same clothes over multiple days. Or she could have switched clothes on the same day, but seven photographs over two separate days seemed like a safe bet. Why were these all Nicholas Gossett had?

Daisy's voice filtered into the room. "Okay, it'll only be a minute. I'll be right there. Thank you for your understanding."

I set the photographs down and picked up the articles.

There was a newspaper wedding announcement for Carol Cutler to Vance Mallory. It showed a smiling picture of my mother and her husband. The clipping mentioned their private ceremony on the San Juan Islands. The wedding date was written in red ink in the upper corner.

Another newspaper clipping announced the latest Seattle Police Department recruits to graduate from the academy. I was pictured with eleven others. My name was underlined in blue ink and the date was written in the upper corner.

Daisy returned to the room. "We need to go back to the shop. One of my regulars from Canada just stopped in. We can take the scrapbook with us."

I shuffled everything back into the folder.

"Now that you've seen his stuff…"

I expected her to ask if I now thought Nicholas Gossett was my father. I wasn't ready to answer that.

"If Nick took off, you know, like he got tired of me or something—" She pointed to the file. "Don't you think he would have taken his scrapbook with him?"

I closed the file and held it with both hands. "Yeah," I said. "I think he would have."

She frowned. "Thank you for saying that. I was starting to think I was going crazy."

***

Corporal and I sat in my truck while Daisy dealt with her Canadian customer.

There were moments when I missed smoking; this was one of them. I had snacks in the truck for stakeouts, but a cigarette provided a tool for decompression that peanuts didn't. Smoking was psychological as much as it was physical. Hell, it was probably symbolic, too.

The act of pulling out a cigarette, lighting it up, and that first long inhale allowed for a mental pause. An interruption in one's intellectual spiral, so to speak. However, that was probably the addiction speaking, hoping I'd scamper off to the store and buy a pack to satiate a silly desire for a symbolic pause.

I checked the rearview mirror for signs of the red Honda. It was nowhere to be seen. Perhaps I was worried for nothing. I opened the folder and returned to the articles.

A small article titled *Veteran Officer Terminated for Improper Conduct* caught my eye. It appeared to have been printed from *The Seattle Post-Intelligencer*'s website. I carefully read the piece since I'd never seen it before. It contained the Seattle Police Department's statement about my firing. The chief was quoted as saying, "John Cutler's conduct was detrimental to the organization. His actions were not reflective of who we are or how we want to be seen in the eyes of the community."

That was a horrible remark to see attached to my name. I read it aloud for the dog to hear.

"What do you think?" I asked Corporal.

He yawned.

"I don't know," I said. "Stings worse than that."

There was also a quote from the union president. "At this time, we do not expect to challenge Mr. Cutler's termination."

No shit, I thought. I ran from Seattle with my tail between my legs. Why would the union waste any effort or money on a guy detrimental to the department? Especially one who wasn't willing to stand and fight?

There were other articles printed from the internet. One *Seattle Times* piece showed my name pursuant to the death of a councilwoman and her husband. A number of years ago, I returned to Seattle to help a former lover and wound up investigating her murder.

Several articles were from *The Spokesman-Review*. My name popped up in stories related to cases I'd been involved with as a private investigator.

One *Seattle Times* article from earlier this year concerned a Democratic fundraiser held in Seattle. Carol Mallory was quoted as saying "this is the most important election of our lifetime." My mother was prone to hyperbole.

Unfortunately, the printouts told me little about Nicholas Gossett except he monitored my mother and me. Had all the articles come from physical newspapers like my mother's wedding announcement and my graduation photograph, then I could imagine Nick was in the Seattle area when those events occurred.

My mother married while I was in the academy, so the two events were linked in time. Most of the articles came from the internet. Nick could have read those from anywhere in the world, at any time.

I closed the file and set it on the dashboard. I reconsidered the photographs of my mother and me.

Assuming Nick had taken them, was he really my father? Is that why he followed us around via the internet? If that was the case, who the hell was Gabriel T. Baldwin, the man listed on my birth certificate?

As much as I didn't want to, I needed to call my mom. I pulled out my cell phone and flipped it open. My mother's phone rang several times and eventually went to voice mail. I didn't leave a message. Either she would see I called, or I would call her again later.

I was about to put my phone away but decided to text my daughter. It was her preferred method of communication, but repeatedly tapping various numbers to get letters to pop up was a pain in my ass. I was getting better at it, but I missed the days when my daughter enjoyed talking to me.

I finished the message and hit send. THINKING OF YOU. LOVE YOU - DAD.

She should be in school, so I didn't expect a reply.

LUV U came almost immediately.

Patiently, I replied, AREN'T YOU IN CLASS?

Y.

WHY ARE YOU TEXTING ME THEN?

BORED.

My thumb bounced around the keyboard. I made repeated corrections before I sent my next message. WELL, I DIDN'T MEAN TO INTERRUPT YOU. HAVE A GOOD DAY.

U TYPE 2 MUCH. LOL.

I snapped my phone closed.

Motion in the rearview mirror caught my eye. A patrol car pulled onto Metaline Street and crept up behind my truck. Instinctively, I put my hands on the steering wheel. My Glock was in the glove compartment.

Corporal sat upright and looked out the back window.

A deputy stepped out of the car and adjusted his duty belt. He was a bald man with wraparound sunglasses. His tan and green uniform fit snuggly. He silently closed his door and stepped toward the front of the car.

He noticed Corporal and me sitting in the truck and paused. His gaze flicked to the license plate before proceeding toward the bookstore. As he walked, he keyed his microphone.

"That's right," I muttered. "Run the plate."

The dog shifted in his seat to watch the deputy ascend the steps to the bookstore.

Chapter 5

I took the dog for a walk. We left the truck in front of the bookstore, so Daisy would know I intended to return.

Corporal and I headed toward the appropriately named Riverside Drive, then walked north for a couple of blocks. Two properties impeded our route along the river since they ran all the way to the water.

Wealthy locals, I thought. Always ruining it for everyone else.

The dog and I meandered around those properties to Main Street and followed it until Linton which also dead-ended into the river because another property went to the water. Riverside Drive, while promisingly named, was short and disappointing.

We returned to Riverfront Park, and I let the dog off his leash. Corporal bolted away. Like before, no one else was there.

My phone rang, and I pulled it from my pocket. It was my mother.

It sounded noisy wherever she was. "Is everything okay?" she asked.

"Yes—"

"I was surprised to see you called." Other voices in the background of wherever she was made it hard to hear. I covered my open ear with my hand. "Is everything okay?" she asked.

"I want to ask about my father."

She sighed. "Johnny." The little happiness in her voice faded. "I don't have time for this nonsense. I'm at an executive meeting, and we just took a break."

"This is important."

"Oh hi, Helen," my mother said away from the phone. "You're looking so much better. Yes, of course. Give me just a moment and I'll be right over. Yes, just a moment, dear."

Across the way, Corporal darted about with his nose to the ground.

My mother returned to the phone. "Nothing is ever important when it comes to that man. I must go."

"Hold on," I said.

"Not now."

The call abruptly ended, and I snapped the phone closed. "That was helpful."

Corporal trotted over. I clipped a leash to his collar, and we headed back to the bookstore.

Daisy McLaughlin walked with the deputy along South Main Street. It appeared as if they might be returning from her house. They watched Corporal and me approach from the opposite direction. The cop asked Daisy something, and she nodded. The length of chain from her belt bounced on her leg.

Outside Sturdy Goats Reading Company, I put the dog inside my truck and joined the two. They stood on the bookstore's small lawn.

The deputy's silver name tag read *Wolfe*. He was roughly forty years old, and he wore his sunglasses pushed on top of his bald head. Wolfe held a notebook and pen in his left hand but hooked both thumbs over the top his duty belt. The deputy's relaxed stance tried to affect a sense of nonchalance, but his watchful eyes said something different.

Daisy motioned toward me. "This is John Cutler."

I nodded.

"Deputy Wolfe," he said.

He didn't bother to offer his hand, and neither did I.

His gaze returned to Daisy. "Has Mr. Gossett exhibited any signs of confusion lately?"

"Like Alzheimer's?"

The deputy shrugged. "Possibly. Maybe he had an adverse reaction to medication. Was he taking anything?"

"No. Nothing. He didn't have any food allergies either."

Wolfe casually jotted something on his pad. When he looked up, he asked, "You're sure he isn't drinking?"

Daisy's face darkened. "I already said he wasn't."

Wolfe's attention returned to his notepad. "That's what happens most often in cases like this."

"He isn't," she said emphatically.

The deputy looked up and his eyes cut to me. "Recovering addicts slip, and they go missing. We see it all the time."

"That's not what's going on here," Daisy said. She crossed her arms. "I'm telling you, something happened to him."

"Okay." The deputy flipped back through his notes. "To confirm, he's been gone four days now, and he doesn't have any family to stay with."

She shook her head.

"No friends locally?"

"Not really. I already checked with everyone I know."

"What about a car?"

"He sold it to the mechanic shop. It was going to cost too much to fix."

Deputy Wolfe tapped his notebook with his pen. "You two didn't fight?"

"Nick and I never argue. Not even about trivial shit."

The deputy waved toward the highway. "People hitch up and down Thirty-one."

Daisy's face reddened. "He's not hitching."

"Has he seemed depressed?"

"He's not depressed."

"Maybe he needed to get away to clear his head."

"For four fucking days?" Daisy blurted.

The deputy shrugged.

"If he wanted out," she continued, "he would have told me. Why won't you believe something bad happened?"

Wolfe looked at me with raised eyebrows. "There's no evidence of foul play."

"Except the man is missing," I said.

The deputy's brow furrowed, and he returned his attention to Daisy. "I'll file the report."

"He would have taken his stuff," she said.

Wolfe smirked. "Not necessarily. Depressed people make irrational decisions."

"I swear. He wasn't depressed."

The deputy handed her a tan card. "That's your report number. I'll enter his information into the system and write a report. We'll start looking for him." He headed toward his car.

Daisy shook her head. "I'm not sure why I got my hopes up they'd help."

"You're human."

We stayed on the lawn as Deputy Wolfe drove away.

"The situation would have been different," I said, "if this was a kid or an elderly person with dementia. Or somebody he felt was important. I'm sure the deputy would have swung into action."

"Why are you defending him?"

I smiled softly. "I'm not. I'm trying to think this through critically."

"And I'm not?"

I motioned in the direction the deputy had driven. "He's probably dealt with a few missing adults in his career. Besides the dementia cases, what he's probably found are wives who left because of abusive husbands, or husbands who split for younger girlfriends."

Daisy crossed her arms. "I'm the only younger girlfriend Nick has."

"What I'm saying is, Deputy Wolfe probably has not had a successful history with missing person calls. Had he, he might have handled this one differently."

"Maybe." She headed toward the bookstore, dragging the heels of her combat boots as she went. "Want some coffee?"

"Yeah, but I'm going to grab Nick's file from the truck. You said you had a scanner in your office?"

She paused at the front door and looked back. "Bring it in."

Daisy disappeared into the bookstore.

***

Daisy set *The Newport Miner* on the scanner and closed the lid, then pressed Start. The machine whirred to life. When she straightened, she bumped into me. "You want this one printed too, right?"

"If you don't mind. The others can just be scanned."

"What about the photos?"

"Scan those, too."

We were in the cramped upstairs office of her bookstore. In most homes, it would be considered a child's room, but Daisy had a large desk and several bookcases. There were multiple boxes of paperbacks. An eclectic mix of posters hung on the walls. There was hardly any room for two adults to stand. We'd already bumped into each other twice. It seemed several degrees warmer upstairs.

Daisy watched the thin bright light proceed across the scanner. She absently tugged and twisted the padlock hanging below her exposed belly button. Her jeans bunched underneath the metal links.

"Mind if I ask a question?" My voice sounded strange.

Her eyes moved to me, but she quickly noticed my focus was on her hand. She stopped pulling on the lock. She suddenly seemed embarrassed by the attention. "I'm sorry."

"For what?"

"Nothing." She dismissively waved a hand. "It's a reminder."

The scanner stopped and reset. Daisy's hands shook as she settled them on the keyboard. She typed something, backspaced to correct an error, then hit Enter. When she straightened, she lifted the machine's lid and removed the newspaper. She folded it and carefully set it aside.

She opened the manila folder and removed the top article. It slipped from her fingers and fluttered to the floor. Daisy hurriedly picked it up and set it on the scanner. Her hand trembled as she reached for the mouse. The scanning process started anew.

"Everything okay?" I asked.

"Yeah, sure." She didn't look at me. Instead, she pulled the folded Newport Miner closer to her. With her free hand, she grabbed the padlock. "It reminds me I'm in a committed relationship."

"You need that?"

"More than you know." Her eyes shifted to me, and her cheeks flushed. The look she had yesterday was back. The lioness once again watching the zookeeper, but it felt like the cage door was open, and no safe measures lay between the two of us.

My pulse raced and my mouth went dry. I had no business having the thoughts I did. Not only was she another man's woman, but I was in a committed relationship. I'd like to think her being a client mattered, but I'd already violated that unspoken rule before.

I should have turned and left immediately, but I didn't. Instead, I stared into the predator's gaze and asked, "Did Nick insist on that getup?"

"I did." Daisy's knuckles whitened as she clutched the padlock. The chain tightened around her waist. She didn't wince. Instead, her eyes narrowed. The pain was enjoyment now. "It's hot up here." Her voice was a throaty rasp. "You should probably wait outside."

Something in the way she spoke broke my spell. Not because it wasn't sexy nor because I wanted something to happen. Both of which were true. Instead, Daisy's voice sounded like a woman perilously clinging to her last hope.

I left the office and headed down the stairs.

***

I freed Corporal from the truck. He bounded off the seat and waited for a command.

"Fall out," I said.

He wandered into the bookstore's yard and peed on the first bush he found.

I scanned the neighborhood but didn't see the red Honda. Maybe I was worried for nothing. Perhaps I wanted someone nefarious to jump out of the shadows and scare me. That way, I had something to hit. The idea of a runaway father returning after nearly forty years was ludicrous. It was the stuff of soap operas and bad Lifetime movies. I needed my father like I needed a venereal disease.

Daisy raced back into my thoughts, and I turned to the bookstore with an expectation she would step out at any moment and laugh. A part of me expected her to say her unbalanced act upstairs was a joke, that she was putting me on. I knew it wasn't.

There was something wrong inside her, and she'd developed an unconventional way to contain it. I'd heard of self-help behavioral treatments before. Some smokers snapped rubber bands on their wrists. Anxiety sufferers held ice cubes. Punching pillows and ripping magazines were even supposed to be options.

Daisy had a strange magnetism. She was attractive, but not beautiful. Her clothing downplayed her attributes. She certainly wasn't refined. Yet, in the confines of that small upstairs office, something animalistic emanated from her.

Nothing good would have occurred if I had stayed. I had too many positive parts of my life to risk doing something so selfish and shortsighted. Stacy Mathers came immediately to mind. My business came second, and my self-respect came a distant third.

I pulled out my cell phone and called Stacy. She answered on the second ring.

"Hey," she whispered. She wasn't supposed to get personal calls at work. "How's it going?"

"Not so bad."

"You sound strange."

"I'm fine. Just outside."

"Any luck?"

"None."

I leaned my back against the truck and stared at the bookstore. Daisy's predatory gaze returned to my thoughts. A part of me wished I hadn't left the upper room. I wanted to know what might have happened if I provoked the lioness.

Stacy interrupted my self-destructive memories. "What do you think?"

I kicked a tire with my heel. "Nick's missing all right."

"Not that. Is he your dad?"

Dad, I thought. No man would ever be my dad, but that wasn't a conversation for now. She was at work, and I was in Metaline with Daisy McLaughlin.

"I don't know," I said. "There's a chance we might be related."

"For real?" She didn't hide her excitement. "You found something?"

"I don't know what it means." I waved my free hand. "I'm looking into it."

The door to the bookstore opened and Daisy exited. She paused at the door and held up a CD and the newspaper.

"When will you be home?" Stacy asked.

"Tonight."

"See you for dinner?"

"Hard to tell."

"Listen," Stacy said. It sounded like she had rustled some papers. "I gotta go. Be careful, all right?"

"I will."

Daisy started down the steps and stopped on the sidewalk. Corporal trotted over, and she petted his head.

"Hey," I said before Stacy could end the call.

"Yeah?"

"I love you." I had said the words to Stacy before, but I didn't usually say them on the phone. This time they were filled with guilt and said more as reminder not to do something foolish.

"You sure you're okay?" Stacy asked.

"Yeah."

"Well, I love you, too," Stacy said. "Everything will work out okay. Drive safe."

I closed the phone and slipped it into my pocket.

Daisy approached. She stopped several feet away. "Wife?"

"Girlfriend. Just checking in."

She extended both hands, and I took the CD and the newspaper.

"I thought about it," she said. "You should have the paper. It's more important for what you're doing."

"Thank you."

She glanced back at the house. "I'm sorry about upstairs."

"No apologies necessary."

"The tight confines and the heat confused me."

"You're an addict."

Daisy shrugged a single shoulder. "The proper term is problematic sexual behavior."

I held my initial comment. Gary Ackerman would have accused me of having the same affliction. Instead, I motioned toward the padlock. "I've never heard of anyone doing that as a way to control it."

"It's my own invention."

"How's it working?"

"It's supposed to slow me down." She patted her front pocket where I imagined a key was. "Give me a moment and make me think about what I'm about to do, but if I really wanted, I can get my pants off without much struggle."

Her eyes challenged mine, and my pulse quickened again.

Daisy bowed her head and broke our gaze. "Don't ask how I know. I guess the system isn't perfect."

I looked around the town. It was too small of a community to carry a problem like hers.

"When Nick was with me, there wasn't an issue. Not really." Daisy looked up and her eyes flared with the admission. "He and I are open about what I'm dealing with. Talking helps. Besides, he's the beneficiary."

"He's got his own addiction, right?"

"We help each other."

I didn't know much about addiction counseling, but that didn't seem right. "Isn't there some rule about getting involved with another addict?"

"We made allowances since I don't drink and that's what he does." She looked away. "Or did."

"Was there a group in town Nick went to?"

Daisy waggled her hand. "There's one in Metaline Falls." She pointed north. "Around the bend. He went once a week."

"Did he have a sponsor?"

"He didn't want one."

"Is that normal?"

"I don't know. Nick's different." She crossed her arms.

"Did he mention anyone from the group? Like a friend?"

"They're not supposed to talk about anyone. Privacy and all. Nick respects people's privacy. Theirs. Mine. He said if I ever slipped..." She left the thought unfinished, but I imagined what Nick had told her.

"When does his group meet?" I asked.

"Every morning at seven over at the VFW."

"Are they open now?" I asked.

"You a member or something?"

"Hey," I called to the dog. "Fall in."

Corporal trotted over. I opened the truck door, and he jumped up.

Daisy shoved her hands into pants pockets. "Again, I'm sorry about upstairs. Getting overheated is sort of a trigger."

"It's okay. I understand."

She studied me closely, but it wasn't with the predator's gaze. Her eyes softened as she discovered a truth that I didn't want her to know. "You've got your own demons, don't you?"

I closed the passenger door as dopamine surged through my system. It was time to leave.

Chapter 6

Surveying Metaline Falls took less than ten minutes. My first time through the town was more about sightseeing, trying to assess how it flowed. This time around, I paid more attention to identifying landmarks and businesses.

Daisy clouded my thoughts, however.

A darkness lay hidden in my soul. I thought I had banished it or, at least, garnered control of it. Some women brought out the worst in me. They carried something innate I couldn't identify when I was younger, but I saw it now. Each bore a level of recklessness. Some hid it better than others, but they all were dangerous under the façade.

Even Stacy had found my darkness upon our first encounter. She encouraged my madness by insisting I slip in and out of her house after her children had gone to bed. I remained a secret lover for some time, and I loved that illicit feeling. Our relationship turned into a form of domesticity, a part-time family. When Stacy warmed to the idea of a full-time relationship, I thought it was something I needed. Getting comfortable was what a lot of men wanted from life, and it should have brought me a sense of stability.

I believe that's why Maria wouldn't marry me when she discovered her pregnancy all those years ago. She saw something most women missed or ignored—I'd never be content. Maria backed carefully away from me like I was a ticking bomb. Based on some of my behavior, maybe she was right.

It's not that I made inherently dangerous choices because of women. They couldn't convince me to jump out of an airplane without a parachute or rob a bank. However, my thoughts often became jumbled when the wrong one came around, and my decisions soon become suspect.

My love life was littered with broken relationships built on unfulfilled hopes and unrealized lies. Yet, it didn't feel like an addiction in the way Daisy battled.

A psychologist might peel back all the layers to point out my mother as the origin of my behavior. I didn't want my mother linked to the romantic matters of my life. I was responsible for my own actions. Me alone. Yet, there was something reassuring in acknowledging Carol Cutler could have played a part in screwing up her son.

The Veterans of Foreign Wars building sat at the triangular juncture of Fourth and Third Avenue. I parked alongside the building and left the dog in the cab.

I pulled open the door and entered a small lobby. Ahead were shiny hardwood floors and clean white walls lining a long hallway. At the opposite end of the corridor stood three flags—the American, the Washington, and the VFW. Rows of glass cases lined the wall on the right. Each contained military paraphernalia, no doubt donated by the post's members. On the left wall was a variety of doors.

To the immediate right was an entry to a bar. The lights were low. Neon beer signs reflected off the chrome legs of the chairs. A television news channel competed with a radio and voices drifted out.

The bar didn't seem like a good starting point for an AA meeting, so I entered the hall.

In the second office, a man in his early seventies sat behind a desk. He looked up and smiled when I entered.

He wore a light sweater, and his silver hair was cut in a businessman's style. "Can I help you?"

"I'm looking for whoever runs the AA meeting."

The man checked his watch. "You're early. It doesn't start until seven." He motioned around the corner. "But you're in the right place. Takes place in the assembly hall."

"Across from the bar?"

The man's smile faded. "It's not ideal, but beggars and all."

"Do you run the meeting?"

His smile returned. "Oh no, that's Lane. Lane Daubel."

"Where can I find Lane?" I asked.

"He's a cook over at the diner."

I cocked my head.

The man smiled politely and raised an apologetic hand. "Fifth Street Diner. It's a hole in the wall, but you can't miss it. Been in this town forever."

"Thank you." I nodded.

"Good luck with your journey."

I returned to Fifth Street and parked in an angular parking spot. It seemed a modern convention for such a small town. Perhaps a city planner saw it on a vacation somewhere and thought the Metaline Falls residents should park their cars at an angle, too.

The Fifth Street Diner was in a multi-tenant building easily a hundred years old. The second story might have held apartments above it. An insurance agency sat on the left of the restaurant. A real estate company occupied the space on the right.

Inside the diner, two booths were occupied by older men drinking coffee. Their plates were empty and pushed to the side. A server who appeared to be in her mid-fifties stood behind the counter. She flipped through a magazine.

No wall separated the kitchen from the counter area. A heavily tattooed man in a white uniform cleaned a grill with a scraper. Grease and other food stuff covered his apron. A white cap sat cockeyed on his head.

The server straightened as I approached. "Just one today?" she asked.

I pointed toward the cook. "I'd like to speak with Lane."

At the mention of his name, the cook turned in my direction.

The server looked over her shoulder. "Someone for you."

Lane Daubel stepped away from the grill. He must have been a couple of inches over six feet. Even in a cook's outfit, he was an imposing figure. Suspicion filled his eyes, and he clutched the scraper like a hatchet.

"I'm looking for Nick Gossett," I said.

Lane's face relaxed, and he returned to the grill. "Can't help you."

"I'd still like to ask you a couple questions."

The cook loudly slapped the edge of the scraper against the grill. "What'd I say?"

The men in the booths turned to watch us now.

"Take your drama outside," one of the older men said.

"Yeah," another growled. "We'd have stayed home with our wives if we wanted this kind of nonsense."

I leaned slightly to get Lane's attention. "Nick is missing," I said.

"Who are you?"

"John Cutler."

He continued scraping. "Never heard of you."

"I'm a private investigator."

Lane stopped cleaning and eyed me.

One of the elderly men muttered, "He's a detective."

"Yeah," another added, "A real life dick."

The old men chuckled amongst themselves.

"Daisy hired me," I said.

Lane's eyes narrowed. "How'd she get you involved in this?" He clutched the scraper like a hatchet again. I expected him to throw it at me.

"She's paying me."

One of the older men asked, "How much does a detective make?"

"Daily rate plus expenses is what Jim Rockford always said," his buddy replied.

"I could go for some of that."

The old men chuckled between themselves some more.

Lane's shoulders relaxed. "Where are you out of?"

"Spokane." I thumbed over my shoulder like an idiot. "I drove up for the day to see what I could learn."

The cook considered me for a moment, then his eyes cut to the server. "I'm gonna take a break."

She shrugged and returned to her magazine. "Fine by me."

Lane tossed the scraper onto a nearby counter and waved for me to follow. He headed toward the rear exit.

***

Lane Daubel lit a cigarette and inhaled. When he offered me the pack, I shook my head.

"One vice for another," he said. He closed the box and slid it into his pocket. His shoulders flopped onto the building's rear wall. The back door to the restaurant remained open in case he needed to return.

Behind us was a cluster of trees. Next door was a large apartment community. It seemed recently built, probably with some government assistance.

"How long has Nick been missing?" Lane asked.

"Four days now."

Lane turned his head and spat on the ground.

"How often does he show up for the meetings?" I asked.

"We're not talking about that." Lane rubbed a thumb over his lower lip. "Anything talked about in group is off limits."

"Does he have a sponsor?"

Lane inhaled on his cigarette. "How do I know you're for real?"

I opened my wallet, removed a crumpled business card, and handed it to him.

He flicked it with his finger. "Cutler," he said.

"That's right."

"There are some Cutlers up in Newport. Any relation?"

"Not that I know of."

A dog barked from somewhere. I wondered if it was Corporal. He usually didn't get excited about people walking by the truck. I was probably wrong.

Lane tucked the card into his back pocket. "What was your question?"

"Does Nick have a sponsor?"

"It was nothing official, but I guess you could say I am."

"Could Nick have slipped?"

"Anything's possible." Lane tapped his cigarette and knocked ash from its end. "But I'll tell you this much. If he did, it would surprise the hell out of me. The guy seemed the least likely to regress of any person I've ever met."

"Why do you say that?"

"He was focused on sobriety like it was a singular mission."

"So, meetings were important?"

Lane studied the burning end of his cigarette. "You keep asking questions I don't feel comfortable answering."

"Because of the group?"

"It's anonymous for a reason." Lane flicked his cigarette into some gravel. "A person needs to feel safe to share within our group. That security is tenfold in the sponsor relationship. I already violated it by saying what I said."

"He's missing. Maybe he told you something that could be important to finding him."

An elderly woman walked along the tree line with a cat on a leash. She waved at us, and I returned the gesture.

Lane dug the box of cigarettes out of his pocket. "Let me ask you a hypothetical."

"Go ahead."

"Let's say you weren't a religious man, but you feared the existence of God." Lane pulled a cigarette from the box. "And you did something horrible in your life that you tried to cover with self-destructive behaviors."

I cocked my head.

Lane lit his cigarette and exhaled. "You wake up one day with the realization that your addictions have a stranglehold on your life. Maybe you're tired of waking up beside your toilet. Maybe you're sick of lost nights. So you turn to an organization that believes in God's grace for help. Following so far?"

"Are we talking about Nick?"

"We're talking about you," Lane said. "This is a hypothetical. Remember?"

"Yeah, all right."

He continued. "So this organization that you turn to requires you take responsibility for your actions. Soon, you clean up and fly right, but you can never fully be accountable. You can't make amends for the one thing you've done in your life which led you down this dark path in the first place. Because if you do, it means going to prison. What would you do, Cutler?"

What had Nick done? I wondered.

"I see your wheels are spinning," Lane said. He inhaled on the cigarette, then exhaled.

"Did Nick tell you about something?"

"If he had told me, I wouldn't tell you. Group, remember? This isn't about him. This is about you."

He smoked his cigarette and stared into the woods.

I studied him for a moment. "The hypothetical me?"

"Uh-huh."

"I admitted something illegal?"

Lane kicked a stone. "If you admitted something illegal, I would go to the police."

"So, the hypothetical me alludes to something bad happening and I feel terrible about it?"

The cook inhaled on his cigarette. "That's how I'd see it playing out."

I crossed my arms. "Why would the hypothetical me keep coming to the meetings?"

"Because you're a hard-headed sort."

That hit close to home.

Lane flicked ash from his cigarette. "You won't go to church, but you want to be around people experiencing some of the grace you're seeking. It gives you hope there might be something good after all this." His hand floated into the air. "Up there."

"Would the hypothetical me have just wandered off?"

"If you went back to drinking..." Lane rolled his cigarette between his thumb and forefinger. "Maybe. Who knows? But don't take your eye off her."

"Daisy?"

Lane cupped the cigarette and pointed its butt at me. "A woman like that doesn't go unnoticed in a town like this. You aware of her problem?"

I stared at him.

"So you are. When you add that in, tom cats come from all around." He waved the cigarette's butt in a circle. "You get what I'm saying?"

The server stuck her head out the back door. "Lane, you got two orders now."

"On it." He tossed the cigarette to the ground and mashed it with the toe of his shoe.

"Just a couple more questions," I said.

Lane headed toward the door. "You can wait for my next break, or you can come by after I get off at seven."

He stepped into the building, and I followed him.

"When's your next break?" I asked.

"Depends on how many customers," he said over his shoulder. "But I need this job."

Lane stepped into the kitchen and moved to a sink where he washed his hands.

I headed toward the door. Either I could wait around for Lane's next break, or I could return when his shift ended. I hadn't expected to be in the Metaline area that late but plans change.

Outside, I headed toward my truck.

A red Honda drove slowly by.

I stopped and bent to make eye contact with the man, but he refused to look my way. I hurried to my truck, hoping to give chase, but the left side tires were flat. A gaping hole was in each.

The parking spot next to my truck was open. Perhaps a vehicle had been there earlier. Maybe even the red Honda.

I squatted near the back tire of my truck and considered the brazenness of stabbing two tires in daylight. Anyone could have seen it happen.

Had the driver of the red Honda done it? I assumed so since I'd now seen him twice. Perhaps he pulled into the spot next to my truck, walked around his car, and flattened two tires with quick thrusts of a knife.

Who was the driver of the red Honda, and why did he want me slowed down? Was I being foolish by applying coincidence to this situation? Maybe he wasn't the one responsible for slashing my tires. When I was a cop, I hated coincidence. That powerful emotion borne out of a need to control everything. The longer I've been away from the job, however, I've started to believe in the occasional flukes. Sometimes, strange events happen. I won't subscribe to the idea of fate, but an accidental happenstance doesn't seem so farfetched.

In a couple of small towns like Metaline and Metaline Falls, what were the chances I would see the same Honda twice? Probably high. Maybe I didn't even have to believe in flukes, just simple probability.

An older male with a leashed pug walked by on the sidewalk. He stopped and considered me. "Got a flat?"

I raised an eyebrow and fought against asking what his first clue might have been.

The older man moved closer. A pot belly pushed against his white T-shirt. Tan shorts struggled to contain his ample hips. Black socks slouched below his ankles and his leather sandals looked newly bought.

From inside the truck, Corporal stared at the little black dog. He had moved into the driver seat to get a better look. Yet, he remained quiet.

The barking I heard earlier was probably his. He had seen the person who damaged the tires and tried to alert me.

I stood and faced the Shepherd. "Good boy," I said.

Corporal's attention never left the smaller dog.

"Got a spare?" the old man asked.

"Won't do any good." I motioned toward the second tire. "Two of them are flat."

He whistled as he scratched his belly. "Got into something bad, huh? Well, the best auto shop around is Red's over in Metaline proper. I went to school with the original Red. Good man. His son ain't so bad, neither."

The pug panted. His bug eyes watched me with hopeful curiosity.

"He'll have some tires for you." The old man stepped back and tugged on the leash. "Come on, Edgar. Let's leave the man to his business."

The little dog huffed after his owner.

I returned to the diner and asked the server for a phone book. She eyed me with mild suspicion.

"Got a flat," I said.

"Need a mechanic, huh?" She reached under the counter. "Best one around is Red's."

"Guy outside told me the same thing."

She tossed a thin phone book onto the counter. "Well, there you have it."

***

Corporal and I stood on the sidewalk. I put a leash on him even though the dog didn't need one. He was trained, but people prefer to see controlled animals. An unleashed Shepherd tends to make people nervous.

I was hungry and thirsty. Perhaps I should have waited inside the restaurant. I could have ordered something.

"You're probably hungry, too," I said to Corporal.

He ignored me and watched a pickup drive slowly down Fifth Street.

The front door to the diner opened, and Lane Daubel stepped out. He wiped his hands on his dirty apron as he approached my truck. "Someone took offense to your parking spot?"

"Something like that."

"Two of them. Hell's bells. That's gonna be expensive." He pulled the cigarettes from his pocket. "Nice dog. He bite?"

"Only when I tell him."

Lane smiled with the cigarette clenched between his teeth. "Only when you—" He shook his head. "Remind me to play nice with you."

"Back on break?"

He pulled the cigarette from his mouth. "I figured we could continue our conversation while you're waiting."

"Did Nick ever mention any trouble?"

"Trouble how?"

"I don't know. Was he being followed?"

"Not that I know of. What makes you think that?"

"Just wondering."

Lane inhaled on the cigarette, then looked toward the sky as he exhaled. "Talking about someone in the program feels like a betrayal," Lane said. "I'm only doing this because he's missing."

"I understand."

"I tried calling Nick before I came out here, but he's still not answering." Lane rolled his cigarette between his thumb and forefinger. "You asked about trouble. He once said it followed him like an old friend."

"Did he elaborate?"

"Not really. When it came to his past, Nick was secretive."

I motioned toward the back of the building. "What about my hypothetical self?"

Lane smiled knowingly. "Let's skip all that. Your tires got me thinking there might be something else going on."

"Did Nick ever tell you what he felt bad about?"

He shook his head. "Nick wasn't secretive about committing sins while on the sauce, but where and when those transgressions happened, he kept in his vault. That's normal. A lot of us are that way when we're in front of a group. If I say I robbed a bank, but you don't know where and when it happened, did I really rob a bank?"

Lane had a point.

He inhaled on the cigarette again. Wisps of smoke escaped his mouth as he spoke. "Some folks may open up in a one-on-one setting, but not Nick. I always felt like I did way more talking than he did, which is strange for a sponsor to do."

"I'm confused," I said. "Did he or did he not confess something horrible?"

Lane tapped the end of his cigarette, knocking ash from it. "Nick never said exactly, but he said something bad happened and he had to leave Canada."

There was no use in wondering what might have caused Nick to flee the country. The possibilities were too wide.

"He also said his trouble didn't start then," Lane said. "It sounded like it started way back when and followed him into Canada."

"From the states? Did he tell you when or where this trouble started?"

Lane shrugged. "He never said."

"Did he tell you what he did while in Canada? For a job, I mean. How he survived."

"He said he worked under the table mostly, because he wasn't a citizen." Lane brought the cigarette up to his lips but refrained from inhaling. "I didn't ask what exactly, but I got the feeling it was mostly labor jobs, backbreaking stuff."

"Why did he come to Metaline?"

"His car broke down, but it's as good as anywhere else to live." Lane sucked on his cigarette. "Unless you want action, then you probably want the big city life like Spokane."

A rickety tow truck from Red's Auto Repair pulled onto Fifth Avenue.

"This is probably for you," Lane said.

The tow stopped behind my pickup. The driver's door opened, and a long-haired man hopped out. He was in his early forties and wore a long sleeve shirt, jeans, and boots.

"Hey, Junior," Lane said.

"Lane," the operator said. "How's your sister?"

"Still mad at you."

"Can't say as I blame her." Junior eyed me. "This your truck?"

"That's right."

"Someone did a number on her. Got a spare?"

"Underneath."

Junior put his hands on his hips. "Here's the plan. We'll put the spare on, then I'll tow you back to the shop. We'll get you a couple replacements and fix you up. Have it done in an hour or so."

"I appreciate that."

Junior eyed Corporal. "Does he bite?"

"No," I said.

Lane motioned with his cigarette. "My sister would pay for that dog to bite him in the ass."

"Stay out of this," Junior said.

"She'd double it if the dog bites him in the dinger." Lane laughed.

Junior pointed at the cook. "Go sling some hash."

Lane tossed his cigarette into the street. "Good luck with your hunt, Cutler."

Chapter 7

Corporal stood next to my chair and watched the traffic pass by on Washington 31. We were the only two in the small lobby of Red's Auto Repair. Three chairs lined the window. The linoleum floor was scratched and dented from years of abuse. The business smelled like all auto shops—a mixture of grease, gas, and body odor.

There wasn't a television or radio in the waiting area. No out-of-date magazines were left behind for anyone to peruse. The white coffee pot looked as if it hadn't been cleaned in years and the black liquid it held smelled burned.

I had already checked the pop machine on the outside wall. All flavors were empty—likely picked clean by travelers who noticed its existence.

An air gun rattled from inside the nearby maintenance bay as a local country station loudly played. I slid down in my chair and rested my head against the back of my seat. I prefer soul or hip hop and can tolerate older rock and roll. Country music gives me a headache.

Junior entered the lobby singing along with the radio. "Well, I'm not big on sausage gravy."

Those didn't sound like the words to the song we'd been listening to, but I didn't correct him.

He wiped his hands on a grimy towel. "You're fixed up."

I stood. "How much do I owe you?"

Junior walked around the counter. "Shouldn't be too bad. Got a couple tires, some labor, and the tow." He pulled out a pad of paper and a calculator. "Gimme just a second."

A semi with a loud engine drove by.

"You new to town?" Junior didn't look up when he asked the question.

"I'm looking for someone."

He paused now. "Who's that?"

"Nick Gossett."

He furrowed his brow. "You his son or something?"

"I'm a private detective."

His eyes flicked to the dog, then to the repair bay. "You don't look like a private detective."

"How should they look?"

Junior shrugged. "They seem more glamorous on TV."

"This is as glamorous as it gets."

He returned his attention to the pad of paper. "I heard Nick was missing."

"How'd you hear that?"

"Small town."

"You know him?"

His head bobbled. "I know Daisy." His eyes flicked up and met mine. "I mean, I knew her." He grunted. "I mean—"

"I know what you mean."

"Now listen, Mister. I don't know what you might have heard…" His voice trailed off, and he stared at me.

"Why don't you finish that thought?"

Junior set his pen down. "Daisy's a nice woman, and she can do whatever she darn well wants."

"That's very progressive of you."

He crossed his arms. "I got no problem with Nick. He seemed like a nice person, and if that's who Daisy wants to be with, that's good enough for me."

"Did someone else have a problem with her being with Nick?"

Junior set his hands on the counter and leaned forward. He looked southbound on the highway. I recalled there were a host of businesses in that direction as well as the fire department and the border patrol office. "Some guys weren't happy she took herself off the market." Junior's gaze dropped to his pad of paper. "Daisy was the most popular girl in town, if you know what I'm saying." He shook his head, seemingly ashamed of his revelation. "I shouldn't spread gossip like that."

"Sounds like that gossip was out in the open."

"Shouldn't be our business."

I narrowed my eyes as I thought, but Junior read the action wrong.

"I like feet," he said.

"Excuse me?"

"Nothing." He rolled his palms upward. "It's just the women I've told have made fun of me."

The song on the radio ended and switched to an advertisement for a local bank.

Junior scratched his head. "Daisy was nice about it. Not that we ever did nothing. She just let me talk about it. I really appreciated that about her."

"Are there any guys in town who got upset about Daisy's involvement with Nick?"

"Some. Sure."

"Who?" I asked.

Junior scrunched his face. "Well, you know how it is. Being in this business, most of what I hear is rumor and innuendo, but from what I understand, some of the border boys were none too pleased. But those border fellas can't help themselves. They aren't too shy about what they say when the beer flows at The Hairy Man."

"The Hairy Man?"

"It's a play on the Bigfoot legend. People around here get pretty excited about it. Metaline Falls even has an annual festival."

"Anyone of these border boys I should talk to in particular?"

"Macon Young. He's a real piece of work."

I nodded. "I already met him."

"Well, then you know." Junior's gaze lowered to his pad of paper. "If you talk with them—"

"Yeah?"

"Would you do me a favor and keep my name out of it? I don't need the hassle. They don't have any real jurisdiction over us, but they act like they do, if you get my drift."

"Do any of them drive a red Honda?"

Junior cocked his head. "Not that I know of, and I'm pretty sharp on cars." He started adding up the total. "Why don't I throw in the tow for free? Since you're helping Daisy and all."

"I'd appreciate that."

He smiled. "Sure." He finalized a number, and I handed him a credit card.

After we settled the bill, Junior escorted me into the shop. The truck looked as it had prior except with two new tires. The spare was back in its rightful place. "I put the new ones on the back," he said, "so both old ones are on the front."

I nodded my thanks.

Junior pulled open the driver's door. The keys were on the seat. I grabbed them and motioned for the dog to jump in. Corporal hopped up.

"Hey," Junior said. "Good luck finding Nick. I hope everything is okay." He smiled awkwardly. "Tell Daisy I said hi if you don't mind."

"Sure."

His expression melted. "It's not that way. I just worry about her is all."

Junior stepped away from the truck and I backed out of the shop.

***

The bell tinkled when I entered the Sturdy Goats Reading Company.

"Be right there," Daisy McLaughlin said from the office. Something heavy dropped to the floor, and she hurried down the office steps. Her jacket was off. The padlock and chain link tail bounced as she went. "I was sorting through books to keep my mind busy."

"I need a better understanding of your situation."

She paused after she came off the last stair. "Which situation is that?"

I pointed at the padlock.

Her hand absently grabbed it and her expression hardened. "What about it?"

"Does everyone in town know about your—" I paused for a moment to find the right word and settled on, "Condition?"

"No, and if you're implying I've slept with every man—"

I lifted my hand. "I'm not."

"That's good because I haven't. I wouldn't." Tears welled in her eyes and her knuckles whitened around the lock. "Who said that stuff?"

"A mechanic named Junior."

"Him?" She turned her face away. "What did he say?"

"He said you were sweet. That you were nice."

Daisy relaxed and let go of the lock.

"He also said there were some guys in town who weren't happy about you and Nick getting together." I pointed at the padlock again. "I'm guessing that has a lot to do with it."

"My choices weren't always so good."

"Would any of those bad choices want to hurt Nick?"

She shook her head.

"What about the guys from border patrol? Big Dog?"

Daisy's face hardened. "I said never to call him that."

I lifted my hand in an apologetic manner.

"Junior talked about them?"

"Sounds like the others were, too."

Her face soured, then she shook her head. "They wouldn't hurt Nick."

"How do you know?"

"I know."

I crossed my arms. "Explain what happened so I can understand."

She lowered her gaze to the padlock. "We had a thing."

"You and Macon?"

Daisy gripped the lock. "Him and his friends. It was dumb, I know."

"What happened?"

Her head stayed down, but she lifted her eyes to meet mine. "What do you think happened?"

"If you want my help, I need to know the score."

Daisy's gaze dropped, and she twisted the lock. "We got together. Sometimes just a couple of us. Sometimes all of us. But they have wives to go home to."

"And Nick ruined that?"

She twisted the lock as far as it would go. Her wrist shook from the pressure she maintained. The metal chains bit into her waist. Tears streaked down her face.

"Daisy?"

With a gasp of air, she released the lock. The color returned to her knuckles. She inhaled like a fighter at the end of an intense round of throwing punches. "The town whore was off the market."

"Did someone say that?"

She shook her head. "They didn't have to. I knew that's what they were thinking."

We stood in silence for a moment. Upstairs, there was a pitter-patter of little feet. I assumed it was the cat.

Eventually, I asked, "What's it all about? Why do you do it?"

Daisy didn't look at me.

"Is it about sex?" I asked.

She sniffed as a tear rolled down the bridge of her nose. "Not really, no."

"Then what?" I asked.

Daisy rubbed her face. "Adrenaline mostly, I guess. About doing something no one else does."

"Is that why you look so happy?"

She looked up, and her face pinched. In a moment, she laughed. The chuckle only lasted a moment before it turned into sobs. She turned away as she fought for control.

Hagrid wandered down the stairs. The cat paused long enough to consider Daisy before darting into the *Romance/Sci-Fi* aisle again.

"The adrenaline," Daisy said with her back still to me. She slammed a fist into her leg. "It's supposed to cover up the loneliness." Daisy hit herself again. "The unworthiness." Her hand remained on her leg. "That's what a counselor once said, but it never works. Only the shame remains, which is a goddamned anvil, dragging me down." Daisy slowly shook her head. "Then the adrenaline returns and rescues me from it all." She pounded her fist on her leg again.

"A hell of a cycle."

Daisy turned. "Nick saw it for what it was." Tears welled in her eyes. "He loved me for who I was, not for what I did. He told me not to feel any shame." Her hand dropped for the padlock, but she didn't touch it.

"And you wear that not only for you, but so everyone in town sees what it represents?"

She inhaled deeply. "You must be a detective."

"Tell me about these border guys."

"I already said they wouldn't have anything to do with Nick going missing."

I nodded. "I hear you, but did they ever give you or Nick a hard time about being together?"

"Sometimes." She shrugged. "But it was never threatening or anything. It only happened when they ran into one of us at the store or the coffee shop. Just shitty little comments was all."

"You probably ran into them a lot around here."

"We tried to keep to ourselves, but yeah. It's hard not to run into people you don't like in a town this size."

"Did Nick go places by himself?"

"Sure."

I cocked my head. "So, it's possible he ran into your border buddies when he was alone."

"He never said if he did."

"Maybe he didn't want to worry you."

Her eyes narrowed.

"Let me ask you something," I said. "Junior knew about Nick going missing. Lane Daubel, too. Do you think everyone in town knows?"

She slowly nodded. "I've asked around, so yeah. Probably."

"If that's the case, have any of the border guys come sniffing around? Because if I had interest in a woman and her old man took off, the first place I'd go is—"

Her face flattened. "Macon Young," she said. "Quinton Akre, Lonnie Shank, and Bodhi Foster. They don't live in town, but they all work out of the customs office."

I pulled out my notebook. "Give me those names again." She did, and I jotted them one by one. When I finished, I looked up. "Junior said they drink at The Hairy Man."

"That's where I met them."

"Do they have a normal night they meet at the bar?"

"Pick one. Doesn't matter. Usually one of them is there. It's their hangout. Their workdays overlap, so one or two guys will be there. You'll rarely get all four."

"What time do they go?"

"Depends on if one of them has the early shift. The border is only open from eight until eight. The earliest one would arrive is five. Latest would be eight-thirty."

"The border isn't open twenty-four hours?"

She shook her head. "Not enough traffic."

I checked my watch. It was nearing five. "I'll be back at six to pick you up. Make sure you eat something."

"Where you going?"

"To rent a room."

She thumbed over her shoulder. "You can stay at my house. I've got the extra room."

It only took her suggestion that I could stay in her house for dopamine to course through my system. "Not a good idea," I said.

Daisy frowned and her eyes darkened. "That won't happen again."

"People talk," I said, blaming my decision on someone else. "Let's keep it professional. That way there aren't any worries."

***

"Are you headed home?" Stacy asked. Her voice was low because she was still at the office.

"I'm going to get a room and stay the night."

"Things are going well?"

"Someone slashed my tires."

She inhaled sharply. "For real? Are you okay?"

"It's fine. I've gotten them replaced."

"Do you know who did it?"

"No."

"That's why you're staying?" she asked.

"I'm still trying to figure out what happened to Nick Gossett."

"Any leads?" she whispered.

"Maybe."

"Listen," she said. "I've got to go. Call me later when I'm at home."

***

"How many nights?" the motel clerk asked.

"Just one."

I was at the Metaline Motel, located on Highway 31. It was a two-story affair with exterior access to each room. The parking lot faced the roadway. The motel wasn't built for long-stay comfort; it was built for quick convenience. Get a few hours of sleep and get back on the road.

The clerk was in her mid-forties, with graying hair and a softening face. She had pretty eyes, the type that still carried the hope for something better in life. Her name tag read Susan and was attached to her green plaid shirt.

"Driver's license and credit card."

I pulled them from my wallet and set them on the counter. Susan slid them closer to her computer. Her fingers danced over the keyboard. "You're that detective people are talking about."

"People are talking?"

"Oh my God," Susan said. "Like a bunch of hens." She tapped the Enter key twice, then stopped. "That didn't make much sense, did it?"

I shrugged. "I got the meaning."

She chuckled. "I'd say talking like a bunch of old ladies, but that sounds terrible now that I'm—" She blushed. "Well, I'm not going to tell you how old I am."

I smiled. "We're the same age."

"Hardly." Her finger touched my driver's license. "I got you by half a dozen. The rooms are non-smoking."

"No problem."

"There's a smoking area out back." Her eyes drifted to the window. "Pets are fine, but I need to charge you a deposit."

"I understand. Let me ask you something."

"We don't charge it against your card. It's just a hold until we check the room."

I waved away her explanation. "You know why I'm in town?"

"People say you're looking for Nick." She turned away from the computer. "Is he really missing?"

"That's the way it looks. Did you know them—Nick and Daisy, I mean?"

"Only a little. Saw them around town. You know. At the store and the bar and such."

"Any opinion?"

"Lots of them."

"Care to share?"

Her smile was reserved. "If I'm being honest, the age difference sort of bothered me. He's old enough to be her father." She entered something on her keyboard. "Then again, he's a handsome man. If he showed me the kind of attention he showed her..." Susan looked at me and an embarrassed smile formed. "I probably wouldn't have a problem with the age gap then."

"Anything else?"

"Not really. They seemed happy when I saw them. It seemed unfair how others treated her."

"Like how?"

She looked both ways before speaking, but we were the only two in the lobby. "It's hard to be a woman like Daisy, free with herself, in a town like this. Everyone knows what everyone else is up to. The old timers think the worst of her. The single men think she's the greatest thing since sliced bread. Hell, some of the married men probably thought so, too. Most of the women hated her because of that."

"What about you?"

Susan's eyes softened. "I don't hate her one bit. If anything, I feel sorry for Daisy."

"How so?"

"She found a guy who loved her for who she was, and now he's gone missing. What could be more terrible than that?"

"You're a romantic, Susan."

She reached under the counter and pulled out a Harlequin romance. "Guilty as charged."

Chapter 8

Daisy McLaughlin climbed into the truck and closed the door. "Where's the dog?"

"At the motel."

I accelerated from her home.

After she slipped her seatbelt on, her gaze dropped to the burrito sitting on the armrest. I stopped at a gas station on the way over.

"Dinner?" she asked.

"Did you eat?"

She looked out the window. "You said to, so yeah. I would have made you something."

"It's all right."

We stopped before entering the highway and I waited for a slow-moving semi heading north. A line of cars followed it.

"You staying at the Metaline?" she asked.

I kept my eyes on the traffic. "Why do you ask?"

She didn't respond, so I turned to look. Daisy was looking the other way. I turned back to make sure the roadway was clear.

"It was a polite question," she finally said. "Making conversation. Don't worry. I'm not trying to sleep with you."

I accelerated onto the roadway. "Yeah, the Metaline."

"Was Susan working?"

"Uh-huh."

"She's nice."

"Seemed that way."

Daisy continued to look out the passenger window. "Not many women who like me around here. She always has. At least, I think she has."

"How do you run a small-town bookstore if most of its citizens are at odds over you?"

She faced me now. "I'd go broke if I relied only on local sales. Online sales help a ton as do out-of-town buyers, but you've probably already figured that."

I hadn't.

We rounded the highway's bend and crossed over the Pend Oreille River before entering Metaline Falls. The Hairy Man sat at the corner of Grandview and Fifth Avenues. Its parking lot was partially full of dusty pickup trucks, muddy Jeeps, and rusty sedans.

I parked on West Fifth with a view of the lot and turned off the engine.

When I made no move to get out, Daisy asked, "We're not going in?"

"Do you see any of their rigs?" We were looking for Macon, Quinton, Lonnie or Bodhi. The border patrol agents she'd known intimately.

She cocked her head and scanned the lot. "No."

"Then we'll wait out here."

"Why can't I call one of them and ask to meet?"

"Have you called any of them since you and Nick started?"

Her brow wrinkled. "No."

"Then we call as a last resort," I said. "Whoever you call might know something is up."

"I could pretend it's for something different."

"There are already enough people talking in town. If word hasn't gotten to them, it will."

"Do you really think they're involved?"

I eyed her. "They were giving you and Nick a hard time."

"You're taking it all wrong. It wasn't like that. They were just making shitty comments. You know, jealous snipes. That sort of thing."

"We have to start somewhere." I checked my watch; it was a little after six. "What time do they show up?"

"This is the hangout. One of them should be here soon. Trust me."

"How do you know?"

She eyed me. "The Hairy Man is a cop bar. Border patrol and customs for sure, but the sheriff's guys come here, too. And some Canadian cops will come down for a drink. Not often, but it happens."

"So, women looking for cops?" My voice trailed off.

"Yeah, and cops looking for women. You understand what happens."

My attention returned to the bar. I hadn't imagined a cop bar possible out here in the sticks, but why shouldn't it?

We had a hangout like The Hairy Man while I was with Seattle PD. Women looking for a good time frequented it, too. We rewarded them with pet names like chippies, badge bunnies, or holster sniffers. No cop dared fall in love with a chippy since she'd likely been with many guys on the job. Besides, those women were interchangeable—available for the cost of a few drinks and a well-chosen war story. I was never sure what the women got out of the deal except for drunken sex with egomaniacs.

The situation with Daisy and the border agents wasn't made possible only due to her addictive behavior. The law enforcement culture fostered that type of knuckle-dragging behavior.

Daisy twisted the padlock, and the chain tightened around her waist. Her words from earlier came back to me. Adrenaline covered her loneliness and unworthiness until shame ultimately smashed the illusion. Then more adrenaline was needed to hide the emotional wreckage, and the process started again.

How many women were caught in a cycle like Daisy? Was hers more pronounced? Or was she only more honest about it?

I reached for the burrito and her nose crinkled.

"That's not good for you," she said.

"So are a lot of things."

I bit into it.

***

Fifteen minutes later, a blue Chevy pickup pulled into The Hairy Man lot.

Daisy pointed. "That's Macon's truck."

"Big Dog," I muttered.

Her lip curled. "Don't ever."

I raised my hand apologetically. "I forgot. I'm sorry."

Macon Young slid from behind the steering wheel and closed the driver's door.

"Stay here," I said.

Daisy looked surprised. "I'm not coming?"

"No." I slipped out of the truck.

She leaned across the front seat toward me. "But I could help."

"Not really." I closed the door.

***

Dive bars don't start out that way. At some point, they were new, with fresh equipment and up-to-date furniture. Customers walked into those bars upon their first openings and uttered something like, "Nice place." It had been many years since someone had done that to The Hairy Man.

The bar stunk like stale beer and dirty ashtrays, even though the state outlawed indoor smoking several years prior. Beer signs hung about the joint and gave it a neon glow. A single pool table stood in the back, along with a *Terminator 2* pinball machine. Now and then, the machine would flash, and Arnold Schwarzenegger would utter a digitized version of, "*Hasta la vista, baby.*"

Overhead, Def Leppard's "Photograph" floated from a seat of speakers. I wasn't a fan of rock and rock roll, but it was hard to grow up in the eighties and not know that band.

Macon Young rested his back against the bar as he chatted with two twenty-somethings. He wore blue jeans and a T-shirt that looked painted on. The women both sported jean shorts and half-shirts. Macon dangled a bottle of Kokanee between two fingers. The women held bottles of Mike's Hard Lemonade.

I approached the three.

Macon's gaze cut to me, and he stopped talking. The two women eyed me with curiosity.

"Hey, Big Dog," I said.

He considered me for a moment until recognition set in. "Find your book?"

"I did."

"What'd you get?" A cocky smile formed.

"It's that one about an unfaithful husband. You might have heard about it."

Macon's expression melted, and he eyed the girls. "Give us a moment."

They glanced at each other, then walked away without complaint.

The bartender approached and asked, "Get you something, bud?"

I shook my head. "I won't be long."

He nodded. "Holler if you change your mind."

Macon kicked his bottle back and took a deep pull. That's when I noticed he didn't wear a wedding ring. After he swallowed, he asked, "Who the hell are you, buddy?"

I opened my wallet and removed a crinkled business card. I only had a couple left.

The border agent briefly considered it, then tossed it on the bar. "Private investigator. So I guess you didn't find a book today."

"Daisy hired me to find Nick." I picked up the business card and put it back in my wallet. Waste not, want not.

Macon cocked an eyebrow. "The old boy still hasn't come home, huh?" He lifted his bottle, realized it was empty, and shook it to get the bartender's attention.

"So, you knew he was gone?"

"It's a small town. People can't fart without everyone knowing about it."

"Is that why you don't live in Metaline?"

"What do you know about it?"

I glanced around the bar demonstratively. "I know your wife's not here."

Macon pressed the head of the empty beer bottle against my chest. "Best shut your mouth before you get my fist in it."

The bartender wandered over to deliver a fresh beer. "Problem, Big Dog?"

"Nope," Macon said. He set his empty down and deftly picked up the new one. "Just a disagreement with my ol' buddy here. Ain't that right?"

I nodded once.

The song on the radio switched to a classic Duran Duran song, and a woman elsewhere in the bar whooped.

The bartender snatched the empty bottle and switched his gaze to me. "Still nothing?"

"I'm good."

"Shout out if anything changes." He wandered off to help a customer who had just entered the establishment.

Macon leaned in. "Spouting off about my marriage isn't going to ruin my night. Those girls know."

"Fair enough."

"But I don't like some asshole thinking he can talk about my wife."

I lifted a contrite hand. "I'm trying to find Nick. Daisy mentioned you gave him a hard time."

Macon leaned an elbow on the counter. "Gimme a break. It wasn't that bad."

I stared at him.

"Listen, the old guy rolled into town and ruined a good deal for me and the boys, probably for some other guys, too. If you think I'd risk my career by harassing some guy over the town pin cushion, you got another thing coming."

My face warmed. I don't know why his words bothered me, because Daisy wasn't the type of woman whose reputation needed protecting. However, there was something in the way Macon talked about her that made me want to hit him.

"You got something going on with her, too?" Macon asked. "I see you getting all worked up right now." He smiled as he leaned in. "Let me clue you in, bud. She threw the pussy around like it had an expiration date. Then Nick showed up, and she started wearing that stupid chain like it was some kind of chastity belt." He barked a demeaning laugh. "What the fuck does she think this is? The Middle Ages?" Macon took a healthy swig of beer. "Well, he's not the white knight she thought he was. I'll tell you that much."

"What do you mean?" I asked.

Macon looked over his shoulder at the two twenty-somethings. He lifted his beer. "Almost done," he called.

They waved back. One of them asked, "Should we order you another round?"

"Definitely!" Macon laughed as if we were old friends. He faced me. "As you can see, Daisy's easily replaceable." A leer developed. "These two are half her age." His expression flattened. "Of course, they won't do half of what she did."

The desire to punch him intensified. "What did you mean by the white knight comment?"

"Like I should do your job?" Macon sounded like Ackerman. "Go ask Daisy. I already told her all this."

"You told her what?"

Macon tapped the head of his bottle into my chest. "I don't work for free, asshole. And I'm not doing your job either. Now, fuck off. I've got better prospects."

He turned and headed toward the women huddled at the opposite end of the bar.

***

I hopped into the truck and pulled the door shut.

"What'd Macon tell you about Nick?" I asked.

Daisy's brow furrowed. "What?"

"What did he tell you?"

"Nothing."

"He told you something." I pointed toward the bar. "He just told me he did. He said Nick wasn't the white knight you thought he was."

She shook her head. "He told me lies."

"Then tell me those lies."

Her face pinched. "Why should I? It was all bullshit. He wanted to break us up." She tugged at the length of chain dangling between her legs. "He wanted me to take this off."

I hit the steering wheel with the palm of my hand. "Just tell me what he said!"

She pulled back and leaned against the passenger door. "You don't get to talk to me that way."

I reached for the key and the engine fired up. My left hand strangled the steering wheel. I dropped the truck into gear and stomped the gas pedal. We headed toward the highway in silence.

As we rounded the bend, I saw Metaline up ahead. If I wanted answers, I needed her to talk with me. I inhaled deeply. "I apologize."

Daisy shook her head.

"Really," I said. "I apologize."

She stared out the window and her fingers played with the length of chain. "I've done a lot to lower myself—" Daisy faced me now. "I know that's what I'm doing, even when it's happening. I'm not stupid. It doesn't take a college degree to see what's going on in my head, but no man lays a hand on me in a way I don't want, and no man talks to me in a way I don't want."

"I've already apologized. Twice."

"That's different than saying you're sorry." She studied me. "Like I said, I'm not stupid."

I left the highway and pulled up to her house.

She put her hand on the door handle.

I asked, "What did Macon say?"

"He would say whatever it took to get what he wanted." Daisy nodded as if she was convincing herself of something. "That's what a man like him does." She yanked open the door and stepped out. Her gaze held mine. "I probably should have known that going in."

She slammed the door and walked toward her house without looking back.

***

I sat on the edge of the hotel bed and ran my fingers through Corporal's hair. He stood before me. I'm sure he was hungry. I needed to go out and get him some food. I hadn't thought I'd be spending the night, so I didn't think to bring any.

"Maybe we should take off," I said to the dog.

He yawned.

There was no reason to stay in Metaline.

I didn't officially have a client, which meant I was wasting time and money traipsing around Northeastern Washington, looking for a missing man.

It seemed as if my unofficial client wasn't fully truthful with me. Macon Young had told her something about Nick she didn't believe. Whatever it was, she found it so unbelievable that she wouldn't share it with me.

I grabbed Corporal's ears like motorcycle handlebars. "Vroom." I tilted the dog's head left and right as if I were slaloming through corners. He suffered the indignity with a stoic calm.

Had Daisy told Nick about Macon's claim?

I stared at the dog. "Well?"

He didn't provide any answers.

I let go of his ears and pulled out my phone. Daisy didn't answer my call.

"Shit."

The activity log flashed up, and I saw the history of that day. I immediately placed another call.

She answered on the fourth ring. "Hello, Johnny." Usually, she answered with false excitement, but my mother was sedate now. "I was wondering when you would call back. What's this about your father?"

"Have you ever heard of Nicholas Gossett? Goes by Nick."

Cars on the highway hummed by. Voices outside in the parking lot drifted up to my room. A door slammed down the hallway. I strained to hear any sounds from my mother's side of the call.

"Hello?" I asked.

"Where did you hear that name?"

"A woman asked me to find him. She says *he* is my father."

"He's not your father. Gabe was." Her words were sharp, but there was an odd familiarity in them.

"But you knew Nick?"

She clicked her tongue. "I don't have time for this."

"Make time, Mom."

"Van and I are heading out for dinner. Here he is now."

"This is important."

"Not to me. I must go."

"Wait."

She exhaled heavily. "What is it?"

"Tell me about Nick."

"Another time."

She hung up and the little screen flashed the finality of my mother's decision.

I redialed her number. It rang twice before going to voice mail. I dialed her a third time. This one went directly to the message.

I snapped the phone closed and squeezed it. Anger and hatred flashed through my body. I wanted to throw the phone and smash it into a thousand little pieces, but that felt too small. I wanted to put my fist through a wall, but that still seemed inadequate. I wanted to burn the world down to show my mother how much I despised her.

Corporal jumped back as I unexpectedly stood and walked from the room.

***

I drove southbound on Metaline. I didn't know where I was going, but I just wanted to get out of my room. The U.S. Customs and Border Patrol building passed by on my right. I spun the truck around the first chance I had and headed north.

Macon's pickup was gone from the now-crowded parking lot when I got to The Hairy Man, but I hoped that he might have been inside. He wasn't. I wasn't looking for a conversation. It was stupid and childish. I couldn't hit my mother, so I wanted to punch the next best option.

Overhead, a rock song I heard back in high school played. I couldn't remember its name and was thankful for that.

The bartender approached as I slid onto a stool.

"You're back," he said.

"Whiskey and a beer back."

He nodded and wandered off.

My anger flared as I caught my reflection in the mirror behind the bar. I turned away and scanned those in attendance. They were an eclectic group of drinkers. Many were in their fifties, but most appeared to be about my age. One of the younger blondes from earlier remained.

Blue jeans and flannel shirts seemed to be the required attire for the men. I was underdressed in a T-shirt.

"Here you go," the bartender said.

I dug into my pocket and laid a fifty on the counter. "Bring another."

"Of which?"

"Both."

He slipped the bill from the bar. "Rough day?"

I stared at him.

"Have at it," he said.

When he stepped toward the cash register, the mirror reflected my image. I didn't look away this time. My anger slowly dissipated and was replaced by self-pity.

John Cutler, I thought. *Conqueror of no worlds. Son to no man.*

I grabbed the shot and kicked it back. The whiskey burned on the way down. The bartender had poured from a cheap bottle. I took a swig from the beer and cooled my throat.

The twenty-something eased onto the stool next to me. She rested her arms on the bar. Her eyes were at half-mast and her smile was mushy. She hunched like a prize fighter at the end of a ten-round bout. Our eyes met in the mirror's reflection.

"Is you," she said. Her words slopped together.

"That's what I've been told."

She faced me and caressed my arm. "You're Macon's friend."

"I wouldn't go that far." I didn't turn to her. Instead, I chose to stare at myself in the mirror.

The woman examined me as if I was a prize bull at the county fair. She sat straighter and thrust her breasts out. Her half-shirt tightened, and I turned to confirm my suspicions that she wasn't wearing a bra. A little roll of fat bulged above her jeans. It was oddly sexy, and I stared longer than necessary.

I turned away, sipped my beer, and berated myself for being a lech. "Where's your other half?"

"Our house." House sounded as if it had sprung a leak.

"They left you alone?"

Her lip curled. "I don't do three-ways."

The bartender returned with the shot and beer. "Second wave, bud." His attention slid to the woman. "Drink some water, Holly."

Her eyes closed, and she crinkled her nose. "I already did."

"Drink some more."

"*You* drink it."

He walked off.

Holly's hand snaked around the shot glass. "Thanks for this." It came out as a single, slushy word.

"You probably shouldn't," I said and reached for the whiskey.

She kicked it back before I could take it from her.

Holly shook her head and tossed her blond hair about. She tapped the shot glass twice on the bar and hollered, "Delta Phi!"

The other conversations in The Hairy Man stopped and the bartender's gaze whipped in our direction. I shrugged apologetically. The mirror mocked me.

Holly wiped the back of her hand across her lips. "Are you—" She hiccupped and fought back an obvious wave of nausea. She turned her head and covered her mouth.

I pulled the second beer closer and now held both.

When she recovered, Holly turned to me. Her eyes momentarily unfocused when she asked, "Are you married with Macon?"

"I barely know him."

She caressed my arm like I was a dog. "That's good." Her words dripped from her lips. "Married men are gross." Holly reached for the second beer and her hand draped over mine.

I glanced around and several of the other patrons watched us.

The bartender returned with a glass of water and set it next to Holly's elbow. "Leave him alone, Holly, and drink this."

She turned to him slowly. "What is it?"

"Gin and tonic."

Holly pulled her hand from mine and reluctantly scooped up the glass of water. Her lip curled after she sipped it. "Too much tonic." She sipped it a second time and her eyes narrowed. "You work with Macon?"

"No."

She drank deeper from the water. "But you're border patrol?"

I shook my head.

Holly studied me through narrowed eyes. Her lips pursed. "What do you do?" The question dribbled out.

In my younger years, I would have said something cute. Holly was a woman who wanted attention, and the younger version of myself would have happily given it to her. I walked into The Hairy Man looking for trouble, and there might have been none bigger than Holly.

"Well?" Holly asked.

"I'm a father," I said. If she thought married men were gross, I figured that answer would really put her off.

"Aw. That's nice." She leaned in closer. "Daddies are nice." An aroma of sweet perfume encompassed her. "Where do you live?"

"I'm passing through."

I lifted a hand and caught the bartender's attention. He was taking an order from another patron.

Holly tried to whisper in my ear, but she slipped off her stool. "Whoops." Water sloshed from her glass and over her hand. She smiled at the others in the bar, then turned toward the mirror. She stood behind me. Our eyes met in the reflection.

"How 'bout we go outside, Daddy?" she whispered. Her breath was hot in my ear.

I waved at the bartender again. He headed in our direction.

"I'll go down on you in your car." Holly closed her eyes, and she reached around my waist.

I pulled her hand from my lap. "She needs a ride home," I said to the bartender.

Holly's eyes popped open, and she jerked her hand back. "No, I don't. I'm fine."

The bartender frowned. "You're cut off."

"I didn't do nothing."

He pointed to a table near the entrance. "Go sit down."

Holly slapped my arm. "Thanks for nothing." She wobbled away.

Why'd she have to be drunk? I thought. If Holly had been reasonably sober and made those advances, I'd have taken her up on the offer. Of course, if she had been reasonably sober, she would never have approached me. It was a Catch-22. In a fit of anger, I wanted to cause myself self-harm, but I wouldn't do it at the expense of a drunk, young woman.

The heightened emotions of the day jumbled me up. The confusion about my long-missing father. My mother's evasiveness. Daisy's hyper-sexuality. All of them competed for attention.

The bartender shook his head. "Sorry about that."

"Happen often?" I asked, hoping to leave my thoughts behind.

"They're home from college," he said. "Holly and her type come up here because they hear we attract cops."

I feigned surprise at the news. "Cops? Here?"

He rolled his eyes. "Beggars can't be choosers. Most of them are okay. The retired guys hang out and tell old war stories. They're pretty fun. It's the young guys who come in looking for trouble that bother me."

"What kind of trouble can you find around here?"

The bartender glanced at Holly.

"Got it."

His attention returned to me. "So, what brought you in?"

"Wanted a beer," I said.

"To town."

"A guy is missing. I've been hired to find him."

"You some sort of private eye or something?"

"That's right."

"What's this fella's name?" the bartender asked. "Maybe I know him."

"Nick Gossett. He's new to the area."

The bartender shook his head. "Doesn't ring a bell." He lifted his arms above his head. "Hey! Anyone seen or heard from Nick Gossett?"

Everyone turned our way. Several expressions were blank, but most shook their heads.

"Nick?" the bartender repeated. "Gossett? Anyone?" He turned to me. "We tried."

"Cocksucker," Holly said from her corner.

"Quiet, you," the bartender said, "or I'll make you wait outside."

"She going to be all right?" I asked.

He nodded. "Their families live in Ione, and those two share an apartment that their parents pay for. Rich girls home for break. Taylor said she'd come back for Holly in a bit." The bartender rolled his eyes and leaned in to share some gossip. "Taylor took off with one of the local border agents, a notorious poon hound."

"That happen often?"

"Look around, man. It's a cop bar. Single women come here for a reason." He tapped the hardwood counter. "Some married women, too." He shrugged once. "What can you do?" He walked off before I could answer.

***

I filled a paper bowl with kibbles and put it on the floor near the door. I had stopped at The Falls Market and picked up a couple of items before heading back to the hotel room.

Corporal sniffed the food.

"It's all right," I said.

The dog finally stuck his snout in the kibbles and ate.

I grabbed another bowl from the sack and filled it with water. As soon as I put it down, Corporal moved to that. He quickly emptied it, and I refilled it.

While he continued to eat, I sat on the bed and stared at my reflection in the quiet TV.

I avoided a meltdown tonight.

Had Macon Young been at the bar, I would have found every reason to encourage a fight. If I couldn't have convinced him to throw the first punch, I might have done it myself. Brawling with an off-duty border agent would end badly. Win or lose, I would have landed in the county jail.

I would have fought with him, anyway.

Had Holly not been so sloppily drunk, I might have accepted her proposition to go outside for a quickie. The fall-out from that decision wouldn't have been a night or two in jail; it would have had lasting repercussions. I'd return home to Stacy with guilt borne of my choices. I'd look into my girlfriend's eyes and tell her I loved her, all the while knowing I'd broken the seal on my commitment.

You're no good, Johnny. My mother's voice rang in my ears. *You're just like your father.*

When my relationship with Stacy started, it was one of convenience. She didn't have time to meet men, so she called under the guise of wanting my opinion on her divorce. Her sister had slummed with me. I was too low class for her to show to her friends, but just right for late night booty calls.

Stacy didn't see me as low class, but she wanted me to remain a secret. We soon fell into a rhythm I found acceptable. She'd call, and I'd sneak over at night, so her children remained unaware of their mother's lover. I'd leave before either child awoke in the morning. Those clandestine hookups were fun but not enough to keep me devoted. There were other women.

Once Stacy felt safe enough to introduce me to her kids, we became exclusive. I stopped looking for other beds to fall into. Remaining faithful felt important. It was expected in a relationship and not something I should pat myself on the back for.

But the desire to go outside with Holly tonight lingered.

A tingling remained in my chest, an aftereffect of the dopamine. My fingers twitched and my legs were restless. My anxiousness had little to do with the promised pleasures of a drunk twenty-something. My unrest had everything to do with the fall that would come after.

I wanted those negative consequences more than the ones that would follow a brawl with Macon Young. It had been some time since I burned my world down. I did it in high school. I did it when I was with the police department. It happened more than once since I moved to Spokane. Right now, I wanted to show the world it couldn't hurt me. Only I could hurt myself.

It was stupid and immature, but I didn't care. It was an itch I couldn't scratch.

I thought about Daisy and her chain link belt. I imagined her twisting the padlock. My pulse accelerated, and I wondered what she might be doing right now.

Corporal wandered over and sat next to me.

"What?"

He stared at me.

"I'm not going to call her."

The dog didn't move.

"Besides, it's not like the guy is my dad."

Corporal moved toward the door.

"Right."

I slid off the bed and grabbed the plastic bag from the grocery store. We headed outside.

***

The dog wandered about, sniffing bushes and rocks. He took longer than normal, probably happy to be outside after being cooped up in the truck and a hotel room for most of the day. We were on the backside of The Metaline Motel. Halogen lights illuminated our activity. Clusters of bugs flew near the bulbs. Figures walked by windows, and someone stopped to watch us occasionally.

Traffic whizzed by unseen on the highway. A noisy semi passed. A rumbling motorcycle soon followed. I wondered if those sounds would continue through the night.

My phone rang, and I pulled it from my pocket. "Hey," I said.

"How's it going?" Stacy asked. She sounded different, as if she might be laying down.

"I'm outside with the dog, letting him do his business."

"Well, there you go." Her speech pattern was slower than normal. "I wanted to call before it got too late."

I checked my watch. It was a little after nine. "Going to bed?"

"Already there. The kids have brushed their teeth and are in theirs. I'm bushed. Calling it early since you're not here." She moaned.

Corporal finally found a spot and hunched.

"Are you feeling better about what you're doing?" she asked.

"About the same."

I didn't feel like bringing up the conversation with my mother. I certainly didn't want to recycle those emotions. I was already struggling with the aftereffects.

Burn my world down, I thought. *What an immature asshole.*

"Feel like talking about it?" she asked.

"Not really."

"If nothing breaks loose tomorrow…?" Her question hung in the air.

"I'll be home."

"That's good. I'm better with you around." She moaned again—a woman struggling to stay awake. "I'm gonna go to sleep. Love you."

"I love you."

I hung up and shoved the phone into my pocket. I yanked the plastic bag from my pocket and squatted near Corporal's deposit.

"It's nice to see someone actually picking up after their dog."

I looked over my shoulder.

Susan, the desk clerk, stood on the sidewalk. A slouchy purse was slung over her left shoulder and a set of keys dangled in her right hand. No longer hidden behind the front counter, I could see her completely now.

She had full hips, and her green plaid shirt was untucked. I'd forgotten how attractive she was.

"You'd be surprised," Susan said, "how many people never pick up after their dogs."

"I can imagine."

I'm not sure what possessed me to grab the plastic bag before leaving the room, but I was glad I did. I scooped Corporal's warm mess and turned the bag inside out.

The dog trotted over to Susan, and she petted him.

"Big plans for the night?" she asked.

"You're looking at it." I walked over to a trashcan, lifted the lid, and tossed the bag inside. "What about you?"

She opened her purse to reveal the romance novel she had shown me earlier. "I'll finish this one and start another." She closed the purse. "Honestly, I figured you'd be the type out looking for trouble."

I smirked. "I went looking for it. Didn't find any."

Susan smiled broadly. "Maybe you weren't looking in the right places."

"No?" My pulse quickened. "Where should I have been looking?"

Her cheeks flushed, and her smile faltered. Susan looked down at the dog and she stuck her hand in his fur. "Any luck on finding Nicholas?"

"Not yet."

"Is there anything I can do?" Her head popped up, and she clutched the purse to her chest. "With the search? I have a computer, you know?" Her face reddened further, and she lifted her chin toward the building. "In the office."

The itch that couldn't be scratched screamed for attention. "You want to maybe get a drink instead?" I asked.

Susan furrowed her brow. "I can't." She shook her head once. "It's not right. You're a customer." Then she backpedaled several steps. "Thank you, though. Really." She turned and hurried toward the parking lot.

I lowered my head. "Son of a bitch," I muttered.

You're no good, Johnny.

Chapter 9

I woke up disoriented when a semi roared by.

It was dark, and the red lights on the clock were blurry. 5:23 a.m.

I grunted and fell back onto a crumpled towel. I still felt tired. I had flipped and flopped for hours courtesy of the bed's overly stuffed pillows. The unreachable itch had lingered while I remained awake, allowing my mind to race. Around one in the morning, I abandoned the pillows and grabbed a towel from the bathroom. I scrunched it up until it proved an adequate substitute.

A night light illuminated the sleeping dog. Corporal didn't stir when I moved on the bed. It was too early for our routine.

The highway traffic was infrequent, but noisy enough that I paid attention to it. It was easy to make out the difference between semis and large pickups. Had it been a consistent hum, perhaps it would have lulled me back to sleep.

When I started wondering where everyone was going so early, I figured it was time to get up. My brain was awake now, and I was cataloging the jobs that required people to work at that time. Garbage collectors. Bakers. Gas station attendants.

Border patrol agents.

I dragged myself out of bed.

***

If Metaline is quiet during the day, it's a graveyard at 6:30 a.m.

The only businesses operating then were the Border and Customs office and A Cup of Happiness. I walked into the coffee shop and made brief eye contact with Brooklyn, the barista. A poppy rock song danced through the air.

Two border patrol agents somberly waited as Brooklyn prepared their orders. They wore the agency's green uniforms and carried tired expressions.

"Still can't believe it," the first guard whispered. He was a thick shouldered man with short, dark hair. His eyes were red as if from crying. "We should be there. Macon was our brother."

The second was tall and lean, the type of build a marathon runner might have. He wore the same uniform. "The lieutenant told us to clear out. He didn't want us down there. And what good could we do? All I know is state patrol better handle this case."

At the mention of state patrol, I moved closer.

Shoulders curled his upper lip. "Our administration won't let the county apes fuck around with this, would they? You know how they'd make a mess of it."

The coffee machine hissed as Brooklyn frothed milk for the coffees.

"Still," Shoulders said. "I don't care about jurisdiction. We should be there in a show of support or something."

"Did Macon have a side piece down in Ione?" Marathon Man asked.

Shoulders shrugged. "Not that I know of."

Brooklyn glanced over her shoulder at the two agents.

Marathon Man looked at his associate. "Maybe she knew."

"Who? His wife?"

"Happens."

Shoulders clucked. "I know, but she wouldn't have done this. No way."

Marathon Man nodded. "For real. Macon would have told us if he had a honey in Ione, right?"

"Of course he would. Air cover, bro."

The two grimaced and shook their heads, obviously lost in their own thoughts.

Marathon Man glanced back and frowned. He didn't say anything but turned back to the front. He leaned closer to his friend. "Someone's with her, right? His wife?"

"I'm sure," Shoulders said dismissively. "Someone."

Marathon wiped his lips. "Whoever it is, let's hope they're not saying anything stupid about him."

"Glass houses," Shoulders said. "Nobody will say shit."

Marathon Man leaned closer to his friend. "If it wasn't a little extra on the side, what was Macon doing down in Ione?"

"I don't know."

"What do you think his wife is going to say to the state detectives?" Marathon Man asked.

"What can she say?"

Marathon Man looked back now. "Help you?"

Shoulders turned fully so I could see his name tag— *Akre*. Quinton Akre. He was one of the men that Daisy said ran with Macon Young. "Got a problem?" he asked.

I pointed at the counter. "Waiting my turn."

Akre scowled. "Do it over there."

I lifted my hands and stepped back.

Marathon Man faced me, and I saw his name tag now—*Foster*. Bodhi Foster. His expression tightened. "Were you listening to us?"

Brooklyn set their coffees on the counter. "Leave him alone. That's my cousin."

They turned to her.

"Your cousin?" Akre asked.

Foster reached into a pocket, but Brooklyn held up a hand. "On the house, because of… Well, you know."

"Appreciate that," Akre said.

"Ditto." Foster lifted his coffee. "So, where's your cousin from?"

"Spokane," she said.

"Spokane sucks." Foster's lip curled as he looked over his shoulder.

I shrugged. If he wanted to goad me into a fight, he missed his chance last night. This morning, all I wanted was coffee. Besides, I knew where the man was emotionally. He'd just found out his friend was dead, and he couldn't do anything to help. Right now, he wanted to hit someone. I wasn't going to sign up for that job.

Acker studied me. "He's too old to be your cousin."

"Are you making fun of my family tree?" the barista asked.

Foster continued to eye me but directed his question at Brooklyn. "What side of the family tree is he on?"

"Why aren't you asking him, Bodhi?"

"I like asking you better."

Brooklyn rolled her eyes but didn't answer.

Akre tapped his friend's arm, then jerked his head. "Let's roll."

Foster nodded. "Some other time, Brooksy."

Brooklyn smiled but her eyes remained flat. "I'll have the coffee ready."

The two border agents left the shop.

"I didn't expect to see you back," Brooklyn said.

"Why not? We're cousins after all."

She rolled her eyes. "They were getting territorial. Hope you don't mind me adopting you into the family."

"I've been called worse than cousin."

A smile hinted at the corner of her mouth. "What can I get you?"

"Black coffee and a muffin."

Brooklyn reached for a cup. "Word around town is you're helping Daisy."

"Small town gossip."

She held the cup under the coffee pump. "Private detective, huh? Is that anything like the movies?"

"Not really."

"You have a gun?"

I thumbed over my shoulder. "In the truck."

"Ever shoot anybody?"

"I once stabbed a guy with an umbrella."

"Jesus." She set the coffee on the counter. "Really?"

"What happened to Macon?" I asked.

"Somebody killed him last night."

"No shit?"

Brooklyn grabbed a muffin and set it on a plate. "That's what his friends said."

"Where'd it happen?"

"Ione."

I pulled out a few bills and tossed them on the counter. "Word around town is Macon and his buddies are a bunch of horn dogs."

Brooklyn smirked. "That's one way of putting it. Macon was the worst of the bunch."

"The Big Dog."

"So you heard." She scooped up the cash.

"What else can you tell me about Macon?"

Her eyes hardened. "You probably know more than I ever will."

"How's that?"

"You're working with Daisy. She has the inside scoop on that clique." Brooklyn put the bills into the cash register.

"Anything you can tell me would be helpful."

"Sorry," Brooklyn said. "I've got work to do." She turned her attention to the back counter.

I grabbed my coffee and muffin and I headed for the door.

"See you later, cousin," she called.

***

Daisy opened the door in a half-shirt and tight cotton panties. Almost nothing was left to the imagination. Her legs were toned, and her stomach was flat.

"What is it?" she muttered as she rubbed a fist into her left eye.

"Macon's dead." I looked directly in the unobstructed eye and ignored the dopamine pumping through my veins.

She lowered her hand. "How?"

"My guess is foul play. He was found last night in Ione."

Daisy crossed her arms over her stomach as if she suddenly realized she wasn't covered. "I should get dressed."

"Probably a good idea."

"Come inside." She backpedaled.

I remained on the other side of the transom.

Daisy took another couple of steps backward. When she realized I wasn't coming in, she turned and went into her bedroom.

I reached into the house, grabbed the knob, and pulled the door closed.

Corporal wandered about the front yard while I sipped my coffee and ate my muffin. I finished the latter by the time the door opened again. The chain was wrapped around her waist and the padlock was back in place. She wore the Army jacket, jeans, and a Def Leppard half-shirt. As usual, her combat boots were untied.

Daisy waved me in. "Bring the dog."

We headed up the steps.

Her gaze dropped to the coffee I held. "I got a pot started, but it looks like you're set."

"I hadn't planned on coming by so early."

Daisy walked into the kitchen. "Brooklyn and I don't get along. Not sure why but I can imagine. We've never really talked about it."

I followed her and sat at the table. Corporal lay on the floor in the living room.

"Why do you stay here if everyone knows your business?" I asked.

"A bigger city only promises more trouble." She checked the coffeepot. It gurgled and was about one-fourth full. "About Macon. What happened?"

"He left The Hairy Man last night with a girl. She lives in Ione."

Daisy turned, crossed her arms, and rested her back against the counter. "How do you know that?"

"I went back to the bar."

"What for?"

I glanced at the ceiling. How could I explain my moment of weakness?

"You went looking for trouble." It wasn't a question.

My gaze dropped to her.

"It's written on your face."

My pulse accelerated.

"I know that look." She shoved her fists into the jacket's pockets. "I've seen it in the mirror."

I looked down at the top of my coffee.

"What happened?" she asked.

"Everything." I paused before adding, "You."

"Me?" She straightened.

It was a dumb thing to say. Before she could ask me to explain, I quickly added, "A call with my mother."

Daisy relaxed. "What'd she say?"

"It's what she wouldn't say. I'm sure she knows Nick."

"Of course she does." Daisy pulled her hands from the coat and spread her arms wide. "He's your father."

I shook my head. "Gabriel Baldwin is my father."

She pointed toward the other room. "Then how do you explain Nick's scrapbook?"

"I can't."

Daisy crossed her arms. "What kind of trouble were you hoping to find at the bar?"

"I was hoping to fight Macon."

"What the hell for?"

"You wouldn't understand."

"Try me," she said.

The coffeemaker percolated behind her.

Daisy grabbed the lock and twisted it. "Did you want to fight him because of me?"

"Not really." I watched the chain tightened around her waist. "Maybe."

"Tell me why." Daisy twisted the lock until she grimaced. "I'll probably understand better than anyone you've ever met."

I met her gaze. "I wanted to burn down my world."

Her hand grew bright red from exertion. "But why?"

"To show it that it can't hurt me."

She held the lock a second longer before releasing it. The tension on the belt eased. "That's a new one."

"Not exactly Man of the Year stuff."

Daisy scoffed. "We're all screwed up, Cutler. Most of us never admit how much."

I picked at my coffee cup lid. "What did Macon tell you about Nick?"

She turned to a cabinet and removed a mug. "It was nothing but lies, so he could get Nick out of the way."

"I still want to know."

"Macon and his cronies liked our setup." She poured coffee into the cup. "Honestly, I was okay with my life like that. I knew my role in their lives." She faced me. "I knew how everyone in town judged me. Maybe I should have worn a big red A on my shirt."

It had been a lot of years since English class, but I got the reference to *The Scarlet Letter*.

"Macon showed up one day to tell me about Nick. He said he couldn't find anything on him. He'd run him through various databases. You know, cop stuff and whatnot. I got upset and told him to stay out of our lives. I should have known he wouldn't."

"What happened?"

She sipped her coffee.

"Macon said Nick stopped existing in the late sixties. There hadn't been any record of him for almost forty years until he wandered into my bookstore."

"What did Nick say about it?"

"He was truthful. He said he'd been living off the grid in Canada. Working under the table, jobs like that."

"Why was he doing that?"

"He'd gone up to Canada to avoid the war."

"He dodged the draft?"

She nodded.

"Why'd he live off the grid? I thought one of those presidents—Carter or Ford—pardoned them."

"He never said why. He just said he did."

I quickly did the math. "The war was a long time ago. He could have come at any time after the mid-seventies. What finally brought him back to the states?"

Daisy stared into her coffee. "An accident."

"What kind?"

"A car accident while he was drinking." She looked up. "That's why he stopped."

"Was someone hurt?"

"A woman. A mother." Daisy set the cup down and crossed her arms. "She died. Nick went on the run after that."

A hit-and-run, I thought. "Are the Canadians looking for him?"

"Nick thought so."

I furrowed my brow. "How'd he get across the border?"

She waved a hand. "I don't know."

"Nick told you about a collision that killed a woman, but didn't reveal how he got back in? The border guards would have asked for identification. He had to show them something."

Daisy shrugged. "Nobody did."

Something didn't smell right. "If he'd been living in Canada all those years, he needed some identification for something. Renting a place. Buying a car. Getting a bank account. Crossing the border."

"I don't know what to tell you."

"What name was he living under?"

Daisy shoved her hands into her jacket pockets. "He lived under a lot of names. He told me that much, but none of those names mattered. Nicholas is his real name."

I almost asked how she knew, but I remembered my mother's reaction. "Why would he tell you his real name? If he'd been living a lie in Canada for all those years, then he kills a woman—"

"It was an accident," she interrupted.

"He comes back into the states and tells the truth to the first person he meets. It doesn't make sense."

"Why are you downplaying what we have?" Hurt registered in Daisy's eyes. "He didn't come back right away. It took him some time to get out of Canada." She turned around and grabbed the coffeepot.

"How long did it take him to get out?"

"Four months." She refilled her cup and set the pot back in place.

"That's what he told you?"

"You don't believe him?" She faced me, and her eyes challenged mine.

"Nick stopped drinking at that time?"

"He stopped drinking a couple months before that. For what it's worth, I believe him. He started going to meetings wherever he was, probably under the other name he had. I never asked those questions. I didn't want to know."

"Why didn't he just drive for the border?"

"I don't know." Daisy appeared frustrated. She looked away and sipped some coffee.

Maybe Nick knew better than to head straight for the border. Or perhaps he needed to get some false identification together in order to cross without incident.

"Did you ever look up this accident?" I asked.

Daisy's face pinched. "Why would I do that? I didn't want to know about it."

I rubbed my chin as I thought. Something was missing from her story. It took me a minute to key on it. "How'd he get money?"

She shrugged. "He worked."

"Doing what?"

"Odd jobs mostly."

"For forty years?"

She shrugged a second time. "What can I tell you? That's what he said. Your father—" Her face softened. "He's a charming man. He told me he lived a lot of years hand-to-mouth, and I believed that, too."

"Did he say where he was from originally?"

"Why would you ask that?"

"Just answer the question."

"He said Coulee City. Why's that matter?"

"Does he have any family there?"

"No," Daisy said. "He's got no family anymore. Nick said he never had any brothers or siblings and his parents died when he was in high school. A train crash or something. You're his only family, whether you like it or not."

I didn't want to argue anymore about my lineage.

"You think he might have headed home?" I asked.

Daisy blinked and considered me. "Wait. You don't think he's missing?"

"Maybe he had to leave in a hurry."

"Without telling me?" Her face pinched. "He wouldn't do that. He would have called."

"Maybe he didn't want to worry you."

Her face tightened, and both hands gripped the coffee cup.

"Back to my question," I said. "Could he have headed to Coulee City?"

Confusion and hurt fought for control in her eyes. "But why?"

"I don't know."

She put the coffee cup on the counter. "It's been a lifetime since he's been there."

My lifetime, I thought.

"He's got no one to go back to." She pointed to the other room. "What about his scrapbook? He would have taken that with him, right? He wouldn't have left that."

I thought about it. "Maybe, but he found most of that stuff on the internet. He could probably do it again." The stuff about my downfall from Seattle PD could likely still be found, and I was certain the recent cases in Spokane were available.

"Some of it was from newspapers," Daisy said. "He wouldn't leave that."

I sipped my coffee. "Maybe."

"Maybe nothing. Those are the only mementos of his past he had." Tears welled in her eyes. "He wouldn't leave the file behind. Why won't you believe me?" She set her coffee down and left the kitchen.

A moment later, she hollered, "No!"

I hurried to the guest room.

Her cheeks were red, and her eyes blazed with anger. "Right there."

The shelf she pointed at was empty.

"The scrapbook was right there!" Her voice rose in hysterics. "Somebody took it."

I left the room. Daisy followed.

"Where're you going?" she asked.

"He's alive," I said. "He's not missing."

She grabbed my arm. "You think he took it?" The emotions on her face showed she struggled to comprehend the truth.

"Who else would want it?"

"Maybe—" Her words cut off as she struggled to find meaning in a stolen folder with my history in it. Her fingernails dug into my arm. "Are you going to find him?"

I pulled free. "I'm done."

"He's your father."

"Listen, lady—" I lifted a finger. "For the last time, he's not my father."

"Then stay because it's your job."

"Yeah? Well, I'm not getting paid." I jerked open the door.

"I'll pay you."

"You can't afford it."

She bounded down the steps after me. "I've got money. My trust fund." She ran around me and held up both hands. "Please stop. There's more than enough for you to find him."

I stopped walking. "Why do you even care?"

"Because I love him."

"If what I think is true, he left without saying goodbye."

"Then something bad has happened."

"He came into your house," I said, "and took his scrapbook without telling you he was back."

She grabbed my arms. "That shows he's worried about getting me involved with whatever's going on."

"He's old enough to be your father."

Daisy's eyes narrowed. "He didn't judge me, and I won't judge him. I want to help him."

I looked over her shoulder at my truck. Corporal watched me.

"My regular rate," I said, "plus expenses."

"I thought that was implied."

"Starting yesterday."

She nodded. "Yeah, okay. Whatever. Do I need to sign something?"

"No, but you need to get ready."

"Why?"

"Because we're going to Ione."

***

Corporal sniffed the bushes outside Daisy's home while I called my mother. She answered on the fourth ring.

"Johnny." Her tone was flat. I imagined her sitting in her kitchen, staring out over the impeccable garden of her Gig Harbor home.

"I need to talk with you," I said.

"Fine."

"Not hanging up this time?"

She scoffed. "Van is on his way to work, and I'm alone. This is an appropriate time for a discussion like this."

My mother was all about appropriateness. She wasn't always that way. When I was little, I remember a different woman. She dressed trendy and listened to folk music. She cursed and smoked and let me eat hot dogs in front of our black and white television. Something changed along the way. She altered her eating habits and refrained from swearing except in those moments when she called me a bastard. Next, she cut her beautiful long hair into a bob and started wearing slacks instead of shorts or corduroys. She dabbled in church for a while, but that didn't stick. The weekend courses on positivity and real estate investing seemed to have a bigger impact than serving the Lord.

I would have blamed her changes on my uncle's murder, but she was already well on the path when that event occurred. Reuben's sudden death might have accelerated her conservatism, but it didn't put her on that course.

"You knew a man named Nick Gossett?" I asked.

"I did once, yes, but that was a lifetime ago."

Lifetime, I thought dryly. Everyone was throwing that term around without much consideration.

I leaned against my truck. "How did you know him?"

She sighed. "How do you think?"

"I don't know, Mom. That's why I'm asking." I kicked a rock, and it skittered down the road.

"He was a friend."

It was my turn to sigh. "What kind of friend?"

"The question you're asking is inappropriate."

A dented pickup drove slowly down Pend Oreille Street. The driver, an elderly man, eyed me, then Daisy's house. I lifted my chin in his direction, but his attention returned to the road.

If she wasn't going to come out and say it, I was going to ask directly. "Were you fucking him?"

"*Johnny!*"

"Don't *Johnny* me, Mom. Your relationship with the truth gets sketchy when things get uncomfortable."

"You're an unbelievable bastard."

"From day one."

Silence descended on our conversation, but she didn't hang up. Corporal flopped in the middle of the yard and rolled on his back.

"Well?" I asked. "Were you—"

"Yes. Nicholas and I were intimate."

The revelation didn't impact me. My mother had many lovers when I was younger. I eventually figured out that the different men parading through our lives weren't visiting uncles.

My mother sanitized her history over the years. She kept no friends who could challenge her revised version of events. Her parents had died, and her brother was murdered so I was the only one who had an inkling of the woman she had been. To the world today, the former Carol Cutler was a pillar of the community. However, to one little boy, she remained an enigma.

"When were you two together?" I asked. "And were you a couple?"

"Why is this important?"

"You know why."

My mother exhaled heavily. "He's not your father. Gabe is."

She was avoiding the answer. I rephrased my question, emphasizing each word. "When were you and Nick intimate?"

"I don't remember the exact dates."

"Was it after I was born?"

Several seconds passed before she answered. "No."

"So, before."

She clucked. "This is like picking old wounds, Johnny."

"I'd rather not have this conversation, either."

"We can hang up now and pretend it never happened."

I barked a single, sharp laugh. "Not a chance."

Corporal shimmied on the ground. The dog was having far more fun than I was.

"Just so I get this clear," I said, "you were intimate with Nick at the same time you were intimate with Gabe."

"I'm not a whore," she snapped.

The silence returned to our conversation.

Daisy opened the front door of her house and stepped onto the porch. She cocked her head as she studied my face. Corporal flipped over and watched her. His tail slowly wagged.

"You look exactly like him," my mother said. "There's no doubt in my mind that Gabe is your father."

"Hold on," I said. "That's how you know he's my father? Because I look like him? You couldn't have known that at my birth. Did you get a paternity test? Did they even do those tests back then?"

"I loved Gabe," my mother said. "I didn't need a test."

Daisy started down the steps.

"But you were fucking Nick, too," I said louder than necessary. I immediately regretted it by the look on Daisy's face.

She stopped before stepping onto the sidewalk. Confusion flashed in her eyes as the dog trotted over to her.

"Why must you be so crude, Johnny?"

"Because I'm angry, Mother."

Daisy lowered her head and sat on the top step. Her hand sunk into the dog's fur.

"Did you love him, too?" I asked.

"Not as much as Gabe."

"Oh, Christ." I pinched the bridge of my nose. "What did you do?"

"When I realized I was pregnant, I ended it with Nick. He wasn't the father."

I squatted and closed my eyes. I was struggling to control myself. I wanted to lash out and yell at my mother. The sanitizing of her history went ever further back than I realized. "How could you know who the father was?"

"Because I knew how the calendar worked."

"It sounds like your calendar was full with both of them."

"I asked you not to be crude." She paused and silence came through the line. Then she brought out an old tool. "A woman knows," she said.

This was the evolution of her bullshit. When I was little, she talked about the universe and its power as her guiding force. For a while, she dragged me to church and decided it was God who told her what to do. When we stopped attending, she announced her womanly intuition gave her authority to make unilateral decisions.

"You couldn't just know that," I said.

My mother huffed. "You're not a woman. You don't know what it means to carry a life."

I lightly punched myself in the head with my free hand—once, twice, three times.

"Gabriel is your father," my mother continued. "You can trust me on that. You look exactly like him. Stop with this nonsense and put it all away. Forget you ever heard of Nicholas Gossett. I have."

A hand rested on the back of my head. I looked up and Daisy stood over me. Her eyes were soft and filled with kindness.

"Do you still have that same email address?" I asked. "The one at AOL?"

"Why do you ask?"

I stood and looked directly into Daisy's eyes. Her hand slid from my head, and she crossed her arms.

"In a couple minutes," I said, "a woman is going to email you a picture."

"What is it? What woman?"

"She's a friend, and it's a photograph from a newspaper. Nick is in it."

My mother sniffed dismissively. "I don't want to look at it."

"I need to know if this is the same guy from your past."

"What if I refuse?"

"Then this will be the last call we ever have." I hung up.

Daisy's lips pursed. "Your mother sounds nice."

I slipped my phone into my pocket. "We need to make a stop before we leave."

"I heard. I'll meet you at the bookstore." She walked away, then turned to call over her shoulder. "I can't wait to learn more about your childhood. It might be even more messed up than mine."

***

We returned to the bookstore, and I followed her inside. Corporal stayed in the truck. She headed up the stairs to her office, but paused when she realized I wasn't following. She looked back to see me standing near the door.

"I won't bite," she said.

I thought I might, and that worried me. I didn't want to be that guy again. I'd tried hard to change over the handful of years. The desire to burn down my world continued to confuse me.

Daisy frowned. "I got overheated last time. It won't happen again. I promise."

I nodded and stepped forward. She turned and finished the trek upstairs. When I made it to the office, I remained in the doorway.

Daisy dropped into her desk chair and settled her hands on the keyboard. After calling up a program, she asked, "What's your mother's email?"

I told her.

"AOL?" She shook her head. "Hello, two thousand late."

"I thought you were a rock and roller."

She glanced over her shoulder and rolled her eyes. "Just because I rock doesn't mean I don't know who the Black-Eyed Peas are. I'm surprised you do."

"Don't judge a book by its cover."

I crossed my arms and leaned against the doorjamb. My gaze flitted about the room while she worked. Above the low bookshelves, various posters hung on the walls. There seemed no rhyme or reason to why they were there. One was from the 1985 Bloomsday race. A faded, crinkled one came from a Bon Jovi concert. The final poster was from the movie *Love Actually*. The first two might have come from her childhood. The film was too new. I wondered what about the movie she liked so much to put it on display.

Flat, unused post office boxes were everywhere. No doubt they were part of her online business. I wanted to know how much money a used bookstore in Nowhere, Washington, could make in internet sales.

"The newspaper photo is on its way," Daisy said.

"Please send the photos of my mother, too."

She glanced back at me. "The files are big. I'm going to have to send them a couple at a time."

I nodded and Daisy turned back to the computer.

"Are we still going to Ione?" she asked as her fingers jumped about the keyboard.

"If there's a homicide investigation going on, they'll be there for a while."

"How do you know?"

"Trust me."

She looked over her shoulder. "Right. I forgot."

I pulled my cell phone from my pocket and called my mother. She answered on the first ring.

"Sturdy Goats Reading Company?" she asked, in wonder. "Where *are* you?"

"Don't bother with that. Just pay attention to the photograph in the article. Is that Nick?"

My mother sounded distracted. "Was there an accident? It says the last name is Grossett."

"Ignore the story and the misspelling. Concentrate on the picture. Is it the guy you remember?"

She went quiet for a moment. "It's been a long time."

"Thirty-nine years. Is that him or not?"

Daisy turned. "All the photos are on the way. Took three emails."

I nodded. "Thank you," I whispered.

My mother sighed. "If I had to guess…"

"I'm asking you."

"That's Nick." She sounded defeated, but it only lasted a moment. A switch flicked, and impatience flooded her voice. "Why can't you leave all this alone?"

"There are three other emails on the way."

"What for?" my mother asked.

"There are photographs in them."

"Of what?"

I bowed my head. "Just look at them."

"Don't take that tone—" The line went silent.

"Hello?" I asked.

I checked the phone to make sure the call was still connected.

Daisy leaned forward in her chair. "Something happen?"

"Hello?" I repeated into the phone.

"They've arrived," my mother said. "The pictures." She sounded distracted. "What was he doing taking these?"

"He was watching you—us."

"I remember this." Her voice softened further as her thoughts traveled back through the years. "We lived in Bothell. With Reuben. It wasn't long. I kept expecting your father to show up, but he never did. It was just you and me, Johnny."

"And Nick."

"He was never part of us. I wasn't seeing him then." The hardness returned to her voice. "Is there anything else?"

"Did Nick and Gabe know each other?"

She inhaled sharply. "Are you crazy? What kind of woman do you think I am?"

"You were a different woman back then."

My mother tsked. "I don't have time for any of this."

"Make time."

"No."

"This is important," I said.

"The past is where it belongs." It sounded as if my mother was now moving about her house. "I'm late for a meeting."

"Don't hang up."

"Goodbye, son."

The call ended, and I stared at my phone.

Daisy stood. "You two need counseling."

I snapped the phone closed. "Let's go."

Chapter 10

It was a twelve-minute drive from Metaline to Ione. The highway paralleled the Pend Oreille River. The truck's radio was off. The only sound inside the cab was the hum of the road and Corporal's excited panting.

Daisy leaned forward to look around Corporal's big head. "I like your dog and all, but why does he have to sit up front?"

"He's not up front."

"You know what I mean."

Corporal rode in the truck's back seat, but he was trying to worm his way into the front. He had a paw on the middle console and his head was level with ours.

I pushed him back with my elbow. "He doesn't ride in the bed. It's not safe."

"People around here do it all the time. Their dogs do, anyway."

"It's not safe," I repeated.

As soon as I put my hand back on the steering wheel, Corporal stuck his head between us again. His panting resumed.

She eyed the dog with mild curiosity. "I thought he followed directions."

"You're in his seat."

"Want me to sit in back?"

"If you don't mind."

Daisy studied me.

"I'm joking." I shoved the dog back again. "At ease," I said harshly.

I didn't know if his previous owner had trained him with a military command to hit the ground. If he had, I didn't know it and we hadn't practiced it. Which meant I was left with the same commands we practiced for other behaviors. None of them calmed Corporal when he was in the back seat. I discovered this odd behavior whenever Stacy rode with us. Corporal became a nervous wreck in the back seat. If he got to sit in the front, he was a happy dog.

Corporal slid off the console and moved to the side window behind me. His panting resumed in my ear.

Daisy twisted under her seatbelt to face me. The shoulder strap cut across her neck, and she pulled it out of the way. "What are we hoping to find?"

"I don't know."

"Yeah, you do. Why won't you be honest with me?"

My thumb bounced on the steering wheel. "I'm hoping we can find the crime scene."

"Where Macon was murdered? What for?"

"Maybe we'll learn something."

She squinted. "You think Nick might be involved somehow?"

"I don't know."

"What do you know?"

Corporal paced from window to window in the back seat as I continued to tap the steering wheel. I kept my thoughts to myself.

"Fine," Daisy said. "Have it your way. What did your mother say?"

"She knew Nick."

"Was there any doubt?"

I shrugged a single shoulder. "My mother..." The unfinished sentence hung in the air.

"Were you worried she'd lie to you?"

"You haven't met my mother."

"Why would she do that?"

"Because Nick doesn't fit her current narrative."

"Which is what?"

"My mother thinks herself an upstanding citizen. One with friends in the right places. Friends who live in gated communities who would never socialize with people like me."

"Or me," Daisy added.

"Maybe those folks think about my mother in the same way," I said. "That she holds some perceived value to their perfect community. My mother wasn't always so squeaky clean. Nick is a reminder of her past—one filled with questionable choices."

Daisy absently tugged on the seatbelt strap. "And she wants to forget those?"

"She's pushed them into the deepest recesses of her closet. I just shone some light on them."

"I can understand her feelings." Daisy faced forward. "If I could forget my past, I would."

We fell silent for a couple of minutes and the humming of the truck's wheels filled the void.

Corporal stuck his head between us and panted. I shoved him back. He bounced from window to window before returning to the middle console. He was like a conqueror hoping to gain ground by repeatedly attacking through a valley. I pushed him away once again.

"I tried to do what your mother did," Daisy said. "I changed my location and got rid of my friends, but my problem followed."

"A bigger city might have a support group for your problem."

"I already said a bigger city only promises more opportunities for trouble." She tugged on the extra length of chain around her waist. "You know, if I was a man, they wouldn't call it a problem."

I casually flicked my hand. "You don't have to call it a problem either. Embrace it if you want."

She eyed me questioningly.

"A person only stops drinking because they want something different," I said. "If they're happy with their lives, they don't give up alcohol."

Daisy smirked. "I see what you're doing."

"I'm not a counselor, but if you like how your life is going—"

She rolled her eyes. "Give it a rest."

"Keep doing what you're doing."

Daisy rested her head against the passenger window. "All right already."

"I'm just saying."

"Since I'm paying you, shouldn't that buy me some peace and quiet?"

Corporal stuck his head between us. His panting seemed even more intense.

Up ahead, the city of Ione waited.

***

We zigzagged through Ione, searching for a crime scene. It had been years since I was in the Seattle Police Department, but there was one thing of which I remained certain. Had Macon been murdered in the night, some part of the investigation was still active.

Perhaps the detectives were fast, and they already investigated the scene and left. Maybe the forensics team processed all the evidence, and the county coroner had collected the body. Even if true, I imagined the crime scene would remain locked down for a day or two just in case someone needed to come back and do a second check.

Corporal panted heavily in the back seat. I looked over my shoulder at him. Was his age the issue or was my lack of working him the problem? His previous owner was a stickler for training. He was a Marine, so he maintained impeccable habits. I played with the dog far more than trained him. Was I doing Corporal a disservice?

When we turned onto Hambrook Street from Fourth Avenue, it was hard to miss.

"There." Daisy pointed ahead.

A Pend Oreille County Sheriff's patrol car blocked our path at the next intersection. Its red and blue emergency lights flicked back and forth.

I backed up, turned around, and headed north on Fourth. When I got to Blackwell Street, I hung a right. When we passed through the next intersection, Daisy and I both glanced south to check out the parked patrol car. Even Corporal turned to look.

Food Court, a local grocery store, briefly blocked our view. After we cleared the building, we entered the partially full parking lot and proceeded through it to the other side. Yellow POLICE—DO NOT CROSS caution tape was strung between sawhorses to block the south exit. A crowd of roughly twenty people had gathered behind the line.

Across the street was The Homestead, a rundown motor lodge with twelve cabins scattered about an office. Each building had once been painted red with black accents. The red had faded and flaked over time to something resembling brown, like dried blood. The black now looked mostly gray. A silver-haired woman in jeans and a droopy Wazzu sweatshirt spoke with a tall man in a sport coat. From this distance, she looked like the sweet grandmotherly type. He held a notepad and jotted things as she spoke.

A maroon unmarked Chevy Impala was parked in front of the third cabin. Its door was wide open. A woman in black slacks and a white shirt exited the cabin with a large brown paper bag.

Behind me, a horn honked, and I checked the rearview mirror. A woman threw her hands in the air then angrily motioned for me to get out of her way. I accelerated to a parking spot that gave us a view of The Homestead.

"What're we doing?" Daisy asked.

"We're watching."

She leaned her head back against her seat. "Is this going to help us find Nick?"

I reached over and petted Corporal who now had two paws on the console. His invasion of the front seat was progressing well. Now that the engine was off and we were parked, his panting had calmed.

"How long are we going to sit here?" Daisy asked.

"As long as it takes."

***

Two women I recognized approached the yellow police line.

"Stay here," I said.

Daisy looked around Corporal. "Where're you going?"

I slipped out of the truck and headed toward the crowd.

Holly wore a tan University of Idaho sweatshirt, blue shorts, and UGGs. Her friend, Taylor, sported a black Vandals sweatshirt, black yoga pants, and leather sandals. Neither had done their hair and their faces were free of makeup. They appeared hungover and clutched iced coffees to their chests.

I was near enough to hear Taylor ask an older man, "What happened?"

"Someone was murdered."

"Do you know who?"

"A border guard."

Taylor inhaled sharply. "Border guard?"

"That's right. Guess that manager—" He pointed across the street. "—heard something and went to check on it and found the dead guy. How 'bout that, huh?"

Taylor whirled to Holly. "You don't think?"

Holly shrugged. "It's probably not. He went home, right?"

"That's right." Taylor nodded. "He went home." She noticed me watching them and cocked her head. "Yeah?"

Holly turned around. "What's your problem?"

"We met last night," I said. "At The Hairy Man."

Her eyes traveled my length. "I don't think so."

"You were waiting for Taylor to come back and pick you up." My gaze flicked to the friend. "She'd left with Macon."

At the mention of his name, Taylor put her hand on Holly's shoulder. "Why're you here?"

"The same reason as you." I jerked my head toward The Homestead.

Taylor's eyes widened. "Is it Macon?"

"I'm afraid so."

She grabbed Holly and collapsed into her arms.

Holly scowled. "Dude. Not cool."

Asking Taylor a question was no longer possible due to her wailing. I stayed focused on Holly. "What time did she pick you up last night?"

She stroked the back of Taylor's head. "I'm not talking to you."

"Maybe I should have a deputy come over and ask the same questions."

"Are you cop or something?"

"A private detective. When did she pick you up?"

Taylor looked up from Holly's shoulder. "A private detective?"

"That's right."

She started crying again and pushed her face into the side of Holly's neck.

"I don't know," Holly said. She caressed Taylor's head. "Eleven, I guess."

I eyed the crime scene. It took maybe fifteen minutes to Metaline Falls from Ione. "Taylor, did Macon leave your house at 10:45?"

"She doesn't have to answer you," Holly said.

Taylor straightened, though, and eyed me. She wiped her nose on the sleeve of her sweatshirt, then inhaled in stuttering fashion. "I picked you up at 10:30."

"10:30?" Holly asked.

Taylor nodded once. "I know because Macon had to get home to his wife by then." Taylor irritably swiped tears away from her eyes. "He left my house at 9:30."

Holly turned to her friend. "It took you an hour to pick me up?"

Taylor's face pinched. "I had to clean up."

"Still." Holly's face reddened. "An hour?"

"You and Macon didn't drive together?" I asked.

Taylor shook her head. "He had to go home to her when we were done." Fury filled her eyes. "I'm so fucking stupid."

"No, you're not," Holly said. She reached out and patted her friend's arm.

"I should have said no." Taylor turned away from us.

I asked, "Did he have any reason to be at the motel?"

Holly motioned toward the west with her iced coffee. "We live back that-a-way. He probably came down this road. You think he maybe saw someone he knew?"

Taylor faced us again and her eyes narrowed. "You don't think he was hooking up with someone else, do you?"

The bartender at The Hairy Man had called Macon a 'notorious poon hound.' Last night, he drove to Ione to hook up with Taylor. Was it out of the question that he had a second woman lined up at The Homestead?

I considered the motor lodge. Perhaps Macon's wife found out about it and killed him. Or maybe the border agent was meeting with a married woman and her husband discovered their affair. Neither was a leap of imagination, but both felt wrong.

Whatever the reason for stopping at The Homestead, it got him killed.

Taylor watched the crime scene. "Where's his truck?" She turned expectantly to Holly. "His truck isn't there." Her eyebrows raised hopefully. "Maybe it's not him."

"It's him," I said. "His killer probably took the truck."

Taylor burst into tears, and she fell back into her friend's arms.

Holly frowned. "Dude, you're an asshole." She patted Taylor's head.

"It was the truth," I said.

"So was that."

More locals approached to watch the crime scene activity.

Holly asked, "Should we maybe go talk with the cops?"

I nodded. "It would help them understand Macon's movements before his death."

Taylor's head snapped up. "Then his wife will know about—" She didn't need to finish her thought.

"She's going to find out one way or another," I said.

The tears started again. "Then everyone will know." Taylor's face pinched.

"That's how it goes."

Taylor wailed into her friend's shoulder.

Holly slowly shook her head. "Jesus, dude. You're the worst."

I left them to decide their plan.

When I climbed into the truck, Daisy asked, "Who are they?"

"Friends of Macon."

She curled her lip. "Please don't ever say that of me."

"That you were friends?"

"He was a terrible person."

"But you two—"

Daisy lifted a hand to stop me. "I know what we did. That doesn't mean I liked him."

"I get it."

"Do you?"

I nodded. "Totally."

Her expression hardened. "Can we go?"

"Not yet. I want to talk with the motel's manager."

Daisy stewed for several moments. "Whatever," she said eventually.

She yanked the door handle and pushed her door open. "I'm going for a walk. All this thinking about Macon isn't sitting well." She slid out of the truck and slammed the door. She headed toward the grocery store.

Corporal jumped into her seat.

I eyed the dog. "That didn't take you any time."

***

Waiting is a skill that can be learned and honed. If it's not practiced, it can certainly be lost. I leaned forward and rested my forearms on the steering wheel. I was better at it now than I had been while wearing the uniform. Back then, I was more about action—waiting

153

seemed like a terrible waste of time. Now, a lot could be gained from standing still.

Across the street, The Homestead's manager ambled back to her office. The detective returned to the opened cabin and talked with a woman in black slacks and a sport coat. She held two more brown bags. I pegged her for another detective or an evidence technician. Since I couldn't see a badge on her waist, I went with evidence technician.

Would Pend Oreille County have a dedicated forensics unit like Spokane and Seattle? I wasn't sure how things worked in smaller counties like this. Perhaps their detectives processed crime scenes. Smaller counties and towns could call in Washington State Patrol for help, but those arrogant bastards proudly splashed their logos over their vehicles, and I didn't see any WSP emblems in The Homestead parking lot.

Considering the woman an evidence technician was probably sexist. I didn't label the guy a forensic geek, and he was dressed exactly like her—slacks and a sport coat. I grunted. I thought myself mildly progressive, but my chauvinism reared its ugly head whenever I let my guard down. I wanted to do better—a guy with a daughter should.

I was about to catalogue my last few days, to see if other sexist thoughts had seeped in. However, Daisy returned from the grocery store and interrupted my self-reflection. She opened her door but didn't climb in.

The dog lay in her seat. I said, "Corporal, get in the back."

"No, it's fine." Daisy's fingers slid into the dog's fur. "I'm going for a walk."

"I thought you had."

She frowned as she lightly tugged on Corporal's ear. He seemed to like it. "Are you staying here?"

"That's the plan."

"Want me to take the dog?"

"If he's good with it."

Daisy leashed Corporal and he hopped out of the truck. The two walked off.

My attention returned to the crime scene. The detectives had disappeared, but the cabin remained open. I assumed they went into the room.

When I was a patrol officer, I developed a certain level of patience. It wasn't a particularly high level of patience, I will admit. I'd sit off a known drug house, waiting for a possible buyer to leave, then pull them over. My wait time was never remarkably long but the rules of engagement, both from the legal system and department policies, provided a framework for me to abide by.

While with the Seattle Police Department, my team and I once watched a murder suspect as he enjoyed a dinner with his girlfriend at a posh restaurant. We had enough probable cause for his arrest, but we didn't want to take him inside the establishment. We were concerned he might turn violent and hurt someone. It was decided to approach him away from others. A supervisor developed the plan. In hindsight, it was the best course of action. No member of the team argued with the ploy and the eventual arrest came off without a hitch. Waiting a couple of hours isn't a remarkably long time, but it feels like watching grass grow when it concerns a murder suspect.

Back at The Homestead, the male detective left the open cabin and crossed the parking lot. He headed toward the motor lodge's office. While he strode, he pulled a portable radio from underneath his jacket and lifted it to his mouth.

The female detective left the cabin with another brown paper bag and walked around the corner. Perhaps she had parked out of sight.

A deputy emerged from the nearby patrol car. He pulled a pocketknife from his pocket and cut the yellow tape from the first sawhorse. Several people in the gathered crowd spoke to him. The deputy ignored their questions as he moved to the second sawhorse and severed that end of tape. He balled the police line and shoved it into his trunk. The deputy picked up both sawhorses and moved them off to the side so the grocery store's exit was free of obstruction. Perhaps a local company had brought the sawhorses out for the deputies to use or maybe an employee of the traffic department had delivered them to the site. However they got there, the deputy wasn't taking them away.

Another patrol car drove by on Hambrook Street. The female deputy behind the steering wheel waved at the one cutting the tape from the sawhorses. She turned right onto Highway 31 and sped south. The first deputy got into his car, executed a U-turn, and headed north on the highway.

Without the forbidden yellow line and the deputies to watch, the crowd began to dissipate.

The female detective returned from around the corner with a roll of police tape.

After I left the department, waiting became a dirty word for me. I was no longer paid an hourly wage to sit around and observe someone else's actions. Observing felt as if I was scared to act. Since I was no longer an officer, departmental policy didn't constrain me. The rules of engagement were my own. Whenever trouble found me, and it certainly did, I could wade in without hesitation. Waiting might have been the better choice, but action felt better.

Opening a private investigator's office brought a new level of introspection into my behavior. Perhaps it was being responsible to a client that reeled in my actions. Maybe it was wisdom gained from getting my ass kicked a few times. Whatever it was, I soon learned sitting still and letting things play out sometimes worked to my advantage.

The male detective entered The Homestead's office. Almost immediately, he stepped out with the silver-haired woman on his heels. The two of them returned to the open cabin. The manager pulled the door closed and locked it. The male and female detectives strung yellow caution tape across the doorway and stapled it into place. They next stuck something in the upper corner of the door and the female detective wrote on it.

"And they're done," I muttered to myself.

The motor lodge's manager headed back toward her office. She stopped to pick up some trash on her way.

Chapter 11

Most of the crowd filtered away. By the looks on their faces, they seemed disappointed something exciting hadn't happened while they were there. No one was arrested or transported from the scene. Macon Young's body likely had been removed before many of the onlookers even arrived.

Crime scenes often start with a bang. They always end with a whimper.

I grabbed the folded copy of The Newport Miner and slipped out of the truck. I was surprised some of the looky-loos didn't immediately run across the street to talk with the manager. Maybe they already knew her and figured they'd get the story sooner or later. Or perhaps it was small-town decorum to allow the older woman time to gather herself before they peppered her with questions. Whatever it was that held those onlookers back, I was the only one who crossed the street.

An electronic bell warbled when I entered the small office. Wood paneling lined the walls, and framed photos of fishermen were nailed into place. A greenish blue shag carpet covered the floor, but a clear plastic mat protected the portion in front of the counter.

"Just a moment," a woman's voice came from another room. It sounded as if her mouth was full.

The lobby was clean and smelled of Lysol. A box television sat in the corner with Jerry Springer on; the sound was turned low. Above, a circular fan slowly stirred the air. A name plaque on the counter read *Betty Sue*.

The silver-haired woman stepped around the corner. She wiped her lips with a napkin and jumped when she saw me. "Shit," she said then coughed. "I thought you were the cops."

From across the street, I thought Betty might be the sweet grandmotherly type. Up close, she resembled something completely different. Her nose was gnarled and pitted from a lifetime of alcohol, her left eye drooped toward her cheek, and a scar called attention to the deep cleft in her chin. For a woman in her late sixties, it was apparent she had lived a rough life.

"They cleared out," I said.

She stood on her tiptoes to look over my shoulder. "Here for a room?" Her voice had a smoker's rasp.

"Just a couple questions."

Betty dropped to her normal height as suspicion clouded her eyes. She balled the napkin and tossed it on the counter. "About?"

"Have you seen this man?" I set *The Newport Miner* on the counter and pointed at Nick's face.

She grabbed the edge of the counter and leaned over the newspaper. "I remember when this happened." She looked up. "Who're you?"

"John Cutler. I'm a detective."

"No, you're not." Betty straightened and her tongue peeked between her lips. "The detectives were just here."

"A private investigator," I clarified. "I've been hired to find this man."

"Likely story."

I opened my wallet and removed the dog-eared business card I'd given to Macon Young the day before. I really needed to find a better way to transport them. I set it on the counter.

The manager strained to examine it. "That means nothing." She looked up with confidence. "Anyone can have those printed nowadays. Scams, you know. I seen it on my shows." She pushed it back toward me.

"My license is hanging in my office. You can come by and check it out if you want."

I reached for the business card, but she slapped her hand on it and pulled it back. Her gaze dropped to the card again. "You're in Spokane? Fat chance I'm going down there to see your business license."

"Was he here?" I tapped the newspaper photograph.

The woman straightened. "Aren't you supposed to bribe me or something?"

"No."

Betty crossed her arms and furrowed her brow. "Them private eyes do that in the movies."

"Some of them also beat up guys to get information."

Her eyes widened and she stepped back. "You threatening me?"

"I thought we were talking about movies."

"I don't think I like you."

"I've been getting that a lot lately."

"You should probably consider why that is." Betty stepped forward, swiped the business card from the counter, and returned to her position out of reach. "Do the cops know you're poking around? They should know about his picture being in the paper."

I lifted *The Newport Miner*. "Was he staying here?"

She flicked the business card with her finger. "They don't know about you, do they, Mr. Detective Man?"

I stared at her.

Betty's shoulders slumped. "C'mon, now. You're not gonna make it worth my while?"

"Being famous for a day isn't enough?"

She chuckled, which turned into a smoker's hack. Her face purpled and she doubled over as she continued to cough. When she finally stopped, she spat into a nearby trashcan. "Who said I'm famous?"

I motioned toward the grocery store parking lot. "Half the town was out there watching you."

"Wasn't half the town."

"Close enough. You'll get a lot of mileage out of this story."

Betty pursed her lips and put her hands on her hips. "Guess you're right. Probably get a beer or two from one of the boys."

"More than one, I'd imagine," I said encouragingly.

A sly grin appeared on Betty's face. "You know that's right."

My gaze bounced from the television back to her. "How about I make it more interesting for you?"

"How you going to do that?"

"What if I give you something better than the murder?"

"Better than the murder?" Betty smirked. "I'd like to see you try."

I tapped next to Nick Gossett's picture. "You'll get to tell people you helped a father and son reunite." The lie tasted horrible in my mouth, but it was better than paying for her cooperation. Besides, I didn't have that much cash with me, and I had no idea how long this manhunt was going to go on.

"He's your father?"

"Long lost."

"Get the fuck out." Betty definitely wasn't the sweet grandmother type. She leaned over the newspaper. "You two don't look nothing alike."

"I take after my mother." Another lie.

Betty's eyes cut to *The Jerry Springer Show*. "Yeah, all right. Fine." Her attention returned to the paper. "That's him."

"He was here?"

"That's what I said. Weren't you listening?" She set both hands on the counter and leaned forward. "Boy, them cops cleared outta here fast."

"How long was he here?"

"Four nights."

"You're sure?"

She nodded. "Of course, I'm sure. I had to show the registration book to the cops and everything."

"What name did he register under?"

Betty eyed the newspaper. "Wasn't Grossett. I'll you that much."

"What was it?"

She eyed me. "I think you should pay for that information."

It seemed as if I was stuck. I reached into my pocket and a smile formed on Betty's face.

"Now, we're talking," she said.

Nick wouldn't register under his own name. He could have picked any random name. I hated to pay for the information, but I didn't see any other way. A thought occurred to me, and I threw it out. "Gabriel Baldwin."

Her smile faded. "He really must've been your father."

I hid my surprise. "Did you ask to see a driver's license or other identification?"

"What for? He paid cash."

I grunted. "Did he have a vehicle?"

"He didn't register one. Didn't see any bags either."

"Didn't you find that strange?"

Betty smirked. "A lot happens I find strange in this business. Staying a few days without bags is pretty mild on my shock meter."

***

After I finished the interview with Betty, I started across Hambrook Street to return to my truck but stopped in the middle of the roadway.

"The hell?" I muttered.

Down the way, a red Honda was parked on the south side of the street. I couldn't be certain it was the same one as before because it was too far away to see the license plate. It might have been a local driver and not someone from British Columbia. I started toward it.

The Honda attempted a U-turn but had to stop short from hitting another car.

"Hey!" I hollered. It was a stupid thing to yell. The driver, whoever it was, wasn't likely to stop because of me. I ran with the newspaper clutched in my hand.

The sedan backed up a few feet, stopped again, then drove away. I got close enough to confirm its British Columbia license plate. The car swung onto Central Street and disappeared north behind the grocery store.

I sprinted as fast as I could, but by the time I made the intersection the car had vanished. It either headed east or west. I assumed it took off for the highway. I continued north to the next intersection, but it was hopeless.

The Honda was gone.

***

I returned to the grocery store parking lot and approached my truck from the rear. Daisy and Corporal stood near its front and watched The Homestead.

"Let's go," I said.

She spun around. "Where'd you come from?" When she saw my expression, she asked, "Everything okay?"

I yanked open the driver's door and tossed the newspaper onto the dashboard. "Get in."

Daisy walked to the other side and tugged open the back door. Corporal hopped in. He immediately tried to climb into the front seat, but I blocked his maneuver.

"Learn anything?" she asked after settling into the passenger seat.

"It was Nick." I started the truck. "He checked in under an assumed name."

"How do you know it was him then?"

"The manager verified his picture." I tapped the newspaper.

She leaned slightly forward as she considered the motor lodge. "What name did he use?"

"My father's—my *real* father."

Daisy flopped back into her seat. We both stared at the motel for a moment.

"Do you think it's possible…?" she started and turned to me. Corporal had stuck his head between the seats again. Daisy lifted so she could see over him. "Did Nick kill Macon?"

I rested my forearms along the steering wheel. "If I had to guess, yeah. I think so."

"But how?" She looked around, then checked her side mirror. "How'd he get here?" Daisy appeared confused. "Nick's not a fighter."

"A man can be lot of things when his back is against the wall."

"How's his back against the wall?"

I cast a sideways glance at her. "Are you sure you've never seen that red Honda before?"

"What red Honda?"

"The one we saw outside your business."

Her brow furrowed. "I'm pretty sure. Why?"

"I've seen it several times since then."

"Someone is following us?"

"Or they're looking for Nick and we keep crossing paths." I shoved Corporal back with my elbow.

"Nick walked from Metaline down here?"

"Maybe he hitchhiked. The Homestead's manager said he didn't have a vehicle when he checked in."

She shook her head. "But it's so far."

"It's nine, maybe ten miles. How long would that take to walk? Three hours or so?"

"I couldn't do that."

"You could if you had to," I said. "Besides, you told me Nick was running to stay in shape."

Daisy's eyes narrowed. "You keep talking about some trouble he's in. What aren't you telling me?"

"I don't know what it is, but a man just doesn't vanish from his home and show up at a motel ten miles away under an assumed name."

"He came back." Her voice was small and childlike.

I kept my thoughts to myself because they would have hurt her feelings. However, she must have read my mind.

Her eyes cut to me. "He came back for his scrapbook, his memories. Not for me."

"He snuck back," I said. "That's twenty miles. He had to walk some of that along the highway, but some of that he walked in forested land. It wasn't an easy hike."

"What are you saying?"

"He could have found most of that stuff on the internet. Why was it so important?"

She turned her attention back to the motor lodge. "The pictures. He couldn't replace them."

I thought about the photographs of my mother as a young woman. "Not the pictures," I agreed.

"Well," Daisy said, "where do you think he is now?"

"He could be anywhere. I think he stole Macon's truck."

Daisy shook her head. "No. No way. Not Nick."

My thoughts drifted to the red Honda. "The hit-and-run."

She faced me. "What are you talking about?"

"Nick was involved in a DUI hit-and-run that killed a woman. You said so."

"It was an accident."

I waved off her excuse. "Nick claimed he left Canada because of a DUI accident. Right? Perhaps the Honda is connected to that. Maybe someone tracked Nick to Metaline."

My voice trailed off as doubt filled my head. Nick lived in Canada under an assumed name. Maybe many assumed names. How would someone track him into the United States?

Daisy rubbed her hands together. "He didn't need to go to jail to feel remorse."

"Huh?"

"The way you talk about Nick. It's like you're judging him for running. You don't know him. He felt remorse for what he did."

"Justice isn't about repentance," I said. "It's about getting what's due. Nick didn't pay for his crime."

"I don't see it that way," Daisy said.

"It doesn't matter how you see it. It matters how the law sees it."

We fell silent for several moments and listened to the truck idle. Traffic zoomed by on Highway 31. Shoppers came and went from the nearby grocery store.

Corporal stuck his head between the seats again and Daisy hugged him. I didn't push him into the back seat, and he didn't try to sneak any further forward. He'd taken enough ground in this battle.

"Where do you think he went?" Daisy finally asked.

"He didn't go north. There's no chance he'd go back to Canada. Who knows what kind of trouble is waiting for him following the DUI?" I motioned toward The Homestead. "The detectives investigating this probably put out an alert for Macon's truck."

Daisy nodded. "The guys working the gates would know what Macon drove. They'd spot it a mile off. So he's heading south?"

"South is a big area," I said. "He could be heading straight south, southwest, or southeast."

"Do you think he's heading home?"

I eyed her.

"To Coulee City?"

"Maybe." I tapped the steering wheel as I thought. "But if he's smart, he'll dump the truck as soon as he can. The longer he drives it, the more risk of getting caught."

"So he drives out of town and dumps it, then hitchhikes wherever?"

"That's an option. If he wanted to make a lot of ground, he could take a bus."

"Don't they ask for IDs and stuff?"

"They're looking for Gabriel Baldwin," I said. "If the cops are looking for him, Nick is safe walking around. Although—"

"Although, what?"

"I wouldn't be surprised if the manager calls the cops and tells them I'm poking around."

Daisy's face pinched. "Why would she do that?"

"To add to her fifteen minutes of fame. I showed her Nick's picture. She remembered the accident. If she tells the cops about that, it won't take them long to birddog the article. Then they'll know what he looks like and his real name."

"What happens then?" she asked.

"They'll put his photo up everywhere. Local news stations, newspapers, you name it. Everyone in Eastern Washington will have an idea of what Nick looks like."

"What are we going to do?"

I eyed her. "Where's the nearest Greyhound depot?"

"There's no depot up here, only a pick-up point. And it's over in Colville."

I dropped the truck into Reverse and backed out of our parking spot. I slipped the gearshift into Drive. Corporal's panting increased.

"You've got a decision to make," I said.

"If we're going after him." She pulled her seatbelt across her chest and clicked it into place. "That's what you were going to ask."

I drove through the parking lot. "That's right."

"As far as I'm concerned, you're still on the clock, so I'm going with you."

We waited at the edge of the lot for a semi with a load of logs to pass by.

"Is that a problem?" she asked.

"Not for me."

I stomped on the accelerator, and we entered the highway.

***

Had Daisy said she wasn't going to pay me to follow Nick Gossett's trail, I would still have gone. I wanted to know how this guy fit into my past, especially after he used my father's name to sign in on the motor lodge's register. I also wanted to know why he photographed my mother from a distance all those years ago. I would have chased Gossett across the west coast to get those answers. Hell, I probably would have followed him all the way to Florida.

"Doesn't it bother you," Daisy asked, "that the cops are looking for your dad?"

When would she let up? "He's not my father," I said sourly.

She waved off my bitterness. "They're looking for your dad, because Nick used his name."

I got her question then. "It doesn't matter," I said.

But it was a lie. Gabriel Baldwin's name mattered to me, especially after I'd just convinced myself that I'd traipse all over the continental United States to find Nicholas Gossett for using it. Why'd I have to act like a tough guy for her? Why couldn't I just be honest?

Daisy hugged Corporal tighter to her. "It would bother me."

I scoffed. "That's because your dad was probably a good guy."

She nodded. "He was all right."

"According to my mother, my father was a douche like Nick."

"Nick's not a douche."

"Seriously?" I eyed her. "He murdered Macon."

Daisy's face pinched. "We don't know that."

"We know he killed a woman in a hit-and-run."

"He was drunk." Daisy's voice was soft.

"A DUI hit-and-run. It sounds douche-y to me."

Daisy looked out the passenger window. "Nick was good to me." Her right hand absently tugged on the extra length of links from her chain belt.

Our conversation petered out then.

We left Highway 31 at Tiger and jumped on the 20. It took us through the Colville National Forest. On another day, I might have commented on the forest's beauty. I turned on the radio but found it mostly static. The couple of stations I did find were talk radio, and I wasn't in the mood to listen to someone's bullshit opinions. I had enough of my own. I clicked it off.

The road rumbled underneath the tires and the rhythm soon became hypnotic. Corporal paced from window to window in the back and continued to pant. Daisy rested her head against the passenger side window and seemed lost in thought.

As for me, I'd stopped thinking about anything specific many miles back. My mind had blanked out and I floated along with the truck. It was a peaceful moment.

"What are you most ashamed of?" Daisy asked.

The question knifed into my tranquility, and I cast a sideways glance. She didn't bother looking in my direction. Instead, she appeared in a trance, staring straight ahead.

We rode in silence for a bit longer before she faced me. "Did you hear my question?"

"I heard it."

"Well?"

"What's this about?"

Daisy moved the seatbelt away from her throat. "I'm asking what you're most ashamed of. I didn't think it was a confusing question."

I rolled a hand from the steering wheel. "I'm ashamed of a lot."

"Welcome to the club." Her eyes bore into me. "Pick one."

"Why?"

"I'm asking."

"I don't feel like sharing."

She tugged on the length of chain. "When I was a teenager, I broke into a neighbor's house and stole a hundred bucks."

Of all the things Daisy recently admitted or hinted at doing, a burglary during her high school years was not the one I'd think she'd be most ashamed of doing.

Daisy motioned at my face. "You thought I was going to say something about sex."

I nodded. "You said your issue was related to shame and unworthiness. It stood to reason…" I didn't finish the argument.

She rubbed her hands together. "My *issue*." A sad smile grew on her lips. "That's a polite way to describe it. Mrs. Anderson was my family's neighbor. She was sweet to my family, especially me. I should never have broken into her house and stolen her money."

"Why'd you do it?"

Daisy's eyes moistened. "My parents said I couldn't have money for some new jeans. Dumb, huh? It turned into this huge fight. A big blow up." Daisy sniffled before continuing. "Anyway, I'd been to Mrs. Anderson's a dozen times. More than that. I grew up next to her. I knew where she kept the cookies. She told me where to find her secret bag of Hershey Kisses. I'd been there so many times I knew she kept a coffee mug filled with cash right there on her kitchen counter." Daisy's eyes unfocused and she pointed just ahead of her as if remembering where the cup used to sit.

"So you broke in and took it?"

Daisy shrugged a single shoulder. "I'm sure Mrs. Anderson knew it was me, but she never said anything. She still invited me over and made me hot chocolate and cookies. I felt miserable every time I went."

"You never made good on it?"

She clasped her hands together. "You mean pay it back? No. I never even thought about it once. Isn't that terrible? I felt shitty about it, but never tried to make amends."

"Did you buy the jeans?"

"I did." Daisy nodded. "But I couldn't wear them."

"How come?"

"Because I would have to tell my mother where I got the money."

"What did you do with them?"

She glanced at me. "Promise not to laugh."

"Why would I laugh?"

"I threw them away." Daisy flashed a half-smile filled with regret. "I was so upset. I didn't know what to do with them."

"Why not return them to the store?" I asked. "Get the money back, and give it to Mrs. Anderson?"

Daisy shrugged. "Then I'd have to admit to everyone what I'd done."

We listened to the hum of the road. How many decisions haunted me because I didn't want to admit what I had done? More than my fair share, I'm sure.

Finally, I said, "I left my daughter in Seattle."

Daisy brought a leg up underneath her to get in a more comfortable position. "You have a daughter?"

"Erin lives with her mother. Maria and I were never married."

"What happened?"

"About Maria? She knew I wasn't husband material." I glanced at Daisy then returned my attention to the safety of the road. "But the reason I left Erin in Seattle was because I got fired from the police department."

"I saw that article in Nick's scrapbook. Was there something more to the story?"

"I lost my head over a woman. To get over that, I moved to Spokane."

"Oh." Daisy briefly looked away. When her attention returned, she asked, "Did you love this woman?"

"More than anything in the world."

"But your daughter—"

I stiffened my arms and pushed back into the driver's seat. "Yeah."

Daisy turned in her seat and faced forward. The road noise overwhelmed the cab again. We drove for a time lost in our thoughts. The memories of selfish emotions crashed inside my heart. I left Seattle because I was embarrassed that I'd been dumped by the woman I loved and fired from the job I prized. The relocation was impulsive and childish. I should have stayed there for Erin. Those actions proved Maria correct. She shouldn't have married me.

There had been plenty of opportunities for me to return to Seattle and build a new life, one closer to Erin. But I didn't. Something held me back. It seemed emotionally safer to keep my kid on the other side of the state.

John Cutler. Father-of-the-year.

When I finally gathered my emotions, I asked, "What was the point of your question?"

"I was thinking about shame. Nick's been living with it all these years. First, for dodging the draft, then the DUI. I can't imagine what it's done to him."

"Nothing," I said. "We humans can adapt to anything, even shame. After a time, we don't even notice anymore."

She rested the back of her head against the seat. Sadness crossed her face as she twisted the padlock. "I guess you're right."

Chapter 12

When we pulled into Colville, Daisy said, "Turn left."

Highway 395 cut through the heart of the town. After being in Metaline and Ione, Colville boomed like a minor metropolis. Car dealerships lined the roadway and battled for attention with the likes of McDonald's and Taco Bell. Walmart and Safeway provided supermarket options.

Daisy pointed to a complex made up of several large buildings. "There."

I turned into the parking lot of Grocery Outlet.

"Go to the back," she said.

We drove past the Chamber of Commerce and a hardware store. I slammed on the brakes. Corporal grunted and flopped onto the middle counsel. His conquest for more territory had been interrupted.

"What?" Daisy asked. "What did you see?"

I turned the car around and returned to the area in front of the hardware store. Near the far edge of the lot was a blue pickup.

"That's Macon's," Daisy muttered. "Nick's here."

"Or was here. Where am I going?"

She turned in her seat and pointed at the large building at the far end of the property. "There's a bus office inside. If Nick was going to buy a ticket, he'd have to get it there."

We found a parking spot near the front of the Rural Resources Center.

"I'll go check," I said.

"I'm going with." Daisy slid off her seat and slammed the door behind her.

I had to hurry to catch her.

The extra length of chain link bounced off her leg. "The more I think about this," she said, "the more pissed at him I get."

We arrived at the entrance. I grabbed the handle but didn't pull it open.

"He could have been honest with me," Daisy said. "No matter what was going on, I would have understood. His shit was no worse than mine."

I wanted to remind her that he likely killed a woman while driving drunk. He probably killed Macon last night, too. As far as I was concerned, there was no way Daisy's sex addiction rose anywhere to the level of Nick's problems.

We went inside. The Greyhound ticket counter was off to the right.

The woman behind the Plexiglas had a round face and short blond hair. She looked like an older, unhappier version of the Dutch Boy from the paint cans. "Destination?" she asked in a bored, detached manner.

"Eleanor?" Daisy asked.

The clerk's eyes narrowed. "Daisy? I heard you moved."

She nodded. "Over to Metaline."

"How'd that work out?"

"Worked out fine."

"One day you was here," Eleanor said. "The next you was gone."

"Needed a change of pace."

Eleanor frowned, which deepened the lines around her mouth. "Oh my God, I hear you. This town." Those two words convened every negative emotion Eleanor felt about Colville. Her eyes shifted to me. "This your husband?"

I moved closer to the counter. "We're looking for someone."

The clerk said, "If you're asking about our passengers, I can't talk about them." Her attention returned to Daisy. "Sorry."

"It's my boyfriend," Daisy said.

Eleanor's gaze flicked to me, then back to Daisy. "Who's this then?"

"A private detective. He works for me."

The clerk lifted out of her chair. Her eyes traveled my length. "He don't look like no private detective."

I asked, "Did you sell a ticket to a Nicholas Gossett?"

Eleanor dropped back to her seat. It groaned in displeasure. "I can't tell you nothing about no one." Her gaze flicked to Daisy. "It's policy."

"It's important," Daisy said.

"Everything is important to someone," the clerk said. "Are you going to buy a ticket or not? Other customers are waiting."

I glanced over my shoulder. No one was behind us. I faced Eleanor again. "When did the last bus leave?"

The clerk pointed upward.

Above the counter hung a bus schedule. Only two buses came through Colville every day. We had missed the first by an hour. It was already on its way to Seattle. The bus coming from Seattle wasn't scheduled to arrive until seven p.m. That one would continue to Chicago.

"Nick went to Seattle?" Daisy asked.

Eleanor said, "If your fella got on the earlier bus, that's where it was headed. Plenty of stops on the way for him to get off, though."

"What's the route?" I asked.

The clerk pointed toward the highway. "Three-ninety-five all the way to Spokane. Switch buses at the depot there and ride the Ninety. Easy-peasy."

"Any stops along the way?"

Eleanor nodded. "Chewelah and Deer Park. Those are the only ones."

I headed for the door.

"You're welcome," the clerk hollered.

Daisy trotted next to me. "What's wrong?"

"Only two buses." I pushed the door open and walked outside.

"What do you mean?"

"Seattle and Chicago. Nick had to have known in advance."

"Maybe he looked it up," Daisy said.

"From The Homestead?" I looked over my shoulder as I walked. "After he killed Macon?"

"I'm not understanding."

I stopped and pointed at the Rural Resource Center. "Nick had an exit strategy. He knew where to go and when the buses ran. Killing Macon wasn't part of the plan, I'll give you that, but he knew how to get out of Metaline and how to do it without a car."

She furrowed her brow. "You're making him sound like a criminal."

"When's the last time you checked a bus schedule?"

Daisy smirked. "I have a car."

"So did Nick."

"It broke down. That's why he sold it."

"Is that why he sold it?" I asked. I tapped my temple. "Think about it. He's involved in a crime in Canada. He gets another car and crosses the border. It breaks down. Maybe he doesn't have enough cash, so he sells it to have some money. Or he sells the car, so he's not tempted to use if further."

"If that's the case, why did Nick stay in Metaline?" Daisy crossed her arms triumphantly. "Why not run to Mexico?"

"I don't know." I started to walk but stopped again. "Maybe Nick thought it best to stop running as soon as he could, right over the border. No one would think he'd do that. I wouldn't if I was on the run. I'd get over the border and run as far south as possible."

"What about me?" Daisy asked. Tears welled in her eyes.

I understood what she was asking. Was she a cog in some larger plan? Had Nick used her? Or were his feelings genuine? I had my doubts but hurting her wouldn't do any good.

"You're right," I said. "That's probably why he stayed." I softened my tone. "He met you and his whole plan got thrown off. He didn't want to run anymore."

An unsure smile creased her lips. "You think?"

"It's as good an explanation as any." I motioned toward Macon's truck. "That doesn't mean he didn't have a plan. Otherwise, this doesn't make sense."

"A plan for what?"

"In case something bad happened."

I headed toward my truck and climbed in. The dog had settled into the passenger seat.

"Get in back," I told Corporal.

He stared at me as if he were an insolent teenager. By dog years, he'd have been a surly thirty-something. Maybe even in his forties. I grabbed his collar and pulled. Corporal reluctantly moved over the console and into the back seat.

When Daisy positioned herself in the truck, she asked, "Who thinks like that? Who has an escape plan ready to go?"

"Someone who has lived through bad scenes."

And spent years living rough and under the radar.

I dropped the truck into Drive, and the truck lurched forward. It stopped just as quickly when I mashed the brake. Daisy was thrown against her seatbelt. The dog slid off the back seat and crashed to the floor.

"The hell—?" Daisy cried.

Ahead was the red Honda. An older white man was climbing out from behind the steering wheel.

I jumped on the accelerator and raced forward.

Daisy grabbed the door handle and her other hand pressed against the dashboard. "Easy!" she hollered.

I pulled the truck in front of the Honda and jammed the brakes. The truck skidded to a halt.

The Canadian stood behind his open car door. He appeared calm, almost unaffected by my dramatic approach. A brown sport coat and white shirt were visible through the window. Below the door, tan slacks and brown loafers could be seen. He casually rested his arms along the top of the door and waited.

"Open the glove box," I said and held out my hand.

"Why?"

"Do it." I anxiously snapped my fingers.

Daisy popped open the glove compartment. Inside was my Glock.

"What're you doing?" she whispered.

"Hand it to me."

Her eyes snapped to the windshield. "Who is he? What's going on?"

"Never mind." I reached across the cab and pulled the gun out. "Stay here."

"No problem, whatsoever."

I slipped out but remained close to my truck. The door hid the gun clutched in my hand. "Why are you following me?" I shouted.

"You going to shoot me, Cowboy?" The Canadian lifted his hands. "I'm unarmed. We've got the right to stand our ground, too, but this would seem over the line, eh?"

"You didn't answer my question."

He rolled his eyes. "I'm not following you. Now, put the gun away before you hurt someone. Let's talk like civilized men."

"Who are you following?"

The Canadian inhaled deeply. "You know what? I tried." He dropped into the driver's seat of his car and pulled the door closed.

"Wait!"

He sat there as I contemplated what to do. I couldn't point the gun and direct him out of the car. I wasn't a cop and had no legal authority to do so. Had we been on a country road, away from prying eyes, I'd have a different opinion of what I could do at that moment.

A dented Mitsubishi passed by on its way to the resource center. The young woman behind the wheel didn't pay attention to either the Canadian or me.

"Shit," I muttered.

"What's going on?" Daisy asked.

"We're negotiating."

"Looks like you're losing."

I set the gun on the seat and closed the door. I lifted my hands so he could see they were empty. "There, you fucking Canuck. Let's talk." I'm sure he couldn't hear me.

The driver's door popped open on the Honda, and the Canadian stood again. "The art of negotiation," he said loudly. "No one is ever fully happy."

Maybe he could read lips.

"If you're not following me," I said, "then you're following her." I glanced at Daisy. She continued to stare through the windshield.

"I'm not following her either, but it seems we're after the same man." The Canadian stepped around his door and approached. As he walked, his eyes alertly scanned me, then the truck. I couldn't blame him; I had just held a gun. When he neared, he stuck out his hand. "Paine Savard."

"I should bust you in the mouth."

"For what?" He lowered his hand.

"Slashing my tires."

Savard narrowed his eyes. "I don't know what you're talking about."

"Sure, you don't."

"Think what you will. Are you going to introduce yourself, or just stand there like a dogger?"

I stared at him as I tried to determine the level of insult dogger was supposed to convey. "John Cutler," I finally said.

Savard stood like a boxer, with his left side closer, ready for a jab. He jerked a thumb toward Daisy. "You're friendly with Nicholas Gossett's woman."

"What do you want with Nick?"

"He killed my niece."

Daisy and Corporal both watched us from the cab. She pointed questioningly at herself, then me. I shook my head. I didn't want her to join us. Not until I had a better handle on the Canadian.

"He tell you what happened in Kelowna?" Savard asked.

"I've never met the man."

"Never, eh?" Savard ran his left hand over his lips, then his eyes flicked to Daisy. "What'd she tell you?"

"Why don't you tell me?"

The Canadian's attention returned to me, and his eyes narrowed. "I already told you. Gossett killed my niece."

"How do you know?"

"I know." His expression tightened further. "And since those K-town cops didn't do shit, we had to get involved."

"We?"

"Her family."

Something in the way Savard said it made my blood run cold. Was his family tied to the mafia or some other criminal organization? As a patrol officer in Seattle, my experience mostly dealt with street gangs. However, as a private investigator, I'd run afoul of several criminal organizations. Some had perceived power, others really had it. Both mattered to the communities they existed in. If Savard was part of an organization like that, could its muscle be brought south of the border?

Savard pointed at the Rural Resource Center. "There's a bus counter in there. The way I figured it, Gossett ran for the nearest terminal." He briefly looked over his shoulder. "With that being the border guard's truck over there, I assume my hunch was right."

I cocked my head. We knew about Macon's truck because of Daisy's previous relationship with the man. It made sense Nicholas had taken it when it was missing from the crime scene, but we had inside knowledge. "How did you know about the border guard and his truck?"

Savard hooked his thumbs into his pockets. "People talk."

"One of the deputies?"

He shrugged but kept his thumbs where they were.

Cops usually didn't talk to just anyone. Even the stupid and lazy wouldn't spout off at a crime scene. There were ramifications for doing so. I quickly ran through the possibilities. He wasn't young nor handsome enough to encourage a female officer to chat him up. Would a male officer have found him attractive? I thought it unlikely. Perhaps he paid for the information. That was a possibility, but I didn't see any cop being foolish enough to take money at a crime scene.

Maybe the Canadian already knew one of the deputies. Odd occurrences happened all the time, but that seemed unlikely. So, what would encourage a cop to share information with a stranger, a Canadian one at that?

Savard's distrusting gaze gave it away. Daisy had called them judging eyes.

"You're a cop," I said.

He raised an eyebrow. "Good guess."

When I knew what to look for, everything made sense. I replayed the scene. He stood calmly behind the open car door as I approached. His gun must have been within reach the entire time. Was it tucked into a door slot? Or was it sitting on the driver's seat?

After I got out of my truck, he continued to remain calm. He likely had a plan if I brought my gun out. Would he have shown his? Or would he have shot me? A foreigner with a gun would be tough to defend. There was a mantra we used to say on the job—better to be judged by twelve than carried by six. I imagined the Canadian thought something similar.

Savard stood with his body bladed. I had wrongly assumed he was a boxer. That stance is a safety technique taught to rookie police officers. It keeps one's gun away from a suspect.

And finally, Savard didn't put his hands into his pockets—only his thumbs. Cops were taught to keep their hands out of their pockets because it slowed reaction time. Hooking a thumb was a psychological ploy. It allowed a suspect to believe the officer was relaxed, yet the whole time they remained ready to fight.

Realizing how ready Savard was for a fight bothered me. I'd been too relaxed. Perhaps I lulled myself with the regional bullshit of Canadians being nice. I shifted my stance and matched his.

Savard smiled.

"How'd the Kelowna cops do a shitty job with their investigation?" I asked.

"If they were my officers, they'd have been disciplined." Savard reached inside his sport coat and removed his wallet. He flipped it open. The small badge on the left had a crown at its top and was inscribed *Vancouver Police*. An identification card on the right side showed a younger Savard. The rank Lieutenant was printed underneath his name. He snapped the wallet closed and returned it to his pocket.

"A little out of your jurisdiction," I said.

"I'm on holiday."

A thought occurred to me. "You said your family was involved."

Savard nodded. "Me and my brothers."

"Where are they?"

"Back home, taking care of our sister—my niece's mother. They're also funding my leave of absence."

"Not a holiday."

Savard shrugged. "A technicality." He motioned again toward the Rural Resource Center. "What'd you learn?"

"What's your plan if you find Gossett?"

"Nuh-huh." Savard shook his head. "You first."

He'd learn the same information we did if he went inside, and it would only take him five minutes. I didn't see the harm in telling him. "The bus for Seattle already left. There's another arriving at seven tonight that'll continue to Chicago."

Savard looked over his shoulder. I assumed he was considering Macon's truck. "The dirty bastard," he muttered.

"All right," I said. "Your turn. What's your plan if you find Gossett?"

"What route is it taking?"

"What's your plan?" I repeated.

"This is where I say goodbye." He patted my shoulder as he walked toward the Rural Resource center. "Good luck."

I reached for him. "Hold on."

Savard jerked his arm free. "Don't get in my way, Mr. Cutler." He backpedaled toward the center. "I'll track Gossett across your country if I must. He's not getting away with what he did."

He spun and headed toward the center. I watched him go for a few seconds, then climbed into the truck.

"Who's that?" Daisy asked.

I started the truck. "The Canadian Mounties."

"What?"

We headed toward the highway.

Daisy looked out the back window. "For real?"

"He's a Vancouver lieutenant, and he's related to the woman Nick killed in the DUI collision."

Daisy's face pinched. "It was an accident."

"Not everyone sees it that way."

"How'd the guy track him here?"

"He's a police officer." I headed toward Highway 395. "And that's exactly what we don't need right now—a cop with an ax to grind."

***

We sped southbound. I wasn't worried about catching the bus in Chewelah or Deer Park since it had an hour head start. However, since it had to make those two stops, I thought we had a chance of arriving in Spokane about the same time.

Even if we were a few minutes late, the bus to Seattle wouldn't depart at the same time as the Spokane arrival. We'd have plenty of time to search the depot for Gossett. But there was something about the bus depot that bothered me. I was about to latch onto it when she interrupted my thoughts.

"What kind of cop is Savard?"

We left Colville ten minutes ago. In that time, Daisy had remained quiet, lost in her reflections.

"He's a lieutenant," I said.

She eyed me. "You said that. What's that mean?"

"It's his rank. If you're asking what he does for their department, I couldn't tell you."

"Do you think he's a good one?"

I frowned. "There wasn't enough time to get a read on him."

Corporal stuck his head between the seats. I pushed him back in frustration. My thoughts about the bus depot were getting further away.

Daisy cocked her head. "Take a guess."

"Savard could be a great guy, but if Nick killed Savard's niece while drunk and ran from the scene, I could see the man wanting to put a bullet in your boyfriend's brain."

Her jaw dropped, and her eyes widened. "You're an asshole."

My face warmed. "Not always."

"From what I've seen."

"Anyway." I fought to keep my voice even.

"Anyway." Her attention returned to the windshield.

My thoughts returned to the bus depot, but I couldn't latch onto whatever concern I almost had before the interruption. Savard was at the edge of my consciousness now. I brought him forward and started to work on that problem. As soon as I did, Daisy spoke once more.

"So, you're thinking maybe Savard is a nice guy?"

I waved a hand. "I have no idea."

"But maybe he is." Her eyes softened as she faced me. "You know, like maybe he's a decent person."

I really wanted a few more minutes of quiet time so I could work out the Savard issue. Daisy wasn't going to allow that. She was upset about Nick and talking seemed to help her process it. If I couldn't work out my thoughts inside my head, I'd work them out with her. "What's his plan?" I asked.

Confusion played across her face. "I don't understand the question."

"Savard's a Vancouver cop, and he's come to the States."

"Yeah, so?"

Corporal's head popped over the middle console, and Daisy scratched behind his ears.

"Back at the Resource Center, I thought he might have a gun, but now I'm thinking he didn't bring one over the border."

"Isn't that illegal?"

"The last time I checked, it was. Maybe the laws have changed, but even cops couldn't do it when I was on the job."

I checked the side mirrors. As fast as we were traveling, I didn't think Savard's Honda would catch up. However, I had no idea what his level of desperation was. Maybe he'd floor it and risk getting arrested for reckless driving.

Daisy's fingers sunk into Corporal's fur. "So, he's down here without a gun?"

"And he's taken a leave of absence to hunt for Nick."

"He told you that?"

I nodded.

"Why would he do that?"

It was a good question. At first, Savard said he was on holiday. Then he made sure to tell me he was on a leave of absence. A vacation implied two things—a need to get away from a job and a definitive date of return. Savard wasn't a man seeking relaxation. He was a man on a mission.

"He wanted us to know how serious he was," I said.

"To find Nick?"

I tapped a thumb against the steering wheel. "That's the next problem. Let's say Savard beats us to Nick. What's he going to do with him? Even if he has proof Nick killed his niece, he's got no jurisdiction here to make an arrest. If he does arrest him, he can't bring him back across the border."

Daisy lifted an eyebrow. "Could an American cop arrest him?"

"If there's a warrant and Canada will extradite, then yes."

"Can we find out if there's a warrant?"

I glanced at her. "We can find that out, but it'll alert the local authorities that Nick's on his way to Spokane."

Daisy's eyes grew distant.

I'd let her out if she wanted, but there was no way I was turning the truck around. I was going after Nick. I wanted some answers about my family. I could talk with him just as easily if he was sitting in the county jail.

"What would you do?" she asked.

***

Gary Ackerman answered on the third ring.

"Hello?" His voice sounded groggy.

"It's Cutler."

"This better be good."

I checked my rearview mirror. I couldn't shake the expectation that the red Honda was going to suddenly appear there. "I need you to run a name."

"We talked about this."

"I know—"

The call ended.

I stared at the phone. "Shit."

Daisy glanced over. "Yeah. The cell service is garbage along here. Try again."

I dialed a second time, and it went straight to voice mail. I hung up and handed her the phone. "Do you know how to text?"

Her face pinched. "I'm not an idiot."

"I know."

She flipped open the phone. "Who am I texting?"

"His name is Gary. It's the last number I called. Ask him to run Nick's name. Spell the whole thing out."

"Duh." Daisy looked up from the cell phone's keyboard. "You want his birthday, too?"

"If you know it. Tell him Nick might have a warrant out of Canada."

Her thumbs stopped bouncing over the keyboard. "This feels weird."

"What does?"

"Asking a cop to run Nick's name."

"You're doing it to keep him safe."

She looked up. "Is that what you're telling yourself?"

I stayed quiet.

"Right," she said and returned to tapping on my phone.

"Tell him we think Nick is headed to the Spokane Greyhound station."

Daisy continued to tap the phone. "Done." She slapped the phone closed and handed it back to me.

It immediately rang. It was Ackerman.

"Hello?" I said.

"I know that wasn't you texting." He still sounded groggy.

"How do you know?"

"Because whoever it was said, 'Thank you.'"

I rolled my eyes.

"What's up with this Gossett character?" Ackerman asked.

"He's the guy I'm trying to find."

"Your father?"

"He's not my father."

Ackerman chuckled. "Are you with the crazy woman right now?"

"I might have been wrong about that."

"Uh-huh. I bet she's attractive, and that's why you're hedging your bet."

I didn't look at Daisy. There wasn't any need for Ackerman to know she was strangely alluring. That hadn't changed from the first moment I'd seen her.

"No comment? So, I'm right." Ackerman's voice changed as if he might have sat upright. "What's the warrant out of Canada for?"

"I don't know if there is one, but he killed a woman in a DUI hit-and-run."

Ackerman whistled. "We could charge that a variety of ways depending upon the evidence."

Had Gossett's crime occurred in Washington State, he might have been charged with Second-Degree Murder or Second-Degree Manslaughter. They'd likely tag on a felony Hit-and-run charge for failing to report the crime.

"I'll run the name," Ackerman said. "You're headed to the Greyhound station now?"

"We're thirty minutes out. We're trying to catch the bus."

"If he has a warrant, I'll text you back."

The phone call ended.

***

Five minutes later, my phone buzzed once. I handed it to Daisy. "Read the text."

She flipped it open. "No warrant. Can't get back to sleep. You're an asshole."

I lightly pounded on the steering wheel with the bottom of my fist.

Daisy closed the phone and handed it back to me. "What's that mean? No warrant. That there wasn't an accident? Or that the woman didn't die?"

"Savard said the local PD didn't do their job, but maybe they did, and the lieutenant didn't like the results."

"I don't understand."

"What if…?" I glanced at her. "And this is a big if so, don't get excited."

"I understand."

"What if Kelowna PD investigated Nick's collision and couldn't find enough probable cause to arrest him?"

Her face brightened, and she shifted in her seat. "So he's not in trouble?"

I slowed for a truck leaving the highway. When it cleared the lane, I accelerated.

"He's in trouble. He was involved in a DUI collision that killed a woman. He failed to stay at the scene. For some reason, the Kelowna investigators dismissed Nick's involvement."

Daisy lowered her head. "Like maybe they didn't know it was Nick?"

Something about that statement struck me as odd. "What do you know about the accident?"

"Nothing."

"What did Nick tell you?"

"Nothing."

I pulled to the side of the road and turned on my hazard flashers.

"Why are we stopping?" Daisy asked.

Corporal moved to the side window facing the road and panted heavier.

"This is serious," I said. "What exactly did Nick say about the accident?"

Her brow furrowed. "He said he was drunk and had an accident."

"Was the victim in the other car, or was she in Nick's car?"

"I don't know."

My face tightened.

"He didn't say," she said. "I swear. Why are you getting mad?"

"This is important. There are two types of hit-and-runs. One where the driver flees in his car. The other where the driver flees on foot. Both result in the same crime, but you can see the big difference, right?"

"The car."

I checked my rearview mirror, waiting for an opening, and entered the roadway. I turned off my hazards.

"So, what are you saying?" Daisy asked.

My hand gripped the steering wheel. "Nick drove off. Maybe there weren't any witnesses and Kelowna PD couldn't find the responsible driver."

"Then what's the problem?"

I thumbed over my shoulder. "If that's the case, how'd Savard end up on his trail?"

Daisy shook her head. "I don't know."

"That's why we have to change the story. Nick fled the scene of the accident and left the car, but Kelowna PD still couldn't pin it to him."

"He was using a fake name on the car registration?" Daisy said.

"Maybe he was driving the woman's car."

Daisy's cheeks flushed as she thought.

"You okay?" I asked.

"I'm realizing I didn't know him as well as I thought I did." She crossed her arms. "I thought he was truthful with me."

"He told you about a DUI collision and that he ran from Canada. That's pretty truthful."

"But I didn't get the whole story, did I? Where was the woman?" Daisy looked at me. "That's what you're asking? Was she in the other car or with him? Or maybe she was standing on the fucking sidewalk for all we know?" Daisy angrily smacked the dashboard. "That seems like it would be important to know."

I didn't need to soothe her hurt feelings. Right now, I was more interested in working out the involvement of Lieutenant Paine Savard. How did he find Nick Gossett who was living in Metaline, Washington?

My gaze dropped to the folded newspaper sitting on the dashboard. I grabbed it and handed it to Daisy. "Open that."

She spread it out.

"When was that picture taken?" I asked.

"A week ago."

I pointed at the text underneath the photograph.

Daisy looked up. "But they spelled his last name wrong, and if Nick was living under a fake name—"

"He wasn't living under a new face," I interrupted. "Somehow Savard knew what Nick looked like."

My thoughts turned inward as the road hummed under the truck's tires.

Daisy had told me Nick was running when the collision on Highway 31 occurred. She said he ran to work off the years of drinking and smoking. What if he was also preparing for a day when he might have to get out of town quickly?

It was twelve miles from Metaline to Ione. Maybe Nick never made that run in its entirety, but he knew how to get quickly out of town. If he trained to only run four miles—two out and two back—then he was prepared to get a third of the way to Ione in a pinch.

And what about the dead woman in Kelowna? If she was in the car with him, had she been a lover like Daisy? Had she known his secret and helped him, regardless?

Perhaps Nick was a user and his feelings for Daisy were less than pure.

I glanced at her. Sadness brimmed in her eyes. I wondered if she now had the same concerns about Nick that I had.

I didn't ask.

Chapter 13

We arrived in Spokane and worked our way down Division Street, also known as Highway 2. The arterial evenly divided North Spokane into west and east sides. Division Street was also the prime retail corridor for the city. Bumper-to-bumper traffic stuttered its way south from Cascade Way, one traffic light at a time. Downtown was still six miles away. The lunchtime crowd impatiently wormed its way back to their respective offices against the ill-programmed timing of signal lights.

"Fucking ridiculous," I said.

Daisy leaned left and right in a struggle to look beyond the vehicles in front of us. "Is there an accident or something?"

"Road construction, most likely."

Daisy pointed ahead. "The bus is probably stuck in the same situation we are."

Her positive spin on our situation irritated me.

Washington State's second largest city didn't have a freeway to serve its north or southbound traffic. The only freeway Spokane had cut through downtown and headed directly west to the political and economic power in the state—Seattle. Olympia might be the capital, but the money lay in the Emerald City. Seattle pulled the strings on the political puppets.

"Is it always like this?" Daisy asked.

"Not always." I stiffened my arms and pushed myself back into my seat. "Only in the morning and after work."

"Lunch, too, it seems," she said.

I never realized how good I had it while living in Seattle. Freeways were constructed whenever new communities sprouted. Anytime a road needed to be repaired, it was. To ease the pressure on traffic, the state threw money at alternative forms of travel like bus and rail because it served multiple communities up and down the I-5 corridor.

Yet Spokane lagged. Construction had begun on the North-South Freeway years before I moved to town. It wasn't expected to finish until 2030. Had this been Seattle, I'm sure the project would have been built by now and the vehicles happily motoring over it every day.

I hadn't fully rooted into life as a Spokane resident, but I had developed one opinion like the locals—a belief the state prioritized projects west of the Cascade Mountains. Every year I remained here, it became more ingrained.

My phone rang, and I answered it. "Hey there."

"How's it going?" Stacy asked.

"I'm in Spokane."

She perked up. "You're back? Want to grab lunch? I was going to get something out today, but I could wait if you want to come by."

"We're heading to the Greyhound station."

"We?"

"Daisy and me," I said. "Nick is supposedly on a bus to downtown now."

"Oh," Stacy said.

"Something wrong?" I glanced at Daisy, who watched me with interest.

"Nothing," Stacy said. "You didn't call this morning."

"I'm sorry. Things went sideways."

"You don't have to explain."

I looked at Daisy again, but this time she stared through the windshield.

"There was a murder," I said.

"Who?"

"A border guard."

"Oh, my god." Stacy's voice rose. "Did it happen near you or something?"

"In a neighboring city. Ione. But I talked with the guard the day before."

"And he's connected somehow?"

"We think Nick is involved."

Daisy shifted her position and looked out the passenger window.

"Holy shit," Stacy said. "You think this Nick guy might have killed the guard?"

"That's right."

"So you probably don't want to grab lunch."

I smiled. "Not right now."

"John?"

"Yeah?"

"Why don't you let the cops deal with this?"

I inhaled as I thought about how to answer. "Because we don't know if Nick's really involved." We knew about the hit-and-run in Canada, but I didn't need to add to Stacy's worry.

"Okay," she said. "Be careful."

"I will."

"Call me later."

***

Daisy and I pulled into the Greyhound parking lot. I grabbed *The Newport Miner* from the dashboard and slipped out. We left the dog in the truck and trotted into the building.

"Look for Nick," I said. "I'm going to find customer service."

Daisy wandered off, her head swiveling as she went.

I headed for the ticket counter. A Hispanic man with puffy jowls and tired eyes greeted me. His name tag read *Juan*.

"Afternoon," he said. "May I help you?"

"Did the bus from Colville arrive yet?"

"I believe so." Juan turned to his computer and tapped the keyboard. He leaned in slightly. "Uh-huh. Yes, ten minutes ago. Bus 186."

"Where do the passengers disembark?"

Juan pointed across the concourse. "Outside."

"And the bus for Seattle. Has it left yet?"

"Not for another hour. It'll leave from the same place." He pointed across the lobby again.

Daisy and I had made up fifty minutes on the southbound bus. They had to stop twice in Chewelah and Deer Park, but perhaps those detours weren't that long. We had our own delays. We had the altercation with Lieutenant Savard and then the quick roadside conversation. Had we not had those, perhaps we could have arrived at the same time.

I jogged across the concourse and shoved open the door. Four buses lined up, one after the other. A five-digit number was printed at the top of each bus. The bus at the end of the line was the only one with its lower storage compartments open. They were all empty. The entry door was secured, and no one was inside. I peered into the windows.

"Forget something?" a male voice asked.

A black man in a gray jacket and flight cap approached. He held a cigarette in his right hand. His silver name tag read *Greene*.

"Is this the bus that just came from Chewelah?"

"That's the one."

"I'm looking for someone." I opened the newspaper and pointed at the front-page picture. "This guy."

Greene inhaled on his cigarette. He twisted his lips to blow the smoke away. "He a friend of yours?"

"I've been hired to find him."

"He in trouble for something?"

I didn't see the harm in being truthful. "Murder, possibly."

Greene picked something small from his lips, then blew it off his fingers. "I seen him. Son of a bitch made a stink to get off the bus."

"Here?" I pointed at the ground.

"Up near the mall." His expression soured. "Like we were a city bus or something."

"Thank you." I started toward the doors and stopped. "Wait. Did he have any bags with him?"

"He's lucky he didn't. I wouldn't have stopped otherwise. We were at a stoplight, and he was bitching up a storm, so I opened the door and invited him to take a flying leap."

"Thank you for your time."

I turned and bumped into Paine Savard.

"Good to see you again," he said. "Your lady friend is inside."

I stepped around him and headed toward the entrance. I glanced back in time to see the lieutenant show the bus driver a photograph. Greene glanced toward me, then he nodded. He pointed north.

"Shit," I muttered and yanked open the door.

***

Daisy stood in the middle of the lobby. She absently tugged on the length of chain dangling from her belt. When I grabbed her arm, she jumped.

"We've gotta go," I said.

"Nick's not here?"

I led her toward the exit. "He got off early."

She looked at me. "Where?"

"At the mall."

"Which one?

"NorthTown." I rammed open the door and pushed her outside.

"Why such a hurry?"

"Savard is here."

She glanced over her shoulder. "You saw him?"

"I talked with him."

"What did he say?"

"Nothing much."

We hustled to the truck.

***

"NorthTown Mall?" Daisy asked. "Why would Nick want to get off there?"

We were again on Division Street, but this time we fought through northbound traffic.

"The driver said he didn't have any bags. Maybe he needs clothes."

She squinted. "Yeah, maybe."

"You don't think so?"

Daisy shrugged.

"Why else then?" I asked.

"Hell if I know." She glanced around. "I'm still getting used to the fact that Nick isn't who I thought he was."

We pulled to a stop behind a line of cars at Maxwell Avenue.

A thought came to me. "He's been gone four days, right?"

"Five. Why do you ask?"

"How often did he go to group?"

Her brow furrowed. "Twice a week."

I looked at her. "Can your phone search the internet?"

"No. No reason to get that up in Metaline."

Mine didn't have it because of the cost. Apple introduced a new phone last year with a touchscreen that my daughter couldn't stop texting about. Thank God, I didn't have to pay for it. However, that didn't help me now.

"Nick got one," she said. "Always seemed like a waste of money to me."

"We need a computer," I said.

The light changed. I crossed a lane of traffic and turned onto Maxwell. We headed toward my office.

Chapter 14

I spotted the red Honda before I pulled onto Spofford Street.

"Shit," I muttered.

Daisy caught me checking the rearview mirror and peeked over her shoulder. "How'd he find where you work?"

"I don't think he did. He must have followed us since downtown." I hadn't seen him, though.

There was a decision to make. I could drive by my house and try to lose him, or I could pull to the curb and talk with the man. Paine Savard was like a rash. Ignoring it wouldn't make it go away. Scratching it would make it worse. Some salve might ease the pain.

I stopped the truck in front of my house. I opened the back door of the truck and let Corporal out. The dog trotted ahead of us as we walked up the sidewalk. Daisy glanced repeatedly at the Honda.

Savard remained in his car. He was on his cell phone. I wondered if he had the ability to run my license plate. I doubted it. But perhaps the man had a connection with someone in the Canadian Border Patrol. How hard would it be for them to talk with their counterparts on the American side of the border? It seemed like a long way to go to run a name. Yet, a man looking for the killer of his niece would likely go great distances.

We entered the house.

"I need to put him outside," I told Daisy and escorted Corporal to the back door. He bounded happily into the yard.

Daisy stood at the front window. "He's still sitting there."

"Let him. He'll come when he's ready."

I dropped into my desk chair and started the computer. As it whirred to life, stupidity washed over me.

"You okay?" she asked. "You look like you want to punch something."

I reached into my pocket and pulled out my flip phone. I shook it. "This."

"What?"

"I thought Nick was working with this, too." I slammed it onto the desk. "The whole time he's running around with the internet in his hand."

"You're giving Metaline too much credit."

"What about Ione? Colville?" I thought about the places the bus had traveled through. "Chewelah and Deer Park. Did the service get any better there?"

Daisy shrugged. "I don't know. Probably not."

"Well, it certainly got better in Spokane."

She hugged herself. "I don't understand the problem."

The monitor lit up. I moved the mouse and started the internet browser. "The problem is we need a computer to do this, and goddamn Nick did it on the run."

"Okay. Shit. Don't take it out on me."

Pressure built in my head, and anger rose within my chest. I shouldn't be that upset. I wouldn't get that way over a normal case. Had it been some other person I'd been hired to follow, I wouldn't have lost any sleep over it. I would follow the trail until it got cold, or I found him. I'd collect my check and move on.

But the proximity to my father's ghost elevated my emotions. The lies my mother told to whitewash her past continued to bother me. And the fact that I had issues vaguely similar to Daisy's concerned me. It all combined to create a confusion cocktail.

I nodded once. "Sorry."

Daisy settled onto one of the metal chairs in front of the desk. "What are you looking for?"

My fingers hopped across the keyboard. "AA meetings near the mall."

"You think he's going to group? Now?"

"You don't?"

She looked toward the ceiling. "He's been doing good. Real good."

"Killing a man is a stressful event."

Daisy's gaze returned to me. "Assuming he did."

"He's on the run. I think it's safe to assume."

Her lips twisted. "He wants to stay clean. I know that much."

"Then that's what we've got to go on."

I tapped the Enter key, and the monitor filled with options. Some groups had clever names such as The Early Bird Gets the Recovery, Oh Come All Ye Faithful in Recovery, and The Big Comeback. Others had more somber names such as Walk in Brotherhood and Ladies of Gratitude. Meeting locations and times were listed.

I scanned the directory to find meetings near NorthTown mall. A couple of locations worked, but only one time fit and it was set to start in thirty minutes. If that's why Nick got off the bus early, we had no time to waste.

"Let's go," I said and stood.

Daisy jumped from her chair. "You found one?"

I opened the door as Paine Savard came up the walkway. He stopped and waited for us to step out of the house. I pulled the door closed behind me. We started down the steps, Daisy behind me.

Savard blocked the walkway. My truck was behind him. The smart move would have been to walk through the grass to get around the man. I wasn't known for making smart choices.

I approached Savard. Just a few minutes ago, I was willing to talk with the man. Now that I had an idea where Nick Gossett might be, I didn't feel like sharing. "Get out of the way."

"Where's he at?"

"We don't know."

"I think you do," Savard said.

"We don't have time for this."

I stepped to the side, and he reached out to stop me. I lazily batted his hand away, which was a mistake. Savard smacked the back of my upper arm with his other hand. My body spun, and he shoved me in the back. I stumbled a couple of steps forward.

I turned and started toward Savard. Blood pounded in my ears. I balled my fists and hunched my shoulders.

"Stop!" Daisy shouted.

Her command gave me pause. I didn't lower my hands, though. Instead, I assessed the situation.

Savard had settled into a fighting stance and was still out of striking distance. His face remained impassive as he raised his arms. The lieutenant was at least ten years older than me, but he remained in good shape. He seemed unafraid of a fight. If the Vancouver Police Department was anything like Seattle's, he had to come up through patrol first which meant he had plenty of opportunities to tangle with suspects.

In other words, I wasn't going to bully my way past Savard. Either I had to fight the man, or I had to reason with him. Time was tight, and I had a choice to make.

The AA meeting might be totally wrong. Nick might have gone elsewhere. If that were true, finding him might be like hunting for the proverbial needle in a haystack. Fighting now would do no one any good.

"Tell me where he is," Savard said calmly.

"What's your plan if you find him?" I asked.

"When I find him."

"Stop it," Daisy said.

I relaxed my hands and my shoulders eased. "C'mon, man? What do you plan to do?"

Savard straightened. "Take him home."

"There's no warrant for him in Kelowna."

His eyes briefly widened. "Even so."

"Even so, what? What are you going to do with him?"

"Take him home and make my argument that he's responsible for my niece's death."

"You're not going to kill him?"

Savard's expression hardened. "I'm a cop. Not a killer. I want him to stand trial for what he did."

"How do you know Nick was responsible?"

"Because he took advantage of her." He shook his head. "It was not a good relationship."

Daisy looked away.

"He was too old for her," Savard continued. "They drank too much. But he wasn't Nick then. He was Jacob Fortin. She had pictures of him on her phone. I got lucky when a friend on the border saw his picture in the paper."

Some pieces of the puzzle clicked into place.

"How will you get him across the border?" I asked.

"Let me worry about that."

The friend on the border, I thought.

I glanced at Daisy. Tears were in her eyes.

"We believe he's headed to an AA meeting," I said.

"All right." The lieutenant backpedaled. "You lead. I'll follow."

***

"What do you think?" Daisy asked.

"About?"

"Savard." She stared ahead. "Do you believe what he said?"

"Maybe."

We sped northbound on Maple Street. It was a one-way arterial with three lanes, so traffic flowed well. I zipped around a late '70s Chevy van riding on a spare tire. Behind us, Savard's red Honda slipped into the available space.

She faced me. "You *maybe* believe he won't kill Nick, and you're still letting him follow us?" Daisy glanced out the back window.

"He won't kill Nick."

"How do you know? You can't know that."

"I trust him."

Her attention remained on the Honda. "Can't you lose him?"

"You watch too many movies."

"I read books."

"Whatever. You read too many books. Losing someone isn't as easy as they make it sound."

The light at Wellesley Avenue flicked yellow, and I slowed. When the light glowed red, I turned right before the oncoming traffic. A Kia slammed its brakes and honked its horn.

"You did it!" Daisy said and dropped back into her seat. "Oh my God!" She kicked her feet and pumped her fists. "You really did it."

I checked the side mirrors. The Kia zoomed by on the left. The driver—a middle-aged woman with long, dark hair—honked right before extending her middle finger. It wasn't difficult to read her lips.

Daisy beamed. "And you said I read too many books."

"It's not as easy as you think."

"You just did it."

My eyes flicked to the rearview mirror.

She spun in her seat. "Are you fucking kidding me?"

The Honda sped toward us.

"Told you," I said.

Daisy settled into her seat. "What're we going to do now?"

"We deal with it. First, we've got to find Nick."

***

The True North Recovery Group met at Journey of the Redeemer, an all-inclusive church. The place of worship sat at the corner of Division and Everett with a view of Franklin Park to the west. If Nick's goal was to attend this meeting, he had exited the bus at Wellesley Avenue and backtracked a half dozen blocks.

Maybe he didn't realize where the church was. Perhaps it took that long to get the bus driver to stop. More likely, though, he waited for the bus to stop at an intersection to make his move. That way, it would be harder for anyone to pinpoint his actual location.

We pulled into the church's lot and parked. I popped open the glove box.

Daisy's eyes widened. "What are you doing?"

"What's it look like?"

"You don't need that."

I frowned. "He killed Macon."

"He's not going to shoot you."

"Because he thinks I'm his son?"

"That's exactly why."

"I'll believe it when I see it." I yanked out the gun and climbed from the truck.

As Daisy hurried around the front, I tucked the Glock into the back of my pants and pulled my shirt over it.

"We're not going in?"

"Not yet. It's better to let Savard blow up out here than inside. Besides, the meeting will go on for a while."

Ten seconds later, the Honda pulled in and parked next to us. Paine Savard jumped out of his car and slammed his door. "The hell was that, eh?" He pointed toward the street. "I almost lost you back there."

"Yeah," I said. "I wasn't thinking."

He moved toward me. "I doubt that."

"We waited here for you, didn't we?"

Savard's brow furrowed as he quickly considered the scenario. In a moment, the anger subsided. "All right. What's the plan?"

"No plan. We go in and see if Nick's here."

"If he is?" Savard asked. "We need a plan."

"We talk with him."

Savard's eyes darkened. "You better not help him get away."

"That's not what I want."

"What about her?"

Daisy looked at her boots. "We're not here to help him get away." It didn't sound convincing.

"We brought you here," I said to Savard. "Keep that in mind."

The lieutenant blinked several times. "Lead on." He scooted us toward the church.

The structure was likely built sometime post World War II. It had none of the beauty some of the earlier churches in the area sported. The brick and concrete building featured sharp angles some might have considered futuristic. Perhaps the architect designed the structure with an eye toward future generations to encourage worshipers to continue to warm the pews. It didn't work. The building still looked out of date.

We climbed the wide concrete stairs and Savard pulled open a heavy wooden door.

"After you," he said.

Inside the lobby, a small reader board announced, "True North Recovery—Crown B."

Crown Avenue was directly to the south, so I headed in that direction. Daisy and Savard followed.

A row of rooms lined the southern wall. The second room's door stood slightly open. A light blue notice stuck on the wall. It read *True North Recovery. Everyone welcome.*

I stepped through the door and moved along the back wall.

Twelve people sat on brown folding chairs. The circle was in the center of the room. More folding chairs were stacked on a nearby cart. A coffee pot and several boxes of cookies were on a plastic table near the back.

Daisy stepped into the room and moved next to me. We shimmied out of the way to let Savard in. The door closed behind Daisy. He hadn't followed her. Perhaps he stopped to use the restroom or take a phone call. Either seemed strange reasons to delay entering after chasing Nick from Canada to Spokane. Or maybe he forgot something in his car. Handcuffs? A gun? It was too late to worry about that.

I scanned the group's participants but didn't immediately see Nick. Due to the circle, a good portion of the group still had their backs turned to me.

"Do you see him?" I whispered.

Daisy held off answering because a woman stood and smiled at us. She had short black hair and wore an oversized gray sweatshirt. "You're welcome to join. Grab a chair and we'll make room." She motioned at the nearby cart.

The rest of the group turned to look at us now.

Daisy bumped my arm with her elbow. "There's Nick," she said softly.

She didn't need to say anything because the shock on Nick's face gave him away. He seemed to have trouble comprehending her presence. Nick's gaze slid to me, and he cocked his head. His eyes filled with doubt.

I still didn't believe the man was my father, yet it was hard not to feel something at that moment. Nick had known my mother when she was young. It was possible he knew Gabriel Baldwin, the man listed on my birth certificate.

My mother's younger life remained mysterious. Maybe all children saw their parents' lives that way. I couldn't ask my father anything about his life and my mother wouldn't share anything about hers. It would upset the narrative she had carefully built.

But I knew things about Nicholas Gossett. He'd fled the U.S. to dodge the draft. However, that was long forgiven, not only by a president I couldn't remember, but by society. No one talked about the Vietnam War anymore and they cared even less about those who dodged its draft. Nick could have returned home at any time, but he chose to stay in Canada until a DUI collision resulted in the death of a woman.

That decision led to the death of Border Agent Macon Young. Nick Gossett had a lot to answer for, but those questions weren't to be asked by me.

Nick said, "They're here for me."

The woman eyed him with kindness. "That's okay. Everybody's welcome."

That's when Paine Savard stepped into the room, and everything went to hell.

***

Nick jumped to his feet, grabbed the folding chair, and awkwardly tossed it at Savard. It flew off course like a giant metal Frisbee. I jerked Daisy to me and pushed her into the wall, putting my back in the path of danger. The chair hit my shoulder and clanged to the floor.

"Stop!" Savard yelled.

Members of the recovery group shouted a variety of unhelpful comments.

I looked over my shoulder in time to see Nick running for the exit with Savard in pursuit.

A counseling group member, a burly fellow with a chin-length beard, hollered, "The fuck, man?"

A clean-cut man in a suit and tie shouted, "Son of a bitch!"

"Language, people!" the moderator yelled. "This is a church!"

Across the room, a door slammed open, and sunlight flooded in. Nick disappeared outside. Savard followed only a moment behind. His shoulder banged into the door right before he vanished around the corner.

I stepped back from Daisy, and she turned. Fear flooded her eyes, but I didn't wait around to help her deal with it. I ran for the exit.

The howling of the recovery group didn't stop. Several of them hurled expletives in my direction as the moderator continued to plead for them to watch their words.

I blasted through the exit, and the door banged on the opposite wall. I stumbled onto the sidewalk and immediately looked for my quarry.

Savard had chased Nick into Division Street. Tires screeched and horns blared as cars avoided hitting them. Metal crunched as a tow truck rear-ended a Subaru.

With the traffic at a momentary standstill, I ran into the arterial. I didn't do it with the reckless abandon that Nick and Savard had.

By the time I made the opposite sidewalk, Savard had caught Nick in the middle of Franklin Park and the two were struggling. Savard grabbed Nick by the wrist while the other man sought to grab anything on the cop for leverage.

The lieutenant kicked at Nick's feet, but to no avail. Savard jerked Nick's wrist to toss the man off balance. It appeared as if Savard was trying to take Nick to the ground—just like a cop would think to do. The whole ugly dance looked like a violent waltz neither was winning.

However, it didn't appear Nick was struggling to get away. Instead, it seemed like he only wanted to keep his footing. His hand would move behind his back and Savard would jerk his arm to throw him off balance.

That's when I realized what was happening. Savard wasn't fighting to take him down. He was trying to stop Nick from pulling out a gun.

"Cutler!" a woman screamed.

I glanced over my shoulder. Daisy stood on the median. Traffic had resumed, and she was stuck on the island until it broke.

"Stay there!" I shouted.

That's when I heard the gunshot.

I spun around.

Savard clutched Nick like a drunken friend at the end of a long night. He slowly slipped to the ground.

I yanked my gun from the back of my pants and sprinted through a series of cars. Several hit their brakes and honked.

"Drop it!" I yelled.

Nick raised his gun as he backpedaled. "You shouldn't be here."

"Drop it, or I'll shoot." I stopped near Savard and lowered to a knee.

"She shouldn't have called you!" Nick lowered his gun but didn't stop walking backward.

I pressed a couple of fingers against Savard's neck. There was still a heartbeat.

"Stop!" I shouted.

"Go ahead and shoot."

When I didn't, Nick turned and ran.

I pulled my cell phone from my pocket and dialed 911.

"Nick!" Daisy shrieked. "Wait!"

She clomped by me in pursuit of her lover, but the chase didn't last long. He was too fast, and she wasn't dressed for a run. Her untied combat boots slowed her down, and the chain around her waist whipped wildly. Nicholas Gossett disappeared into the neighborhood.

My call was answered on the first ring.

"Nine-one-one, what is your emergency?"

Chapter 15

The first officer to arrive drove his patrol car through the park to our location. The vehicle's emergency lights spun, and its siren wailed. It felt as if it had taken them an hour to arrive, but I knew it was only minutes.

Daisy frantically waved her arms. "Over here!" she cried. It was an unnecessary gesture, but she'd never been in a critical incident before.

I kneeled next to Savard with my hands pressed against his belly. Blood seeped through my fingers. "Help's on the way."

Sweat beaded over his forehead, and the color drained from his face. He squinted into the sky. He coughed blood, and I reflexively turned away.

The patrol car slid to a stop nearby, and the driver's door popped open. The officer stepped from the car and drew his weapon. "On the ground!"

I looked over my shoulder. "We called you!"

"He's been shot!" Daisy screamed.

"On the ground!" the officer commanded over the screeching siren.

A second patrol car arrived with its lights and sirens activated. It raced across the grass toward our location.

Things would only get worse now. I'd been in this situation before as an officer.

Reported shootings meant a gun was involved. A bleeding man on the ground meant confirmation of that report. Two screeching sirens only heightened that tension.

Daisy's appearance didn't help the situation. A woman in a faded Army jacket, black half-shirt, and blue jeans might be quirky on a normal day. Add untied combat boots and a chain link belt, and she suddenly appeared like a militant.

We hadn't followed the directions of the first officer. Everything was rendered moot after that. A backup officer had arrived. The first cop's orders were now validated since we were in a standoff.

Daisy only made it worse. She balled her fists and leaned forward. Her face was beet red, and her eyes were wild. She screamed, "He needs fucking help!"

"On the ground!" the officer repeated. He leaned forward and jammed his gun into the air.

The second patrol car careened to a stop on the grass. The driver's door opened, and another officer appeared with his gun drawn. Without hesitation, he shouted, "On the ground!"

With the sirens and the shouting, it was a cacophony of chaos.

"Daisy!" I barked.

"Why aren't you helping him?" she screamed at the cops.

"On the ground!" the cops yelled in unison.

"Daisy!"

Her attention snapped to me.

"Get down!" I hollered.

"What?"

"On the ground!" both officers yelled over the wailing sirens.

I motioned with my head toward the ground. "Do it."

She kept her eyes on me as she dropped to her knees. When she fell forward, she put her arms out to the side.

"It's gonna be all right," I said to Savard, but he didn't hear me. His eyes had rolled back into his head.

"Hey," I said and reached for his neck.

"On the ground!" one of the cops yelled.

My fingers searched for a pulse, but I couldn't find one. Maybe it was faint and the adrenaline surging through my system was stopping me from finding it.

More sirens entered my consciousness. Was the ambulance finally here?

A blow to my right side lifted me off my knees. My temple collided with the top of someone's head before we crashed into the grass. I didn't fight back. I knew better than to do so with a cop, but I tried to protect myself by tucking my elbows into my ribs. Even that was wrong.

The cop kneed me in the ribs. "Quit resisting!" he yelled even though I wasn't. He struck me again, which forced all the air from my lungs. "Stop resisting!"

The officer put his hands on my back as if to mount me for better control. He touched the gun in my waistband and yelled, "Gun!" The cop jumped away and drew his weapon. "Gun!" he yelled a second time. "Get your hands out to the side."

I did as he ordered.

Two other officers sprinted over with their weapons drawn. When they moved from my line of sight, they holstered their guns and grabbed my arms. One of them dropped their weight across my shoulders and handcuffs ratcheted around my wrists.

"Baker-233," one of the cops on my back said.

A radio squelched before a dispatcher responded. *"Baker two thirty-three, go ahead."*

"Two in custody. Scene is secure. Send in the medics."

***

The police closed Franklin Park and left Paine Savard's uncovered body lying in the middle of it. Groups of onlookers stood on the sidewalks and stared at the dead man. Several news crews gathered in the parking lot and waited for a briefing. Across the street, the recovery group stood in front of Journey of the Redeemer church.

I was placed in the first patrol car that had arrived on scene. Daisy was put in the second.

There was no room to sit comfortably due to the thick metal partition between the front and back seats. They were built like that for a reason. Criminal transport shouldn't be a pleasant experience for the arrestee. There also wasn't any air flow in the car. The officer hadn't bothered to turn on the air conditioning. The back of the car stunk like the plastic seat covering and body odor.

The initial officers on scene established an inner and outer perimeter—those two areas that limited who could be in them for investigative purposes. Natural posts are usually used to secure the yellow POLICE—DO NOT CROSS tape. Trees, light posts, or porch supports are great for that. However, the middle of a park created a unique challenge.

Dispatch must have contacted the parks department because a truck arrived with green metal stakes and orange mesh fencing. The officers grabbed the stakes and ignored the fencing. In less than ten minutes, they had established the perimeters.

Occasionally, I studied Paine Savard's body. Holy Family Hospital was less than one mile away. I could have run there in less than ten minutes. Had I not called for the police, could I have carried the man there before he died? Would he have been able to walk there with some assistance?

I twisted in my seat and the plastic seat covering squeaked. Movement was difficult with my hands secured behind my back.

Two mid-thirties men approached. They both wore dark suits and carried spiral bound notebooks. They chatted casually but carried serious expressions. One of them eyed me as they passed. Major Crimes, I thought.

I turned in my seat, which caused the plastic seat covering to squeak again.

The two men approached Officer Brenner, the first patrol officer on scene. I learned his name when he escorted me to the car. At the time, he advised me I was being detained while they investigated the matter further.

Brenner was a taller man. He'd been serious and non-committal while we spoke. However, with the detectives, he smiled frequently. They did not return the gesture. Brenner pointed at me and Daisy, then Savard. The detectives asked a couple of questions, to which Brenner motioned toward the church, then he pointed at me again.

Eventually, Brenner headed toward my car with one of the detectives in tow. The other detective walked toward where Daisy was held. Brenner opened the front door before pressing a hidden button, which popped open the back door.

"Scooch out," Brenner said.

With my hands cuffed behind my back, I wriggled and wormed my way toward the opening by pulling with my legs. When I was near the door, Brenner grabbed my arm and gently helped me to my feet. He positioned me at the back of the patrol car.

"This is Detective Kellmer," Brenner said. "He's got some questions for you."

Kellmer opened his notepad. A Miranda Warning card was paper clipped to the inside. "You're not under arrest, but since you're detained, I need to advise you of your rights."

I could have told him I knew them, but it wouldn't have mattered. Kellmer would still have to jump through this hoop for legal reasons and departmental policy. The dead man off to my left dictated it.

"You have the right to remain silent," Kellmer said. He proceeded to run through the remaining warnings.

While he read my rights, Brenner hooked his thumbs into his duty belt and shifted his weight onto his right foot. He glanced casually around. He wore the bored look many senior patrol officers did. They've seen too much to stay excited for long. I had that look while I was on the job, too.

When Kellmer reached the end of the warning card, he looked up. "Having these rights in mind, do you wish to talk with me now?"

"I do."

He pulled a pen from the inside of his suit jacket. "It's John Cutler, right? And you're a private detective?"

"Correct on both counts."

I waited for him to say that the department has had contact with me before, but he didn't.

"How did you know the victim?"

"Paine Savard was a lieutenant with the Vancouver Police Department." Kellmer must have known that, or he had the best poker face I'd come across. "He was in the states looking for Nick Gossett." I waited a couple of beats before adding, "The killer of his niece."

That was something Kellmer didn't know because his eyebrows lifted, and he cocked his head. He wasn't that good of a poker player. "His niece's killer?"

"Savard's niece died in a DUI collision. Up in Kelowna."

The detective jotted a note and stared at it. "Collision?"

"That's right."

"Most people say accident."

"An accident implies no fault," I said. "Someone is always at fault in a collision."

Kellmer and Brenner exchanged glances. Brenner's face soured, but Kellmer asked, "Were you a police officer somewhere?"

"Seattle."

I expected the detective to ask one or two follow-up questions about my experience on the job, but instead he asked, "How'd you get involved in this?"

"The woman you detained with me is Gossett's girlfriend. She hired me to find him."

"How old is this Gossett?"

"Early sixties." I tilted my head back. "She knows his birthdate."

"Why'd she—" He checked his notebook. "Daisy McLaughlin. Why'd Daisy want help in finding him?"

"Gossett went missing five days ago. Truth is, he's been on the run since the early seventies."

"Draft dodger?" Kellmer asked. "Didn't Carter pardon them all?"

That was the president, I thought. *How could I not know that?* However, I nodded as if I knew the correct president all along.

"Did this Gossett not follow the news?" Kellmer asked.

I shrugged. "Maybe he liked it there."

"It's too cold in Canada," Brenner muttered.

Kellmer glanced at the officer. "Like it's any better here." His attention returned to me. "So Gossett comes down here after the felony collision and is followed by Savard?"

"That's the gist of it."

The detective tapped his pen against his notepad while he thought. Eventually, he said to Brenner, "Uncuff him."

The officer stepped forward. "Turn around."

I did so.

Brenner slipped a key into the cuffs, and they slipped from my wrists one by one.

"Need me any further?" Brenner asked the detective.

"Not for this," Kellmer said, "but I'll talk with you later."

The officer wandered off.

I rubbed my wrists as Kellmer considered his notes. "All right, Mr. Cutler. Let's start from the beginning."

***

The police kept us at the scene for another ninety minutes. Kellmer and his partner conferred with each other repeatedly. During that time, they sent two officers across the street to interview the remaining folks from the recovery group.

When the detectives felt they had the stories straight, Brenner transported me to the department. My clothes had Savard's blood on them, so they were going to take them for evidence. I gave my truck keys to Daisy and explained how best to get to the police station.

An evidence technician met us outside the detectives' unit. She was a serious-looking woman with almond-shaped eyes and dark hair. She had light skin, but her features belied Asian descent.

"This is Ann," Kellmer said.

"We've met," I said.

They both cocked their heads.

"A few years ago, you did a GSR on me with Detective Ackerman."

Ann's eyes widened at the mention of a Gunshot Residue Test, and she turned to Kellmer.

He opened his palms. "He's a private detective. He gets around."

"I guess," Ann said, "but I don't remember that."

They escorted me into an interview room. A set of blue medical scrubs and a pair of flip-flops waited on a table along with a plastic bowl. Several open brown bags were lined up on the floor. A small briefcase was also there.

Ann photographed my front, back, and sides. She paid special attention to the blood on my hands and lower arms. When she finished with the pictures, she let the camera hang around her neck. "The GSR test isn't going to work on his hands and forearms because of the blood."

"What about his upper arms?"

She shrugged. "It might work. He was outside, right?"

Kellmer nodded.

"How important is the presumptive test?" Ann asked.

"It's not the end of the world, but it would be nice."

The presumptive test only took about five minutes, and it wouldn't stand up in court, but it would quickly return a result whether there was gunshot residue on my skin.

"The lab can test his clothes for GSR," Ann said, "and that would be a far truer result. I'd hate to bust open a kit just for the presumptive."

Reluctance flashed through Kellmer's eyes. "All right. We know where he lives if it comes back to haunt me."

Ann faced me again. "Empty your pockets into the bowl, then take off your clothes. Put the shirt, pants, and shoes in separate bags. If there's no blood on the underwear, you can keep them."

"When can I get my gun back?" I asked.

"We're keeping it for ballistics testing," Kellmer said. "Just in case I've read this entire situation wrong, and you killed Savard."

I figured as much. The clothes were never coming back. Not that I'd want them with the blood, but I wanted the gun. I didn't know how long ballistics testing might take, but it would be in my best interest to write off the gun. If I got it back, great. If I didn't, I'd call it a business expense.

"I'll step out," the technician said, "and give you some privacy."

Kellmer watched as I emptied my pockets. "One thing bothers me."

I tossed my wallet and cell phone into the plastic bowl. "What's that?"

"Why'd she pick you? There had to be another detective between Metaline and Felony Flats."

Felony Flats was the nickname the locals gave to my part of town. Every city gave nicknames to their communities, but Spokane seemed especially fond of derogatory terms for its neighborhoods. Dog Town, Vinegar Flats, and Little Africa were a few of the others I'd heard since I moved here.

I kneeled and untied my first boot.

"If not a detective," Kellmer continued, "at least someone who would have helped. She's attractive." He cleared his throat. "Wouldn't seem like she'd have a hard time getting some assistance."

I looked up at him. The way he emphasized Daisy's attractiveness led me to believe one thing about Kellmer. He wore a wedding ring, but plenty of cops were on the make. In my time with Seattle PD, I met plenty of cops who would never consider stealing. They would not lay hands on a suspect in an illegal manner. Those cops spoke about integrity and honor in a way that would make any department proud. Yet they treated their marriage vows like toilet paper.

It made me glad Maria never agreed to my shoddy marriage proposal. I wasn't sure how I'd stand up under that pressure.

I switched my foot and untied the other boot. "She thought Gossett might be my father."

"No kidding?" Kellmer's brow furrowed. "Why would she think that?"

I stood and kicked the boots off. "He knew my mother before I was born. That doesn't mean he's my father, though." I put the boots into a paper bag.

"Fortunately, right?" Kellmer said. "With him being wanted for murder."

I pulled the bloody shirt over my head and dropped it into the second bag. "Yeah."

"Any idea where he might be heading?"

"He grew up in Coulee City, but from what I heard, his family members are all dead."

As much as I wanted to find and talk with Nicholas Gossett, the fact that he killed Paine Savard in a public park showed how little he could be trusted. Besides, he'd already run from a DUI collision. Even though Nick didn't shoot me when he had the chance, who knew what he'd be willing to do if his back was really against the wall?

"You used to be a cop," Kellmer said. "You ever hear of something like this? A draft-dodging killer."

I slipped off my pants and put them into a bag. "The draft-dodger bit is antiquated now. He did that almost forty years ago."

"The sins of the youth, you're saying? Like who we were when we're young isn't who we are today. Doesn't look like you've got any blood on your shorts."

"Four decades is a long time." I grabbed the scrub shirt and tugged it on.

"Almost your lifetime."

I grunted. At least Kellmer saw it the way I did. I grabbed the scrub pants.

"Don't know if I've ever run across a draft dodger," Kellmer said.

"How would you know? They're probably just grandparents now."

He smirked. "Nick Gossett as a murdering grandfather doesn't sound any better than a draft-dodging killer."

"Lucky he doesn't have any kids."

Kellmer shrugged. "That we know of."

I tossed the flip-flops on the floor. "That we know of."

"Let's get you to a restroom so you can wash your hands."

***

It was dark when I walked out of the west doors of the Public Safety Building.

My truck idled in the drive lane and Daisy sat behind the wheel. I opened the driver's door.

"Scoot over."

She did so. As she settled into her seat, her foot kicked something metallic. The sound was familiar, and I looked down. The floorboard lights were on because I hadn't pulled my door closed yet. Underneath her feet was the chain belt and the opened padlock. Daisy nudged them out of the way as she buckled up her seatbelt.

I pulled the door closed and left the parking lot.

***

We headed north on Monroe Street until Indiana Avenue, then cut over to Division, which would eventually turn into the highway. There was no conversation as to where I was taking her. We both understood we were heading back to Metaline.

"Do you want to talk about it?" she asked.

I shook my head. "Not really."

Even at seven in the evening, Division Street traffic was heavy. The lights remained stop and go.

When we passed Franklin Park, both of our eyes went to where Paine Savard died. I didn't ask what she thought about, and she didn't ask me. My hand rested on the flip-down middle console. She covered it with hers as tears filled her eyes. When we passed the park, she looked away, but her hand remained on mine.

After a while, our fingers interlinked.

***

It's a two-hour drive to Metaline. The cab was dark, and the radio was silent. Once we cleared Spokane proper, the road hummed underneath us. Daisy remained lost in her thoughts for some time. Twenty minutes passed when she pulled her hand from mine and lifted the middle console.

"Do you mind?"

My adrenaline spiked. "What're you going to do?"

She unfastened her seatbelt and laid her head on my lap. Daisy curled into a ball like a little girl. I put my hand on her head and felt bad for the stupid thing that I had just thought.

I also felt guilty about it. Stacy entered my thoughts, and I considered calling her. Those considerations disappeared as I stroked Daisy's hair.

Soon, Daisy slept on my lap, and I felt the rhythmic rise and fall of her body next to mine.

***

She awoke and sat upright when I turned onto her street. Daisy rubbed her eyes with the heels of her palms. "Have I been out the whole time?"

I stopped in front of her house. "It's all right."

She dropped her hands between her thighs. "This didn't work out the way I hoped."

"It happens."

Daisy stared ahead. It was a little after nine, but Metaline was already dark. "He's not coming back."

"Not now."

She kicked the chain and padlock with the toe of her boot. "I thought we had something special."

"You did."

"It was a lie." She faced me. "Like him."

I didn't know what to say, so I kept quiet. My hands remained on the steering wheel.

Daisy studied me. "Are you hungry? I can make you something to eat."

The adrenaline returned. She wasn't hinting at anything inappropriate, so why was I hoping something would occur? I knew why. The desire to burn down my world remained somewhere in the back of my consciousness.

"I've got to get going," I said.

"But you've got to be starving."

"I'm good."

She looked down at her hands. "Are you afraid to come in?"

"Yes."

"Nothing will happen."

"I know."

Daisy looked at me. "I don't want to be that person anymore."

"You can be whoever you want."

"That's what they say, isn't it?" She popped open the door and the cab lights activated. Daisy collected the chain and padlock from the floor. She slid off the seat and turned to face me a final time. "Don't forget to send a bill."

I nodded.

"John?"

"Yeah?"

"I really hope he's not your father."

"Me, too."

She gently closed the door. I watched her walk up the sidewalk. She dropped the chain and padlock outside before unlocking her house. When she disappeared inside the house, I left Metaline.

***

The headlights pierced the darkness, and my window was rolled down to let the cool night air rush in. Curtis Mayfield's "Pusherman" blasted through the stereo at full blast. My eyelids drooped and I fought to stay awake.

I mumbled along with the lyrics until it ended. The CD changed to something slow, and I skipped it. "Are You Man Enough?" by the Four Tops started, and I pounded the steering wheel. When it got to the chorus, I sang it as if I stood on the front of the stage.

It didn't help me feel any more awake. This was another one of those moments when I wished I still smoked. Thoughts of Daisy's invitation for a meal invaded my head. It was still ninety minutes until I got home.

If I turned around, I could be at her house in thirty minutes and save myself an additional hour of driving. It was probably safer, too.

I turned down the music and pulled out my phone.

She answered on the second ring. "Hello?"

"Did I wake you?"

"No," Stacy said. She sounded as groggy as I felt. "I'm lying here watching the news about your shooting. Just waiting for you to call. Are you driving?"

"Back from Metaline, yeah."

"Been a long day."

"It has."

I heard the television in the background.

"Are you doing okay?" she asked.

"Tired."

"If you feel yourself falling asleep, you should pull over somewhere."

I didn't think that was a good idea. Too much temptation to turn around. "I don't know," was the best answer I could muster.

"Think about it."

"Okay, maybe."

She must have shifted her position because her voice changed. She sounded more alert. "Are you staying here tonight?"

"I don't think so." A semi came in my direction with its brights on. I turned my head slightly to avoid getting blinded. "I've got to get the dog. He hasn't been fed yet."

"You can still come over."

"I could." It sounded like a lot of hassle, and my lack of enthusiasm came through in those two words.

"It's okay," she said. "You sound wiped out. Call me in the morning."

"I will." I didn't want the call to end but asking her to stay on the line and babble was childish.

"John?"
"Yeah?"
"I love you."
"I love you, too."

***

Somewhere near the town of Elk, my weariness disappeared, and I felt invigorated again. Nick Gossett drifted through my mind, and I wondered where he might be headed.

A part of me thought he would show up at my house. He knew I lived in Spokane; he had articles of some of my higher profile cases. A basic internet search could find my office on Spofford street. Maybe he would try to show up in the middle of the night. Or perhaps he'd hunker down somewhere and show up at the office in the morning.

I imagined the conversation we would have. He'd tell me about my mother. That he was still hung up on her. A part of me really wanted to remember what my mom was like before her metamorphosis. We all change as we grow up, most not so drastically as my mother. Maybe Gossett knew my father. Even one positive tidbit to hold on to would be more than my mother gave me.

After a time, reality set in.

Gossett would not come by my home. He'd had plenty of years to reach out. He would not do it while his freedom was on the line. He'd shot a man in Franklin Park. Maybe he didn't know Paine Savard was dead, but it would only take a cursory glance at the news to learn the truth.

No. Nick Gossett was in the wind.

Chapter 16

I woke up without the aid of an alarm and let the dog out.

It was shortly after six. I started a pot of coffee and took a shower. I wanted a leisurely morning, but my mind whirred with recent events.

After dressing, I grabbed a cup of coffee and a notepad, before sitting at the kitchen table.

My mother answered after the third ring. "You've called more this week than all last year." She didn't sound happy about it.

"What do you remember about Nick?"

"This again?"

I sipped my coffee.

"Why can't you let the past be the past?" she asked.

"He killed a man yesterday."

She inhaled sharply. "What happened?"

The murder caught her attention, and I explained the events at the park.

"And you're okay?" she asked.

"I'm fine, but I need you to tell me everything you remember about Nick."

Silence descended over our call.

"Hello?" I asked.

"There's not much to tell," she said. "I don't know what you're after."

"He was obviously hung up on you. Start there."

"He wasn't hung up on me."

"Are you kidding? He kept photographs of you."

"Some people do that, I guess."

She didn't. My mother removed any memory of a former lover with the precision of a surgeon's scalpel. Old photographs were burned. Mementos were tossed in the trash. Even gifts that had utility were traded with friends. A boyfriend once bought her a new couch. When the two broke up, she swapped it with a friend for a ratty loveseat. She wanted no reminders in her personal space.

"Nick had a copy of your wedding announcement," I said.

My mother clucked. "Where would he get that?"

"The paper."

"Nick was always…" Her voice trailed off.

"Possessive?"

"Obsessive," she corrected. "We didn't look at it as a bad trait back then."

"How did you two meet?"

She sighed. "A party down in Fife. Or was it Kent? Doesn't matter, I guess. I think it was Fife."

"How does my father factor into this?"

"He doesn't. Gabe and I broke up before I met Nick."

"That's it?"

"I'm not comfortable talking about this with you."

"Jesus, Mother."

"Don't take the Lord's name in vain."

I sniffed dismissively. "You said a lot worse when I was a kid."

"I don't need to listen to this. I have things to do."

"Wait." I bowed my head and closed my eyes. "I'm sorry." I hated saying those words to her.

She stayed quiet on the other end of the line.

"I was told Nick had family in Coulee City," I said. "Is that true?"

"He did. Who knows if they still live there?"

"Did he mention any names?"

"Why is this important?" she asked.

"My client hired me to find him." It was a true statement, although the job had ended in the park yesterday.

"Aren't the police looking for him now?"

"The local police, yeah. If he's fled out of the area, they won't find him."

Someone knocked on the front door. Could that be Nick now? Was I wrong in my assessment? Had he decided to show up at my house?

"You should let them do their jobs," my mother said.

I stood. "A name. Please."

"He didn't have any siblings, but Nick had a cousin he used to talk about all the time," she said. "Corwin, I think. Yes, that's right. Corwin Gossett. That's the only name he ever mentioned."

"Thanks. I've got to go."

"Johnny—"

I hung up.

I didn't have a second gun in the house, so I was at a disadvantage. I tiptoed to the front door. An aluminum baseball bat leaned in the corner. I grabbed it and peered through the peephole.

My anxiety waned, and I opened the door.

Sergeant Gary Ackerman eyed the bat. "Good morning, Slugger."

***

Ackerman settled into a metal folding chair in front of my desk. He wore a wrinkled blue T-shirt and faded jeans. His hair was mussed as if he had just come off the graveyard shift.

"Your name came up," he said. "Wanted to stop in and see if you were doing all right."

I spread my arms wide. "I'm in one piece."

"I heard the DOA was a Canadian lieutenant. Vancouver or something."

I nodded.

"He was after the guy whose name I ran?"

"Yeah."

Ackerman's face pinched. "Hope that doesn't come back to bite me."

"Why would it?"

"If someone audits the system and sees I ran a suspect's name hours before he kills a Canadian national. A cop to boot." The sergeant shook his head. "Won't look good for me."

"Probably not. Hey, man, I'm sorry."

"It's my issue," he said. "I understand policy and procedure. I violated it. If I get caught, I get caught. I'll have to take my lumps."

"Couldn't you just say you got word from an informant that Nick might be headed to Spokane and might have a warrant? You checked and he didn't. End of story."

Ackerman eyed me darkly. "That's a lie."

I wobbled my hand. "More a different shade of the truth."

"Sitting in IA, it's a lie. That's something I can't take back. I'll own my screw-up, but I won't lie about it."

"Regardless, I'm sorry."

He glanced around the house. "Where's the dog?"

"Out back." I thumbed over my shoulder. "Want me to get him?"

Ackerman held up a hand. "I'm good. What're you going to do now?"

"Nothing."

His brow corrugated. "It's a police investigation."

"I know."

"If you have any idea where the guy might have gone, you need to tell us."

"I already told the detective what I thought."

"You did?"

I nodded. "I can tell you if you want to know."

"Is it in town?"

"Coulee City."

Ackerman stood. "What am I going to do with that?"

"Thought you might want to know."

"I'm a graveyard sergeant. Not a detective, but I'm glad you let him know." He stopped at the door and looked back. "If you go after this guy, be careful."

I nodded.

Ackerman pointed at the bat. "Take more than that."

***

I started my computer and entered Corwin Gossett's name into the internet browser's search bar. It returned results from Facebook, MySpace, and a smattering of references across the world, including some in Australia. I added 'Coulee City, Washington' to the search bar and that cleaned up the findings.

Corwin Gossett owned CG Contracting, which had received a smattering of reviews. I ignored them, figuring all they would do was distract me from my ultimate objective.

Below was an obituary link from *The Star*, a regional newspaper based out of Grand Coulee. It read:

Corwin Gossett left his earthly home on February 18 after suffering a stroke due to an intracerebral hemorrhage. He lived his whole life in Coulee City, leaving only to serve proudly in the U.S. Army during the Vietnam War.

The announcement included a picture of a younger Corwin in a soldier's uniform. I leaned back in my chair and reread the announcement.

Would Nick have kept tabs on his cousin after four decades? My mother said Corwin was the only family member Nick talked about.

He had printed my history for his file. Surely, he would have kept information on his favorite cousin had he known about it. Why wasn't that in the file?

I studied Corwin's picture. Could a clue to the cousins' relationship lie in the obituary? Corwin served in Vietnam. Nick fled to Canada. Would that push the two apart? If it had, would Nick not know about his cousin's death?

It was possible.

But if Nick knew about Corwin's death, that potential hiding place was gone. That meant he could head anywhere now. That wasn't entirely true, I corrected myself. Nick would not double back to Canada. He would not risk crossing that border again. Not since he killed someone there. Paine Savard's appearance confirmed his need to stay away.

By killing Savard, Nick put an additional bullseye on his back. If the Spokane Police Department hadn't written a warrant for him yet, they would certainly do it soon. That meant he wasn't safe anywhere in America. He couldn't board a plane because he'd need to show his identification. Mexico seemed the natural destination, with an illegal border crossing as the only way across.

So, while Nick could go almost anywhere in the world, getting there was problematic. He'd have to find non-extraditable countries. I didn't know which ones there were, but that was a concern for another day. Nick first had to get out of America. He needed to head south and cross several states to get to Mexico.

He'd been out of America for nearly forty years. As far as I knew, he had no allies.

Going home didn't seem so far-fetched after all.

I cleared the search bar and entered 'Lynnelle Gossett Coulee City.' Was Nick's aunt still alive?

***

After shutting down the computer, I fed and watered Corporal. I didn't take him over to throw the ball. I needed extra time this morning. I planned to leave him in the backyard for the day. The concern about the encounter with the bum a couple of mornings previously had worn off. He'd be fine in the yard for a day.

I called Stacy. She was already at work, so the conversation was quick and quiet.

"Good morning," she said softly.

"Good morning to you."

"What's the plan for today?"

"I'm heading to Coulee City."

"What for?" she asked.

"Nick Gossett might be there."

She didn't respond.

"It's gonna be all right," I said. "If I find him, I'll call the cops."

"You promise?"

"I promise." It wasn't a lie. I would call the cops eventually, but I wanted to talk with Nick Gossett first. There were still questions I wanted answered.

We said our goodbyes, and I told her I loved her. She said it back, but hers sounded filled with suspicion. As if she parroted the words only because I had said it. Stacy wasn't happy I was going after Nick, but I wasn't going to give up the chase.

I grabbed Marvin Gaye's *Trouble Man* soundtrack before leaving the house.

It already seemed like that kind of morning.

***

Coulee City was almost two hours directly west of Spokane on Highway 2. It's an easy drive through farmland with towns like Davenport, Wilbur, and Almira dotting the way.

After shooting Paine Savard, Gossett fled the park. He couldn't return to Macon Young's truck because the cops had seized it as part of the investigation. Detective Kellmer and his partner likely contacted their counterparts in Pend Oreille County and looped them in on the discovery of Young's vehicle.

If my guess was right about his destination, and I could still be wildly wrong, Nick had to figure out a way to get to Coulee City.

I should have checked to see if Greyhound went through the town. Perhaps it did. Or maybe he knew how to steal a car. What aptitudes had the man developed while living on the run for forty years? Savard said he had lived under an alias. How many had he lived under during four decades?

Trouble Man played as the miles clicked off. It's a funky soundtrack to a film I'd never seen. My Uncle Reuben had it in his collection when I was a kid. I didn't appreciate it much back then. I liked the albums with singing in them, so I could participate. I was that odd kid who learned the songs of James Brown and The Isley

239

Brothers while my friends listened to Duran Duran and Def Leppard.

Marvin Gaye's soundtrack was a wonderful piece of driving music. There were few lyrics to battle my thoughts. The album ebbed from fast to slow, just as I imagined the movie might. I've never been much of a film buff, so I never sought out Gaye's inspiration.

Memories of my childhood drifted back. Life was good with my mother when I was young. It felt like us against the world. Reuben was around, but he wasn't much help. He'd drift in for some laughs with my mother, then disappear for a while.

I tapped my hands on the wheel and bobbed my head in rhythm with the soundtrack. Trouble Man, I thought. *What kind of trouble were you in?* The groovy vibe took over and my shoulders got in on the action. I turned up the volume and continued my one-man dance. When that instrumental ended, a slower song started, and memories of my mother entered.

I could never point to the exact time when my mother's attitude shifted, and she started her social climbing. It happened before Reuben's murder, because he stopped coming around as much when she insisted that he behaved differently. They argued more, and she started telling me that he wasn't a good role model. I didn't listen to her. What boy isn't going to look up to his cool uncle?

The changes were noticeable around our house. My mother's friends vanished one by one. Whether she cut ties, or they did, didn't matter. She didn't look back. My mother had her sights set on new associates. She stopped listening to music all together. I was never a big fan of the stuff she liked—James Taylor and his ilk, but at least there was music in the house. Her records vanished before the small stereo moved to my bedroom. She stopped smoking and swearing, then judged anyone who did.

I was outside Wilbur when I passed a hitchhiker. She stuck her thumb out and smiled. When I passed, she spun and flashed me the bird. I laughed, but that happiness quickly faded. I had wondered how Nick might make it to Coulee City and it was in front of me all along.

Had I already passed him in one of the previous small towns?

Or had he hitchhiked through the night? Perhaps he was already there. Was he already gone?

I pulled into Coulee City around ten in the morning. I hadn't bothered to look up directions to Lynnelle Gossett's house. I had only written down the address.

How hard would it be to find her house in a small town like that?

Chapter 17

Lynnelle Gossett lived on McEntee Street at the easternmost edge of town. It took some zigzagging through the various streets before I found it.

It was a yellow two-story house on the corner of the block. The lawn appeared recently cut, but the landscaper didn't trim the edges or shrubs. The result looked like an old man with a fresh haircut but unkempt eyebrows and untidy ear hair. A For Sale sign loomed near the concrete pathway.

Next door, a woman in denim overalls clipped the waist-high hedges along her chain link fence. A red bandanna held her hair in place.

I parked the truck and got out. There wasn't a curb or a sidewalk. I nodded at the neighbor in overalls and headed up the pathway toward the front door.

"No one's home," the woman called.

I turned toward her.

She lifted her clippers in a form of greeting. "Lynn's at the doctors."

I crossed the lawn toward her. "Any idea when she'll be back?"

The woman was in her early sixties with steel-gray eyes. "You wanna look at the house?"

"No, ma'am. I want to ask her a couple questions."

"About?"

How much should I tell this woman? If she grew up in Coulee City, she might remember Nick. They were roughly the same age. Maybe if I handled the news a certain way, it wouldn't matter.

I glanced over my shoulder at Lynnelle's house. "I'm supposed to meet a friend here today."

"Who's that?"

"Nick Gossett."

Her face brightened. "You're a friend of Nick's? Why didn't you say so? It was so wonderful to see him after all these years."

I did my best to keep my expression flat. "When did he get in?"

"Must have been last night sometime. I don't know. I only saw him this morning."

I motioned toward the house with my head. "Is he inside?"

"No, he went to the doctor with her."

I smiled. "He did?"

"He was always so sweet with Lynn. I'm sure they'll be back soon." The woman snapped the clippers over the bush. "You can go in if you want. I'm sure it won't be a problem."

"I appreciate that, but I think I'll wait in my truck."

"Suit yourself."

***

A red Ford Escape turned onto McEntee Street and headed in my direction. Two figures were in the vehicle. As it neared, I could see them better. An elderly woman sat behind the steering wheel while Nick Gossett was in the passenger seat.

We made eye contact as they passed, and he never looked away.

Lynnelle Gossett, however, did not look away from the road. Her focus remained intently on the task of driving. The Escape crept around my truck and onto her property.

The neighbor had remained on her front lawn. Her bushes were fully pruned now, yet she continued to snap the shears like a barber snipping away final errant hairs. She frequently glanced in my direction and did so again when I opened my truck door.

I climbed out of the cab and waited near the tailgate.

The Escape finally stopped near the edge of the house, and Lynnelle got out. She was in her late seventies or early eighties, with wispy gray hair held in place by a blue scarf tied under her chin. A hump on her back forced her to stoop. A gray sweater dangled open over a multi-colored dress.

Nick's head appeared over the roof of the car and his attention immediately locked on me. We exchanged nods.

Lynnelle waved at the woman no longer pretending to trim her hedges.

"Everything turn out okay?" the neighbor called out.

"Best I could hope," Lynnelle said. The elderly woman stepped toward her house.

"You got a visitor." The neighbor pointed at me.

Lynnelle shuffled around to face me.

Nick walked from around the back of the little SUV. "I got it, Aunt Lynn."

She eyed her nephew. "You know him?"

"I do."

"Invite him inside for some coffee." She headed for the door.

I stayed where I was. Just because Lynnelle invited me into her house didn't mean I was moving anywhere. Nick still had a gun and mine was locked up in police evidence somewhere. I brought the baseball bat, but it was inside the cab of my truck. I didn't think he'd shoot me in front of his aunt.

Nick wore the same clothes he was in yesterday at the park. Were they the same he'd worn while he killed

Macon Young? The cop in me realized their evidentiary value. The abandoned son in me wanted answers more.

He walked over and stopped about six feet away. He kept his hands out of his pockets. Nick briefly eyed the neighbor. She had returned to snapping the shears over the already pruned hedges. "How'd you find me?" He kept his voice low.

"Daisy said you mentioned family in Coulee City. My mother said you used to talk about a cousin named Corwin."

Nick frowned. "Corwin's dead."

"I read his obituary. Did you come to pay your respects?"

Suspicion clouded his eyes. "Why are you here? You gonna call the cops?"

"I came for answers."

"About what?"

"Did you know my father?"

Nick's lips tightened. He inhaled deeply and thought for a moment. "How's your mother?"

"You wouldn't recognize her."

"I think you'd be surprised."

I didn't want to hear about a torch he still carried for her. "She never told me about my father. She said he ran when I was born."

"Why'd she say that?"

"Because he did. It hurt her badly. Really messed her up."

Nick's brow pinched with concern. "How so?"

"The mother I had as a kid isn't the one I have today."

"People change." He shrugged. "We all change. Life has a way of doing that."

It was a simple platitude; one he didn't need to share. However, trying to describe how much my mother transformed over the years to this man would be an uphill battle. I tried to focus on the reason I was there.

"I learned my father's name by seeing it on my birth certificate."

"Your mother never told you?" Nick asked.

"She refused to say his name my entire life. That's how much she hated him."

Conflicting emotions seemed to battle for control, and Nick looked down at his feet. "How's Daisy?"

"Confused."

He nodded.

"She doesn't understand why you had to leave."

His nod deepened.

"She doesn't understand why you killed Macon Young."

Nick looked up. "I didn't want that to happen."

"I believe that."

"It's just that he and his friends—" Nick pointed in a direction I imagined Metaline was. "They chided me for getting involved with her." His face tightened. "They didn't appreciate her for who she was." He tapped his chest with his fingers. "I did. I appreciated her."

"Then why didn't you tell her the truth?"

"I did."

I stared at him, and his eyes narrowed.

"You're not talking about the DUI," Nick said.

"I'm talking about Paine Savard. He told me about an alias. What's a draft dodger need aliases for when President Carter pardoned them all? What were you really doing in Canada?"

He kicked a stone and sent it skittering into the street. "Is there any way you'll leave this alone?"

"I think you knew my father. My mother explained a little about your relationship, but she was cryptic. That's how she is. I want someone to tell me the truth."

Nick looked toward the house. "Want a cup of coffee?"

"Not really."

"I'm going to need one for this. Either that or a beer and I'm really trying to stay sober."

He headed toward the house, and I followed him.

"Wait outside," he said. "I don't need my aunt to hear any of this."

***

Nick returned from inside with two cups of black coffee. I never worried about him leaving because I heard him talking with Lynnelle the entire time. He'd left the door to the house open. After he handed me a cup, he pulled the door closed behind him.

We sat on a stair, and he looked out into the neighborhood.

His hands wrapped around his cup, and I noticed bruises and scrapes on his knuckles.

"What's it like where you live?" he asked.

I looked up. "Fine."

"Sleepy like this?"

"Hardly. It's an older part of town. Poor. Some crime."

"You like it?"

I shrugged. I didn't feel like making small talk. "Tell me about my father."

Nick sipped his coffee, then leaned forward. "I should have been him."

"I don't understand."

His head bobbed. "Your mother and me. I thought we were something special." His voice grew wistful. "She was so beautiful. You've probably heard people say how a woman could take their breath away? She didn't do that to me. Rather, she made me nervous. I got too excited around her. All I wanted to do was make her laugh." His voice trailed off, and he searched for something inside his coffee.

"She dated my father before you."

"Gabe was a piece of shit."

"Hey."

Nick sucked his lower lip into his mouth. "Carol broke up with Gabe because he couldn't keep his dick in his pants. At least, that's what Carol told me." Nick set his coffee cup on the step between his legs. "I swore I'd never do that to her. It was the sixties, and everyone was fucking everyone. I thought maybe being committed to her might make a difference." He bowed his head.

The neighbor finally got bored with miming her landscaping duties. She headed around the far side of her house.

"When Carol said she was going back to him—" Nick's voice hitched, and he looked away. He pretended to be interested in a stray dog. When he had control of himself, he continued, but didn't make eye contact. "I believed we'd get married someday. She was that kind of woman. I planned it all out in my head."

Nick picked up his coffee and took a healthy swig.

"I'll give Gabe this; he was a handsome man." Nick cast a sideways glance at me. "You resemble him."

"My mother never kept a single picture for me to compare myself to."

"No?" Nick's brow furrowed. "Huh." He rubbed a thumb along the edge of his cup. "Gabe came up from California somewhere. I guess he wanted to bust out of that whole Haight-Ashbury scene. Thought Seattle would be better, but it had the same problems. War overseas. Young people repressed. The old were in charge." He grinned. "Sounds like today."

My expression remained flat, and Nick's smile melted.

"Why'd my mother go back to my father if he ran around on her?"

Nick's eyes narrowed and studied the house across the street. "She was pregnant."

A car turned onto McEntee Street and pulled into the second house on the block.

"I thought it was mine. Hoped is the better word, but Carol said it wasn't. The timing didn't work out." Nick's eyes grew watery. "But I didn't care. It didn't matter to me. I still told her we should get married." His lips trembled, and he sniffled.

Overhead, a flock of birds flew north.

"Seeing them together," Nick said, "was like a knife in my heart. Every time it sunk a little deeper." His hands tightened around the mug, and a tear ran down his cheek. "I could have been a really good father."

His words carried a strange finality to them.

"Did something happen?" I asked.

Nick set his cup on a step and stood. His cheeks were wet now. "I couldn't get her out of my head. Your mother was really something. I bet the guy she's married to now is really happy." Nick looked down at me. "What's he like?"

"Vance? He's nice."

"Runs a college or something."

"That's right," I said.

"A smart guy, then." A sad smile spread across Nick's lips. "Carol changed her type. Is she still beautiful?"

I told him what he wanted to hear. "Yeah."

Nick gently wiped away the tears from his face. "Can you believe this? Me crying like a baby."

"Tell me what happened."

He rubbed his fingers together. "Gabe didn't deserve her."

The way he said the words cut into me. "Nick."

He held up his hand. "She loved him so much." The tears returned, and he angrily wiped at them now. "Loved him in a way she would never love me, and what did he do?" He swallowed with some difficulty. "I caught him with another woman." He nodded. "That's what he always did."

The front door opened, and Lynnelle stepped outside. "Is everything okay?"

Nick wiped the tears from his cheeks. "Everything is fine, Aunt Lynn."

"But you're crying." She stepped onto the porch. Her gaze dropped to me. "What's going on?"

"We're talking about old times," Nick said, "and it got me sad. That's all."

"Oh, honey," she said. "I certainly understand that."

Nick motioned toward me. "This is my friend, John."

She nodded. "Do you need more coffee?"

"I've hardly touched mine," I said. "Thank you."

"What about you?" she asked Nick.

"I'm good. I'll be inside in a bit."

Lynnelle glanced between the two of us. "All right, then." She returned to the house and pulled the door closed.

"She's worried about me," he said. "She took me to a meeting this morning."

"The neighbor said it was a doctor's appointment."

Nick looked for the hedge-clipping woman. "Lynn lied to protect my reputation. Small town gossip and all." He rubbed his eyes with his palms. "Why don't we go for a walk? I don't want to finish this story where anyone might hear."

He headed for the edge of the property, and I followed.

Chapter 18

We walked over to Washington Street in silence. Our shoes scuffed the faded asphalt as we went. I wasn't worried he would try to hurt me since we remained in a neighborhood. Besides, it seemed as if he wanted to talk.

When I was a police officer, there were a few times when a suspect blabbered on about a horrible crime they'd committed. It seemed a strange occurrence until a detective explained the need for some to unburden themselves of their guilt. The psychopaths and sociopaths of the world have no qualms about what they do. The rest of society carries remorse for their actions. They might try to bury the shame with self-destructive behavior and use tools like alcohol, drugs, or sex to aid them.

I remained quiet as we walked, not forcing the conversation. I had all the time in the world. Unfortunately for Nick Gossett, his world was closing in around him.

When we turned north onto Second Avenue, Nick asked, "What happened to the cop?" He didn't have to explain he meant Paine Savard.

I said, "He died."

If I expected a display of emotion, I would have been disappointed.

"Why were you and Daisy with him?"

"He followed us from Metaline," I said. "He was the uncle of the woman killed in your crash."

Nick's nod was barely perceptible. "I know."

"I didn't care if he or the police caught you. I just wanted to talk with you."

He looked at me out of the corner of his eye. "What about Daisy?"

"She wanted to make sure you were okay. She's worried about you."

"I really screwed up."

He didn't need me to convince him one way or the other.

Second Street curved toward the highway. Vehicles occasionally zoomed by in both directions. We had to raise our voices to be heard.

"So, the cops know it's me?" Nick asked.

"Spokane PD does. They impounded Macon's truck, so I'm sure Pend Oreille County knows it's you now."

"Macon was an accident."

I thought about his injured knuckles. "What happened?"

Nick waved his hands as he spoke. "He showed up at my room a couple nights ago. Smelled like a distillery. How he found me, I don't know. Maybe he saw me outside my room. However it happened didn't matter." He stopped walking. "I told him he could have her. Do you know how much that hurt to say? I knew I couldn't stay in Metaline anymore. Not with Savard after me."

Some seagulls flew overhead.

His face pinched. "The prick said he was going to have her all right. Then he proceeded to tell me everything he and his friends would do with her. What they'd already done. I hit him and he fell. It was one punch, I swear. On a normal day, he could have killed me. Especially if he wasn't loaded. I didn't expect him to go down like that, but he did." Nick snapped his fingers. "Lights out. As if I flicked a switch. He hit his head on the corner of the dresser and that was the end."

Nick inhaled deeply and held it for several steps. When he exhaled, he said, "If I could do that over, I'd take it all back. I shouldn't have gotten mad and hit him. He was drunk, and it was just words. Besides, I wasn't going back to Daisy. I couldn't."

"Because of Savard."

He nodded. "Because of Savard."

The highway loomed ahead, and a small gas station was on our right. Across the road was a large parking lot. The entrance nearest us was blocked by a small white gate.

Nick slowed and checked both ways for traffic. When it was clear, he trotted across the highway. I matched his pace.

"You ever see the lake?" Nick asked.

"No."

We walked around the white gate. "C'mon. I'll show you."

Nick led me through the parking lot. Several RVs, trucks, and cars were in the parking lot.

"Banks Lake," Nick said. "Used to be good fishing when I was a kid." He pointed at a body of water ahead. "Corwin had a rowboat, and we'd get out there with it."

We approached a pathway that allowed us to walk out over the water to a small island. Nick led me to the tip of the rock where a protective railing stood. We stared out over the lake.

Several boats zipped about the water. Others bobbed near the shore; their occupants most likely had fishing lines in.

"It's been a lifetime," Nick said wistfully.

I never noticed how often people used that expression until it coincided with mine.

He turned to me. "I should have turned myself in after the accident."

"Would have saved further deaths."

"It wouldn't have stopped the first."

We stared at each other for a moment.

"I'm sorry, John," he said finally.

I've punched a lot of men in my life for a lot less. "Tell me what happened."

***

"I went to Gabe's apartment," Nick said, "to confront him about what he was doing to your mother."

"What did you expect was going to happen?"

He lowered his head. "I thought he'd back off. Do the right thing."

"Walk away?"

"He didn't love her like I did."

"He knew who you were?"

Nick nodded. "We all knew each other back then." He turned to look out over the lake. "Gabe said I'd better leave them alone if I knew what was good for me." His gaze grew distant. "No offense, John, but your father talked tougher than he was."

I leaned against the railing. "Who started the fight?"

"Does it matter?" Nick asked. "I went there to challenge him. Any court would have said I was the reason it started. Trust me, I've thought about it a million times over the years. I was always guilty."

He wrapped his hands around the railing, and I stared at his knuckles again. How many times had my own hands looked like that? Nick didn't hit Macon Young once. The man might have fallen and hit his head on the corner of a dresser, but not before he was hit many times.

"What did you do afterward?" I asked.

"I buried him."

"Where?"

"Somewhere he wouldn't come back to haunt me."

I considered what I'd learned about Nick from the conversations with Daisy and what little I had gleaned from my mother. Daisy said he'd gone to Canada to dodge the draft.

What if Nick had fled to Canada to avoid prosecution for murdering Gabriel Baldwin? Perhaps he was worried someone might put two and two together. Was he concerned my mother would figure out he killed my father and alert the police? She had already broken up with him. If Nick showed up after the mysterious disappearance of my father, surely that would be a red flag.

Where could Nick bury a body that it wouldn't haunt him? Maybe bury was a euphemism for disposal. He could have burned it, but did he have access to a crematorium? Unlikely. Maybe Nick could have dumped the body in the ocean, but people have washed up on shore before. Disposing of a corpse in a vat of acid seemed too vile and sophisticated.

What if bury wasn't a euphemism and Nick really dug a hole and covered it with dirt? He could have done it in a variety of wooded areas, including the Olympic National Forest. It likely wouldn't be disturbed if he hid it well enough. However, would animals dig it up? Would a hungry bear root around and pull the body from the ground? That would be too big of a chance to take.

Then it hit me.

"You took the body to Canada."

Nick squeezed the railing. "The Canadian guards were pretty lax at the time. With Pierre Trudeau in office, they couldn't ask about our military status if we were seeking permanent residence in Canada. I crossed the border and started a new life."

"And the body?"

Nick inhaled deeply. His face strained and relaxed twice before he spoke. "I drove to a small village you probably never heard of."

"Try me."

"Anmore."

I shrugged.

"I never heard of it either until I pulled off on a trail and buried the body."

"You had a shovel with you?"

"I stopped along the way and bought one."

"Why didn't you come back to the states?"

Nick looked at me like I had asked the most obvious question in the world.

"Right," I said.

He had just murdered Gabriel Baldwin, and the authorities might pin it on Nick if he returned.

"Besides," Nick said. "I was about to finish college. I couldn't put it off forever. Once I did, I'd get drafted. Then I would have had to make a choice. Canada was the best option all the way around."

"Savard said you lived under an alias."

"One of many." He glanced at me. "I keep expecting you to hit me or something."

"I've waited my whole life to get an answer to this. If I'm going to hit you, it's when you're done talking."

He nodded.

"Assuming you don't have your gun with you," I said.

"I ditched that before I left Spokane. Threw it into the river. If the police want it bad enough, they can go find it."

The cops didn't need the gun. They had my testimony as well as Daisy's. I wasn't sure, but I believe there were other witnesses to the shooting. The gun would have been an extra nail in the coffin, but Nick had already dug his own grave.

He put his back against the railing and crossed his arms. "So those aliases. I couldn't come back to the states because I figured everyone knew what I did." Nick bobbled his head. "This isn't easy to talk about with you."

"How'd you get the fake IDs?"

"It wasn't hard back then. You've got to remember there were a lot of men in Canada looking to avoid our illegal war. It wasn't as bad as the media made it seem, but still forty thousand is a lot of men hiding out."

Dodging the draft, I thought.

Nick continued. "Some of the locals weren't too keen on helping us out, especially the old timers who served in World War II. They were vocal about their opposition. But the youth were the same everywhere. Power to the people. Make love, not war." He chuckled. "It's hard to believe we spouted that nonsense."

I wanted to ask how much of it my mother believed in. She gave lip service to democratic causes now, especially after marrying a college president, but she had been an ardent supporter of the conservative agenda during the Reagan and Clinton years.

"Someone always knew a guy," Nick said. "Want to score some weed? So and so knows a guy. Need a fake ID? Some other fella knows a guy. Short on cash? Same story."

"You lost me on the last part."

He kept his arms crossed but shrugged his shoulders. "What skills did I have? No college degree and it's not like I could use the credits I'd already earned because they were tied to my name—my birth name. Things got real, very fast, when I got desperate for money." His voice trailed off.

"You committed crimes?"

Nick shrugged a single shoulder. "Not at first. I borrowed money from a guy to get a place." He smiled, but it was without joy. "A guy. See what I'm saying? I couldn't get any cash from a bank."

"What about your family?" I pointed across the highway. "What about Aunt Lynn?"

"No way. I wouldn't have her know what I did."

"She seemed calm just now. You must have reached out to her at some point."

He nodded. "When Corwin died."

"How'd you know?"

"The best invention ever for me was the internet. When it first popped up, I would go to one of those cafes and pay for an hour. I'd spend the whole time searching for friends and family. There wasn't much on there back then. Things have changed, I'll tell you. What you can find now is crazy."

"So you called Aunt Lynn?"

"I set up a bunch of Google Alerts. Have you heard of them?"

I hadn't, but I got the gist.

"I put one on Corwin and Aunt Lynn. Put them on your mom and you, too." Remorse crossed his face. "Not sure why I bothered keeping tabs on Corwin. He made it clear he never wanted to talk with me again. I called him after I got into Canada. I was afraid the cops might go to him and ask about me, but before I even got a chance to tell him what happened, he called me a traitor. All he cared about was that I went to Canada. He said to never call him again."

"Why'd you put an alert on me?"

Nick's expression softened. "Why do you think?"

"You're not my father."

"I could have been." He uncrossed his arms and shoved his hands into his pockets.

"How'd you know my name? You were gone before I was born."

"Your mother said she was going to name you after John Lennon. Man, she loved his voice. All I had to do was pay to verify your birth record—"

"You saw my birth certificate?"

He shook his head. "Just your listed parents. There's only so much the internet can do."

"You never had any kids?"

"Not with the life I led. I bounced around too much. Never remained in one place for long. Met some ladies. Some nice ones at that. Some not so nice ones, too. When they got too serious, I ended it."

"Don't tell me it was because you still pined for my mother."

"You wanna walk?" He lifted his chin toward the pathway.

"I want you to finish telling me the truth."

He exhaled heavily and looked at his shoes. Nick kicked the toe of one against the other for a moment. When he looked up, his eyes clouded over, and he stared into the parking lot. "I've carried regret my entire life, John. Everything bad that's followed me can be traced back to that night in Seattle. My drinking. The things I did to survive. It's all back to that night."

"When you killed Gabriel Baldwin?"

He shook his head. "The night Carol said she was pregnant with his kid." He tapped his chest. "I loved her. Gabe didn't. End of story." Nick's lips twisted as he fought to control his emotions. "He would have married her. That's what people say you should do." He kicked at an imaginary stone. "He didn't love her. Doesn't that mean something? I loved her, she loved him, and that son of a bitch would only have married her because she was about to have his baby."

I thought about my own life. When Maria ended up pregnant, I offered to marry her. I didn't love her, and she knew it. Thank God she was mature enough for the both of us to say no.

"Life isn't fair," Nick said.

"Pity doesn't look good on you."

His eyes cut to me.

"You've killed three people I know of," I said. "Tell them life isn't fair. Tell their families that."

Nick faced me. "Is this where you hit me now?"

"Don't pretend you know me."

"I read those articles. Sounds like you've had a temper. I just thought—"

I pointed toward Seattle. "I grew up without a father."

"He wouldn't have loved you."

"How do you know? You don't know." My face warmed. "So what if he didn't? At least, I would have known I had an old man. I spent my whole life—"

"My parents died, too."

I leaped forward and grabbed him by the shirt with my left hand. He fell back onto the railing and brought his hands up to protect his face, but he didn't strike me. My free hand remained cocked near my ear, ready to punch him in the mouth.

We stayed that way for several seconds.

"Do it," Nick said.

"Your parents died when you were in high school. It's not the same."

He lowered his hands and gently grabbed my wrist. "You can hit me if you want. It's okay."

"No." I released my grip and pushed him.

Nick sucked his lips into his mouth.

I pointed toward Seattle once more. "That woman you loved? What do you think happened to her?"

"It sounds like she did pretty well for herself."

My shoulders slumped. "You think you helped her? Jesus, man. She's spent her whole life thinking some asshole ran out on her. That she wasn't good enough to keep the father of her child around. Do you know what that did to her?" I tapped the side of my head. "It messed her up."

His gaze drifted toward the nearby dock. A rowboat with a couple of boys headed toward it. "That used to be Corwin and me," he said. "I wonder if they caught anything."

"What's your plan?" I asked.

"I thought maybe I'd go to Mexico."

"I'm not going to let that happen."

Nick inhaled. "I thought as much." He smiled weakly. "Mind if I say goodbye to Aunt Lynn?"

"We've got to go back and get my truck."

He led the way off the small island. His shoulders were hunched, and his head bowed. It was the walk of a defeated man. As we entered the parking lot, though, he straightened. His shoulders pulled back, and he glanced about.

"Don't think about it."

"Think about what?"

"Running."

He slowed his pace, so we were shoulder to shoulder. "I'm too old to run."

"You're never too old to think about it."

Nick made a sweeping gesture. "I was just thinking how beautiful it was here."

The parking lot surface was faded and cracked. Highway traffic zoomed by. Coulee City was ahead of us, and it was hardly picturesque. Banks Lake was nice looking, but it could barely be called beautiful. Maybe Nick wore nostalgia-colored glasses as he thought about his hometown.

Our conversation vanished as we passed through the parking lot and approached the closed white gate we had encountered earlier.

We paused at the edge of the highway. A semi approached from the east while a fast-moving sedan came from the west. The late early afternoon sun hung almost directly overhead.

"Tell your mother I'm sorry," he said.

I turned to him with a snarky reply on the tip of my tongue, but it was already too late.

Nick hopped into the roadway.

***

Everything played out in slow motion. The semi hit its brakes, but there was no chance. Nick hit the grill and immediately disappeared under the eighteen-wheeler. The truck jackknifed on the highway, its tires skidding and smoking from the sudden pressure they were under.

The westbound sedan sped by and continued on its way. Had it been going the speed limit, the car likely would have been involved in the collision.

I ran before the semi stopped moving. When it finally rocked to a stop, I found Nick's bloody body. His head had been mashed by the wheels.

The driver, a burly man in blue jeans and a Harley-Davidson T-shirt, ran around the truck. "Is he all right?"

I didn't say anything. Instead, I stared at the bloody pulp of the man who'd just admitted to killing my father.

The truck driver squatted next to me to investigate. "Christ," he said. "Oh, Christ." He spun and puked on the roadway.

Several people ran toward us from the gas station. One woman was on her cell phone.

"Help is on the way," she said right before she screamed.

I walked to the side of the road and waited. I knew what was coming next.

Chapter 19

"Why didn't you call the police?" asked Washington State Patrol Trooper Joseph Bray.

"My phone was in the truck."

Irritation flashed over the trooper's face. "When you found him, I mean. Why didn't you call the authorities when you found him? You had plenty of time to do that."

Bray was a tall man with an athletic build. I'm nearly six feet, and he stood a couple inches taller than me. His light blue uniform fit him perfectly. He wore his Smokey Bear hat tilted down like a salty drill sergeant.

We stood on the side of the highway. Deputies from Grant County had blocked off the roadway while WSP troopers conducted the investigation. Traffic was rerouted off the highway and through Coulee City.

A crowd had formed in the parking lot north of us. It seemed most of the town had heard about the collision and had come to witness the investigation. Fortunately, Aunt Lynn wasn't amongst the onlookers.

Bray said, "Nicholas Gossett was wanted on a homicide warrant out of Spokane."

I nodded. "I understand."

"Your *private* investigation doesn't come before an active *police* investigation."

The trooper didn't need to convince me. Learning about my father mattered only to me. Catching Nicholas Gossett for the murder of Paine Savard mattered to the whole community.

"You interfered in a police investigation," Bray said with an unconvincing tone. "That's a crime."

It wasn't one that Bray could likely write me up on, so I wasn't worried about what would happen today. If anyone would charge me with that crime, it would be Detective Kellmer. I was more concerned if the trooper was going to say I had something to do with Nick's death.

"You're lucky," Bray said. "The truck driver is adamant you had nothing to do with this. He said the suspect jumped into the roadway on his own volition."

Suspect, I thought.

Cops see the world in black and white. Suspects, witnesses, and victims fall into neat categories. Yet, Nick wasn't any of them in his death; he was a coward. He'd lived on the run for nearly forty years. He'd outfoxed the police because they didn't know they should have been after him. Now that he woke the sleeping dragon, they were about to nab him. He took a chickenshit way out.

"You're free to go." Bray handed my driver's license back. "I hope you've learned something."

"More than you can imagine."

***

When I returned to my truck, Aunt Lynn opened the door to her house and stepped onto the porch.

"Leaving?" she asked.

"Yes, ma'am."

Lynelle looked up and down the street. "Where's Nicky?"

"He's not coming home."

I climbed into the cab.

As I pulled from the curb, Aunt Lynn slowly descended the stairs and looked about the neighborhood. Sooner or later, someone from the small town would break the news to her.

***

Stacy opened the door when I pulled up in front of her house. I got out of the truck and walked to the passenger side so I could let out the dog. I picked him up when I drove through town.

"I was beginning to think I'd never see you again," Stacy said. "I've got a plate ready."

"I'll take it."

Corporal and I headed toward the side of the house so I could put him in the backyard.

"Hey," she said. "Why don't you bring him inside?"

"You sure?"

"Just a few minutes to see how he does."

The dog and I diverted our course and entered the house. The kids bounded into the room and cautiously approached Corporal. He wagged his tail as they patted his head and ran their fingers through his fur.

"I'll warm your dinner," Stacy said. "You keep an eye on the kids."

What she really meant was watch the dog. I didn't worry about Corporal. He had never shown any signs of violence toward anyone except when commanded. He wasn't an attack dog; he only looked and sounded like one. He was well-trained by his previous owner. I hadn't kept up with his training and instead turned him into a buddy.

Stacy clunked around the kitchen while the kids talked with the dog.

"Why'd you name him Corporal?" Hailey asked.

I scratched under the dog's chin. "My friend named him."

She cocked her head. "Your friend gave away his dog?"

"He had to leave," I said, "and couldn't take Corporal with him."

Hailey hugged the Shepherd's side. "I would never give away my dog."

"My friend didn't want to."

Ethan scratched behind the dog's ear but remained mostly silent.

"What do you think?" I asked the boy.

"He's nice."

Stacy stepped into the room. "All right, guys. Give John and Corporal some space. He needs to eat some dinner."

They moved away, and I escorted the dog to the sliding glass door. He bolted around the yard to inspect if anything had changed since our last visit.

A plate sat on the dinner table. Spaghetti and meatballs with a small side salad. A slice of garlic bread was balanced on the edge. I sat and picked up a fork.

Stacy walked away to attend to the children. "Get your jammies on," she said from around the corner, "and brush your teeth."

When she returned, most of my meal was gone. She lifted her eyebrows. "There's more spaghetti if you're still hungry."

I slurped in a wayward noodle and wiped my mouth with the back of my hand. "This is enough. Thank you. Didn't realize how hungry I was."

The last meal I ate was breakfast, and it was nearing eight. I hadn't thought about food for most of the day. Now that everything had settled, hunger returned.

"Want to talk about it?" she asked.

I motioned Stacy toward a chair, and she settled into it.

Stacy knew about Nick's death. I called from Coulee City and gave her a brief rundown. There were a lot of dots that needed to be connected. After that, I had to provide color and context. She listened intently, interrupting only to ask the occasional clarifying question such as "Wait, who said that?"

Midway through my retelling of the past three day's events, her eyes drifted to the clock. She stood and held up a finger. "Hold that." She hurried away to check on the kids.

My thoughts drifted to Nick Gossett and the women he left behind. The most recent would need to come to terms with the fact that she had loved a killer. Daisy knew about Macon Young and Paine Savard. She knew about the DUI collision that cost the life of a young Canadian woman. However, she didn't know about the death of my father. Would I tell her? What would it change?

Understanding how Gabriel Baldwin died might matter to my mother. All these years, she believed my father ran out and left her to raise a child alone. That damaged her in ways that I suspected couldn't be reversed. It likely was the catalyst for many of the changes in her life.

An uneasiness lingered in the pit of my stomach. The deaths surrounding my life could now be traced back to my father. I always thought it started with Uncle Reuben's murder. Then a former girlfriend was killed after she called for help. Two of my friends later died at the hands of others.

Was this my legacy—those close to me often die violently?

That was simple thinking. I wasn't accounting for the lives I had taken. My legacy had the stench of death, but there was something else to it.

According to Nick, my father wasn't a decent man. He didn't love my mother the way a man should. I knew that feeling intimately. Maria and Erin were constant proof of that. There was a string of failed relationships. All of them had a common denominator—me.

Stacy returned to the table and interrupted my morose thoughts of heritage. "I'm sorry about that," she said.

"It's fine."

Her eyes softened, and she rested her arms along the edge of the table. "How are you?"

"Okay."

"Are you really?"

A forced chuckle escaped my lips. "Of course."

"You found out this man murdered your father. I would think that should bother you."

"It doesn't."

Stacy leaned forward. "How does it not?"

I crossed my arms and studied her for a moment. "Who's your favorite actor?"

She flopped back into her chair. "What's that got to do with anything?"

"Or singer," I said. "It doesn't matter. Just name a famous person you've liked since you were a kid."

"I don't know."

I smiled gently. "Think about it. This isn't a trick question."

"I guess I'd say…" Her eyes drifted to the ceiling as she thought. When her gaze dropped to me, she said, "Madonna. I liked her music. Even saw her movies, although they really weren't that great."

"Have you ever met her?"

"I wish."

"What if she died today?"

"I'd be sad." Stacy's brow furrowed. "That's the point I'm trying to make, John. It's okay for you to be sad."

"But you've known about Madonna since you were a kid," I said. "Even though you've never met her, you've seen pictures and videos of her, you've heard her voice, read stories about her. I bet you and your friends even talked about her at times."

She nodded, but it was barely perceptible.

"I never had any of that. For me, my father was a figment of my imagination. A name on a piece of paper. I thought him dead for most of my life. Learning how he died didn't change anything."

Stacy's eyes softened. "But there had to have been a moment of hope."

"A little." I tapped the table with the side of my thumb. "But I kept it in check."

"Sometimes hope is good."

I didn't respond to that.

Stacy stood and held out her hand. "C'mon. Let's go to bed."

"It's barely eight," I said.

"You're going to complain about that?"

I pushed back my chair. "The kids might hear."

"We'll turn on the TV and lock the door."

"What are we going to watch?"

Stacy grabbed my hand and led me to the bedroom. "Three days is too long for you to be gone."

***

Later that night, as I lay in bed, I stared up at the ceiling.

Stacy's body pressed tightly against mine and her hand lay on my chest. Her breath was warm on my shoulder as she snored softly.

My thoughts weren't with her, though. They were two hours north.

I needed to send a bill to Daisy McLaughlin in the morning, and my connection to her would be severed.

Yet, a part of me longed to drive to Metaline and tell her what happened. I could just as easily call her and relay the truth. Seeing her in person plagued my mind. Driving up there was unprofessional. Wanting to see her again was immature.

Would hearing the truth about Nick hurt Daisy? Possibly.

Would it lead to something between us? That's what I hoped for.

As I listened to Stacy breathe, shame washed over me, and it felt comforting. The desire to burn my world down again raged like a recently stoked furnace. I could struggle to contain the longing, but eventually I would let it free. Maybe not tomorrow or the next day, but the release was coming.

As I looked up into the darkness, I knew that was the truth.

Because that was my legacy.

Did You Enjoy the Book?

Thank you for reading *Cutler's Legacy*. I'm always grateful when a reader takes time out of their day to comment on one of my novels. If you do write a review, please email me and let me know. I'd love to say thanks!

About the Author

Colin Conway is the creator of the 509 Crime Stories, a series of novels set in Eastern Washington with revolving lead characters. They are standalone tales and can be read in any order.

He also created the Cozy Up series which pushes the envelope of the cozy genre. Libby Klein, author of the Poppy McAllister series, says *Cozy Up to Death* is "Not your grandma's cozy."

Colin co-authored the Charlie-316 series. The first novel in the series, *Charlie-316*, is a political/crime thriller that has been described as "riveting and compulsively readable," "the real deal," and "the ultimate ride-along."

He served in the U.S. Army and later was an officer of the Spokane Police Department. He's owned a laundromat, invested in a bar, and run a karate school. Besides writing crime fiction, he is a commercial real estate broker.

Colin lives with his beautiful girlfriend, three wonderful children, and a codependent Vizsla that rules their world.

Also by Colin Conway

The John Cutler Mysteries

Cutler's Return
Cutler's Chase
Cutler's Friend
Cutler's Cases
Cutler's Bargain
Cutler's Legacy

The 509 Crime Stories

The Side Hustle
The Long Cold Winter
The Blind Trust
The Suit
The Value in Our Lies
The Mean Street
Murder by Any Other Name
Black and Blue in the Lilac City
The Only Death That Matters
The After-Hours War
The Fate of Our Years
The Night of the Dead Boys
The Path of Progress
When the Wicked Rest
The Golden Witness
The Wasted Pawn

The Flip-Flop Detective

Strait Over Tackle
Strait to Hell
Strait Out of Nowhere
Strait Through the Heart

The Cozy Up Series

Cozy Up to Death
Cozy Up to Murder
Cozy Up to Blood
Cozy Up to Trouble
Cozy Up to Christmas
Cozy Up to Danger
Cozy Up to Terror

The Charlie-316 Series (with Frank Zafiro)

Charlie-316
Never the Crime
Badge Heavy
Code Four
The Ride-Along
The Silence of the Dead

Others

Tales from the Road (with Bill Bancroft)
Some Degree of Murder (with Frank Zafiro)